Garfield's®

BIG FAT HAIRY ADVENTURE

BY JIM DAVIS

ROSS RICHIE CEO & Founder • MATT GAGNON Editor-in-Chief • FILIP SABLIK President of Publishing & Marketing • STEPHEN CHRISTY President of Development • LANCE KREITER VP of Licensing & Merchandising
PHIL BARBARO VP of Finance • BRYCE CARLSON Managing Editor • MEL CAYLO Marketing Manager • SCOTT NEWMAN Production Design Manager • IRENE BRADISH Operations Manager
SIERRA HAHN Senior Editor • DAFNA PLEBAN Editor • SHANNON WATTERS Editor • ERIC HARBURN Editor • WHITNEY LEOPARD Associate Editor • JASMINE AMIRI Associate Editor • CHRIS ROSA Associate Editor
ALEX GALER Assistant Editor • CAMERON CHITTOCK Assistant Editor • MARY GUMPORT Assistant Editor • MATTHEW LEVINE Assistant Editor • KELSEY DIETERICH Production Designer • JILLIAN CRAB Production Designer
MICHELLE ANKLEY Production Design Assistant • GRACE PARK Production Design Assistant • AARON FERRARA Operations Coordinator • ELIZABETH LOUGHRIDGE Accounting Coordinator • JOSÉ MEZA Sales Assistant
JAMES ARRIOLA Mailroom Assistant • HOLLY AITCHISON Operations Assistant • STEPHANIE HOCUTT Marketing Assistant • SAM KUSEK Direct Market Representative • AMBER PARKER Administrative Assistant

kaboom!

GARFIELD'S BIG FAT HAIRY ADVENTURE, October 2016. Published by KaBOOM!, a division of Boom Entertainment, Inc. Garfield is © 2016 PAWS, INCORPORATED. ALL RIGHTS RESERVED. "GARFIELD" and the GARFIELD characters are registered and unregistered trademarks of Paws, Inc. KaBOOM!™ and the KaBOOM! logo are trademarks of Boom Entertainment, Inc., registered in various countries and categories. All characters, events, and institutions depicted herein are fictional. Any similarity between any of the names, characters, persons, events, and/or institutions in this publication to actual names, characters, and persons, whether living or dead, events, and/or institutions is unintended and purely coincidental. KaBOOM! does not read or accept unsolicited submissions of ideas, stories, or artwork.

A catalog record of this book is available from OCLC and from the BOOM! website, www.boom-studios.com, on the Librarians Page.

BOOM! Studios, 5670 Wilshire Boulevard, Suite 450, Los Angeles, CA 90036-5679. Printed in China. First Printing.

ISBN: 978-1-60886-901-5, eISBN: 978-1-61398-572-4

CONTENTS

COVER BY ANDY HIRSCH

DESIGNER GRACE PARK
ASSOCIATE EDITOR CHRIS ROSA
EDITOR SIERRA HAHN

GARFIELD CREATED BY
JIM DAVIS
SPECIAL THANKS TO JIM DAVIS AND THE ENTIRE PAWS, INC. TEAM.

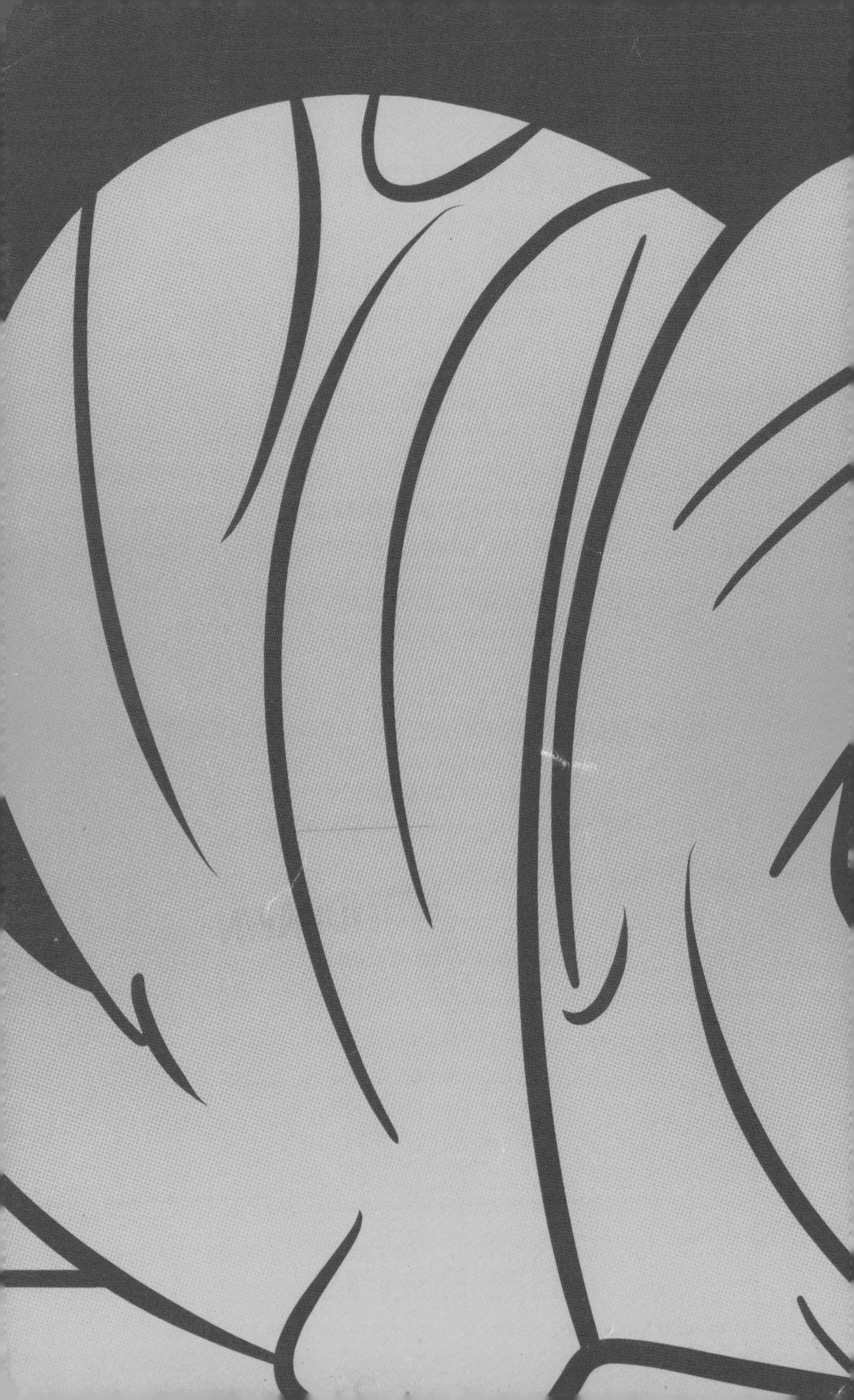

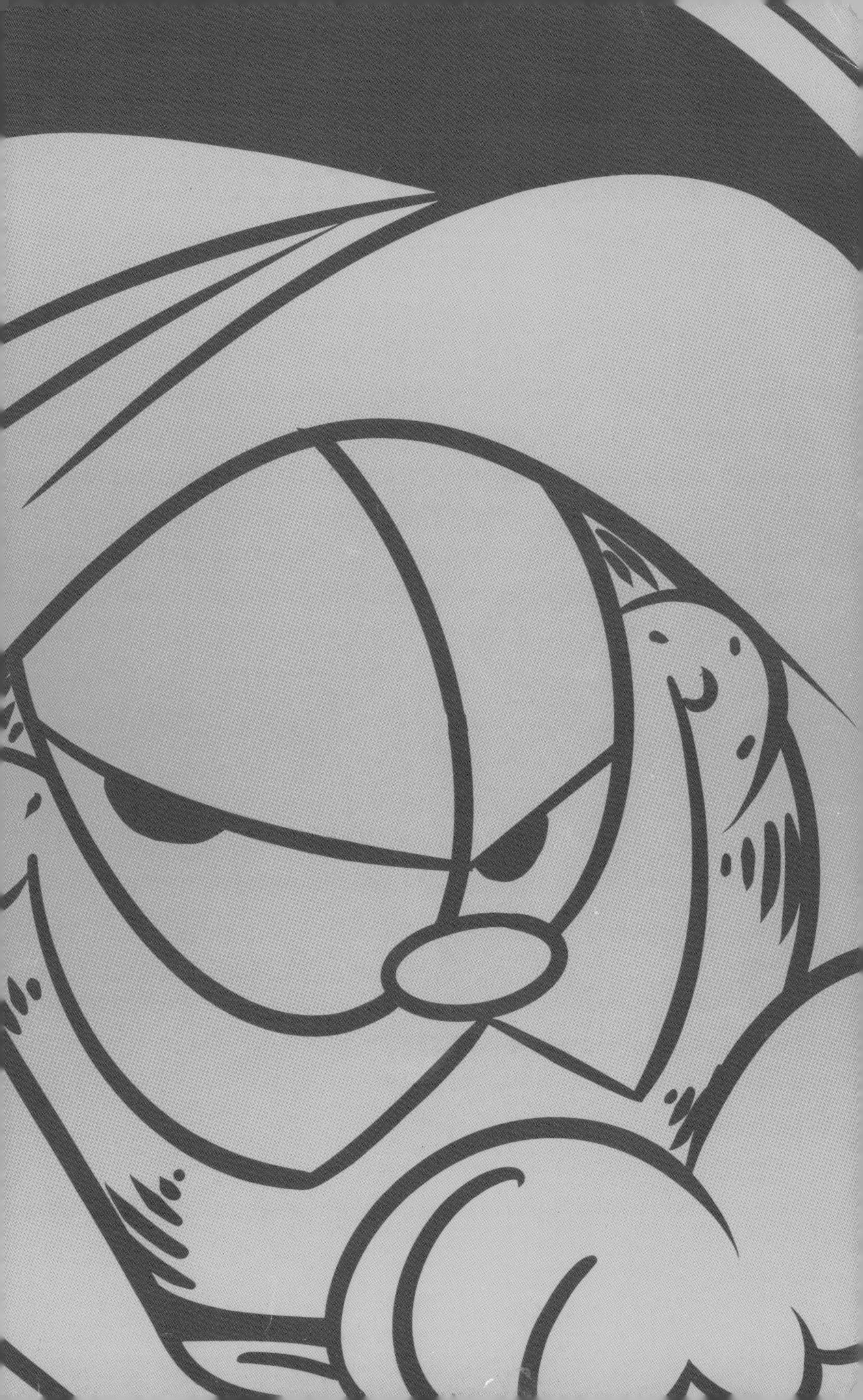

"ODIE'S GOT TALENT"

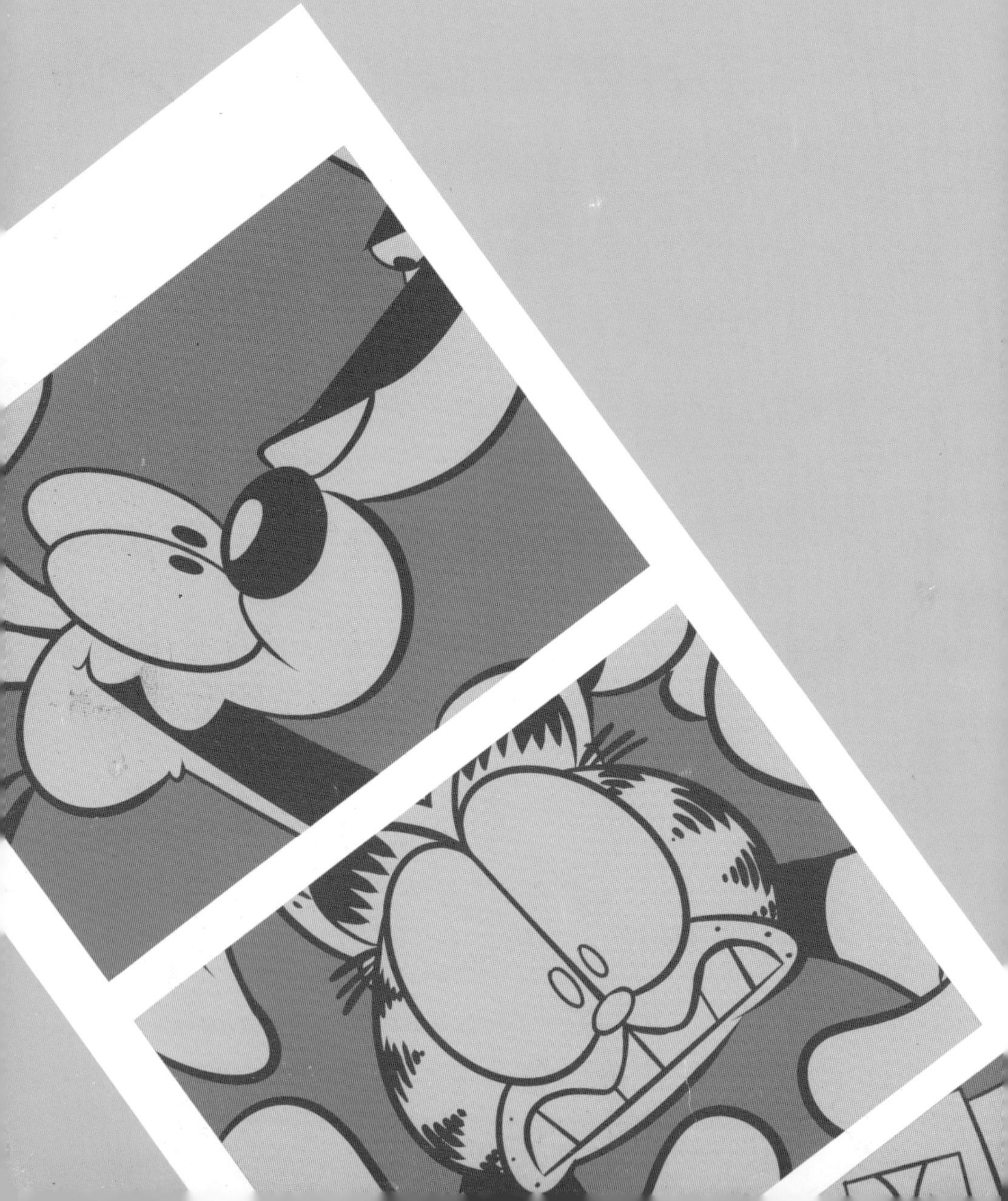

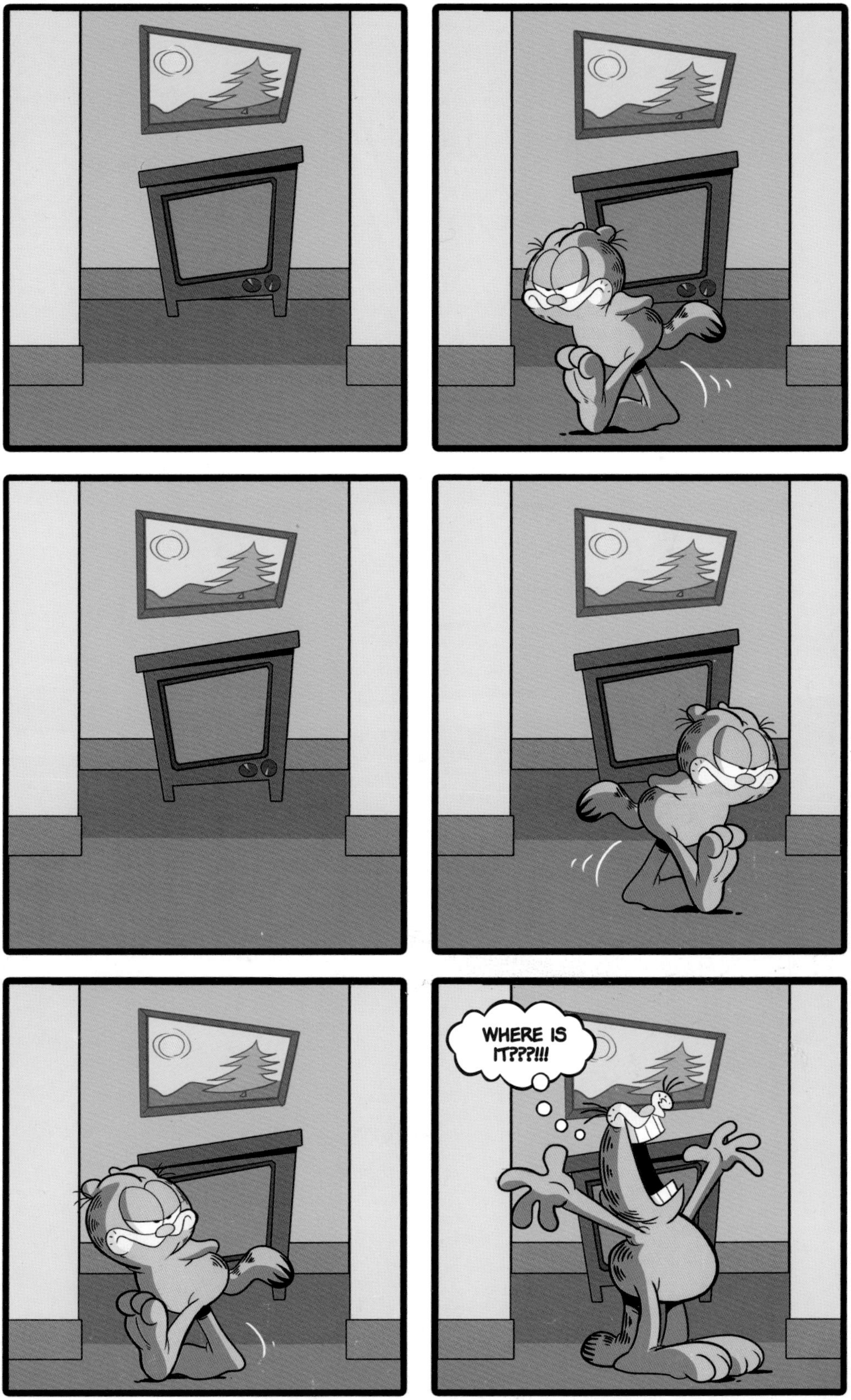
WHERE IS IT???!!!

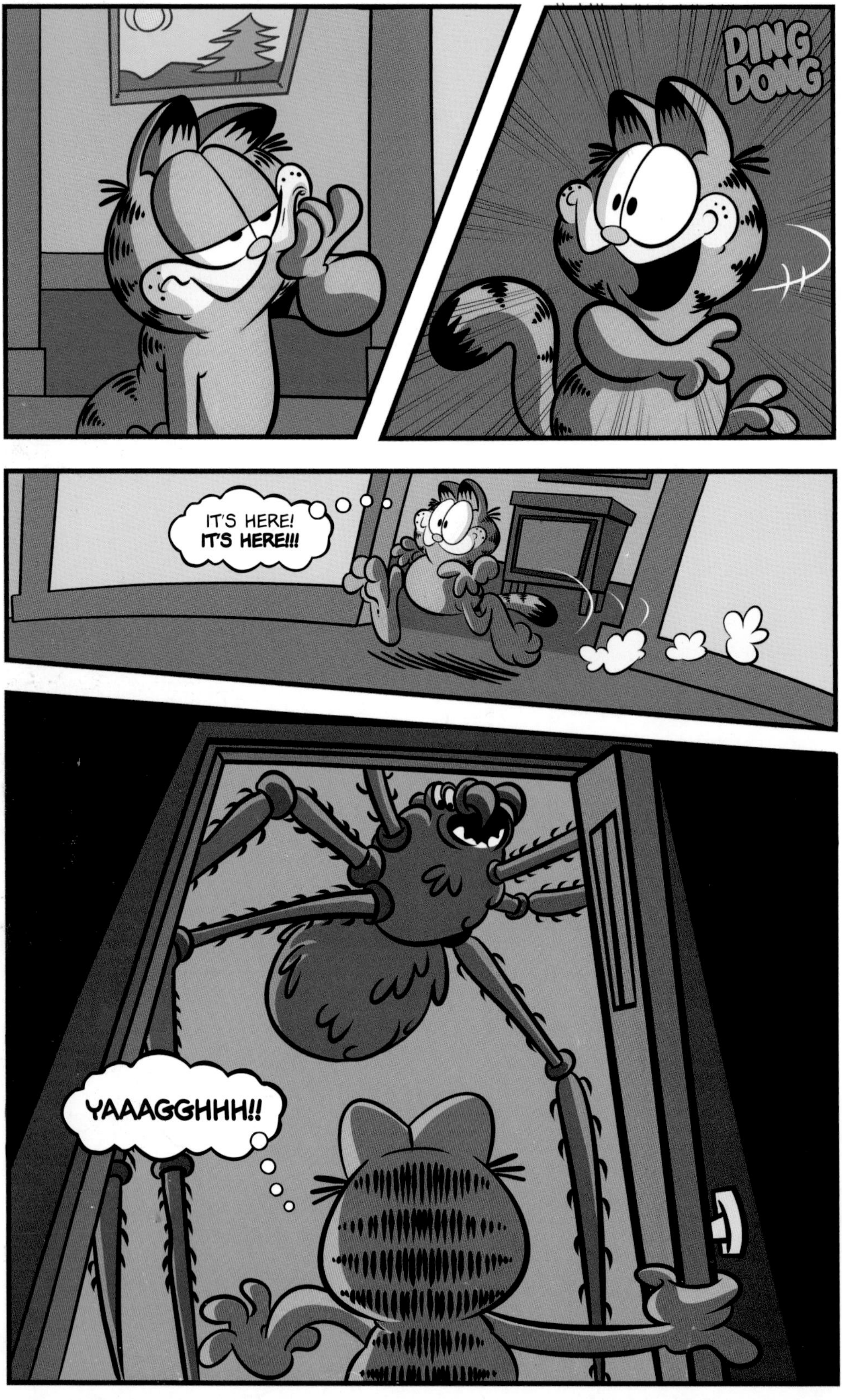
DING DONG
IT'S HERE! IT'S HERE!!!
YAAAGGHHH!!

NO, NO, NO, NO, NO. THIS **CANNOT** BE **HAPPENING.**
SKREEEEE!
OKAY, OKAY. SO IT **IS** HAPPENING!
UM, CAN WE **TALK** THIS OVER? MAYBE IF I **APOLOGIZE** FOR KILLING YOUR BROTHERS AND SISTERS AND UNCLES AND SECOND, THIRD, AND FOURTH COUSINS...
TOO LATE... CAT...
IT ISSS **LUNCH... TIME...**
...AND YOU LOOK SSSSO... **TASSSSTY...**
NO! I CAN'T BE...**SPIDER CHOW!**
EVERY...THING...GOING...
"BLACK..."

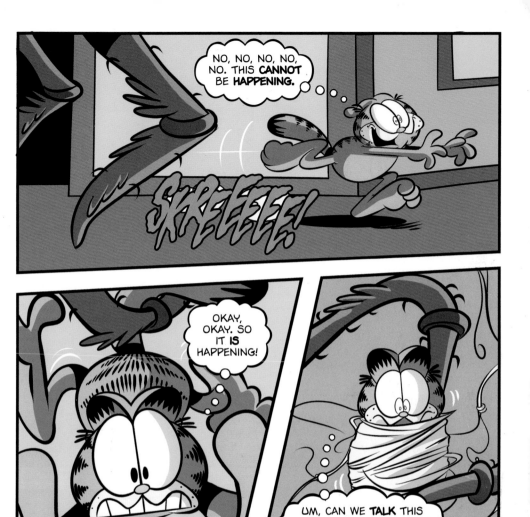

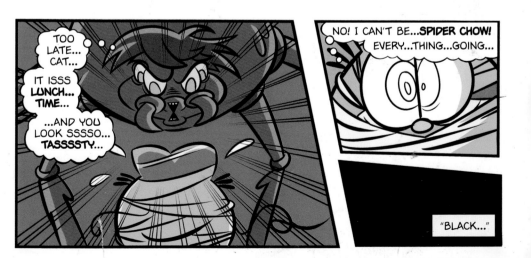

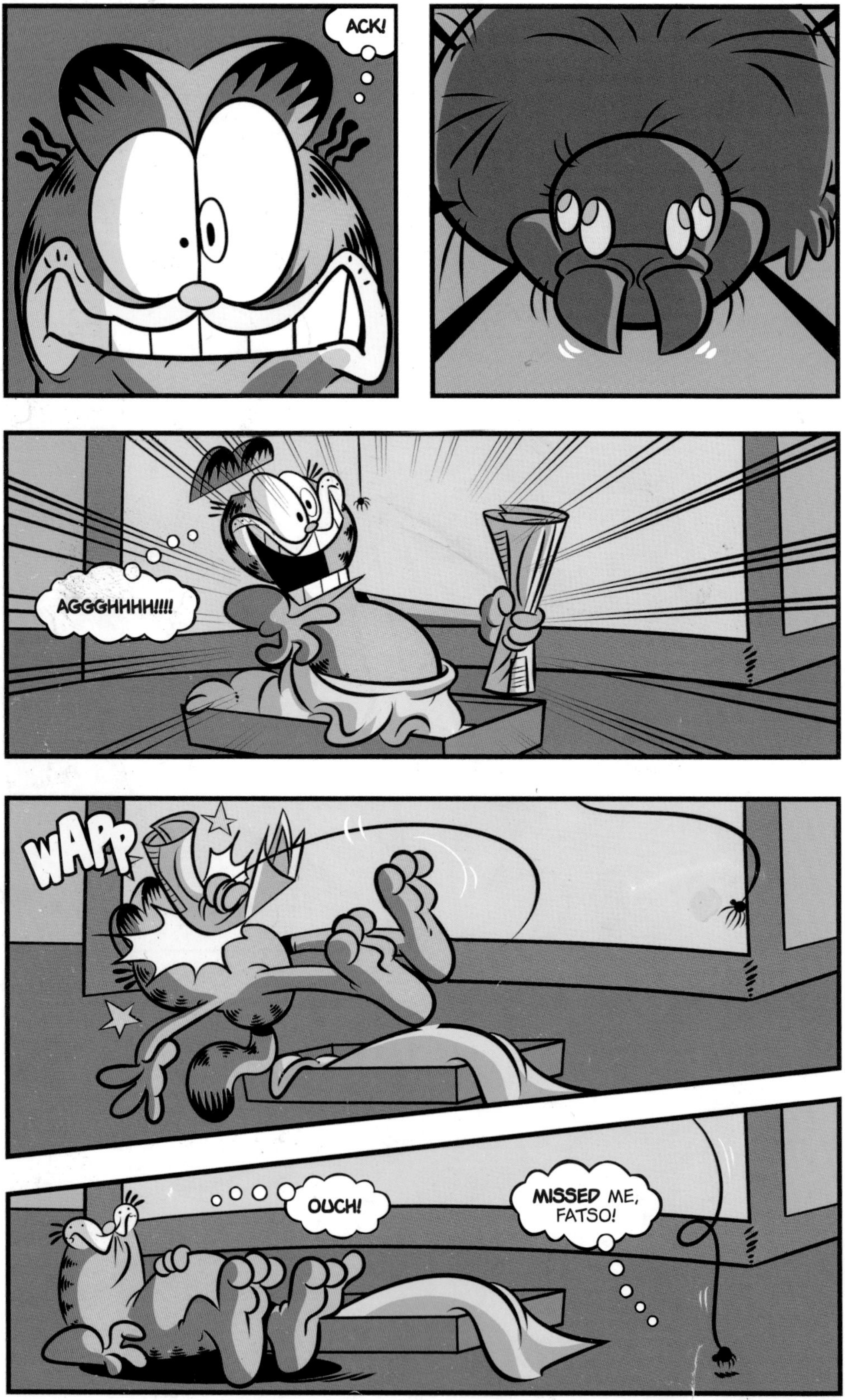
ACK!
AGGGHHHH!!!!
WAPP
OUCH!
MISSED ME, FATSO!

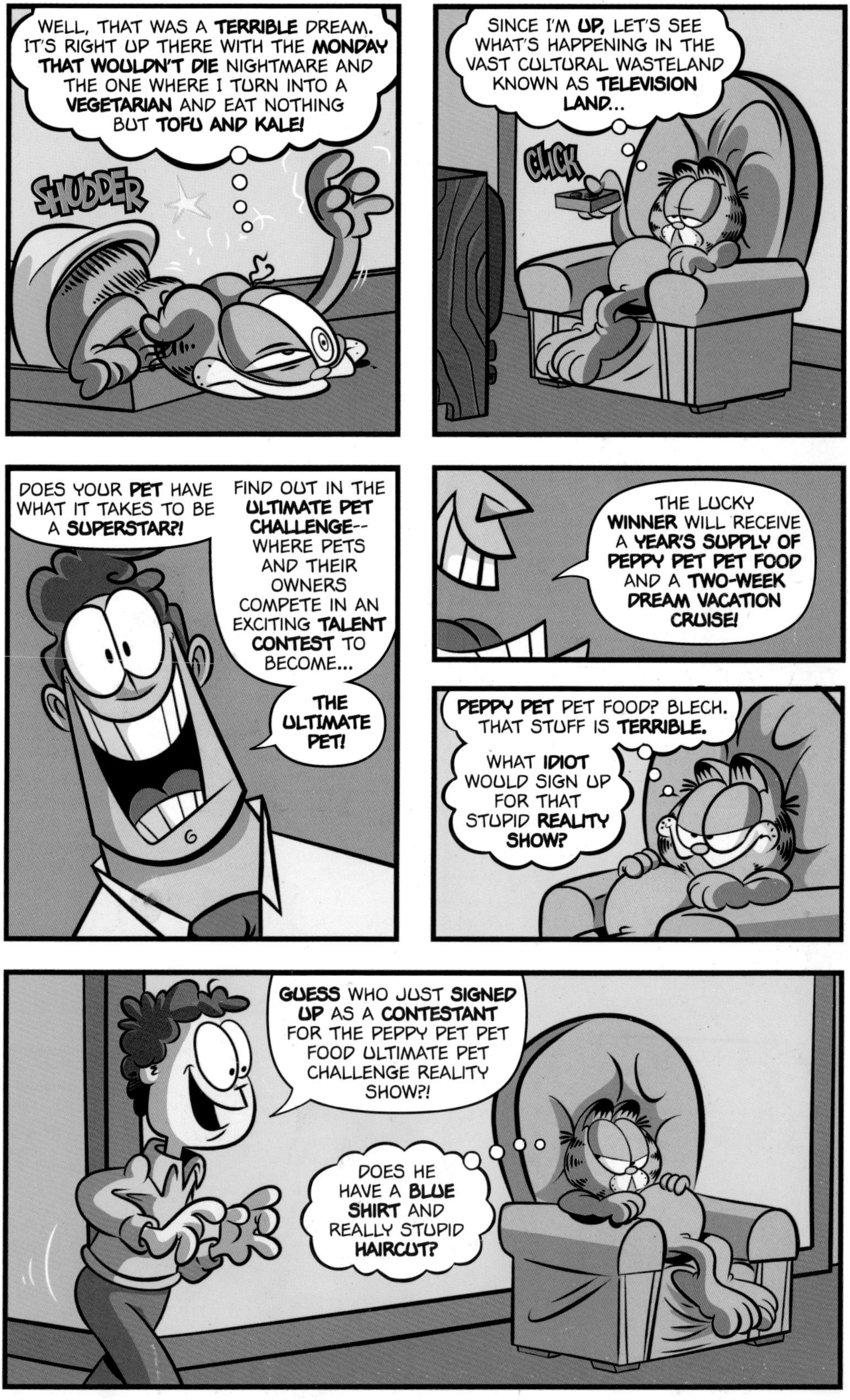

WELL, THAT WAS A TERRIBLE DREAM. IT'S RIGHT UP THERE WITH THE MONDAY THAT WOULDN'T DIE NIGHTMARE AND THE ONE WHERE I TURN INTO A VEGETARIAN AND EAT NOTHING BUT TOFU AND KALE!
SHUDDER
SINCE I'M UP, LET'S SEE WHAT'S HAPPENING IN THE VAST CULTURAL WASTELAND KNOWN AS TELEVISION LAND...
CLICK
DOES YOUR PET HAVE WHAT IT TAKES TO BE A SUPERSTAR?!
FIND OUT IN THE ULTIMATE PET CHALLENGE-- WHERE PETS AND THEIR OWNERS COMPETE IN AN EXCITING TALENT CONTEST TO BECOME...
THE ULTIMATE PET!
THE LUCKY WINNER WILL RECEIVE A YEAR'S SUPPLY OF PEPPY PET PET FOOD AND A TWO-WEEK DREAM VACATION CRUISE!
PEPPY PET PET FOOD? BLECH. THAT STUFF IS TERRIBLE.
WHAT IDIOT WOULD SIGN UP FOR THAT STUPID REALITY SHOW?
GUESS WHO JUST SIGNED UP AS A CONTESTANT FOR THE PEPPY PET PET FOOD ULTIMATE PET CHALLENGE REALITY SHOW?!
DOES HE HAVE A BLUE SHIRT AND REALLY STUPID HAIRCUT?

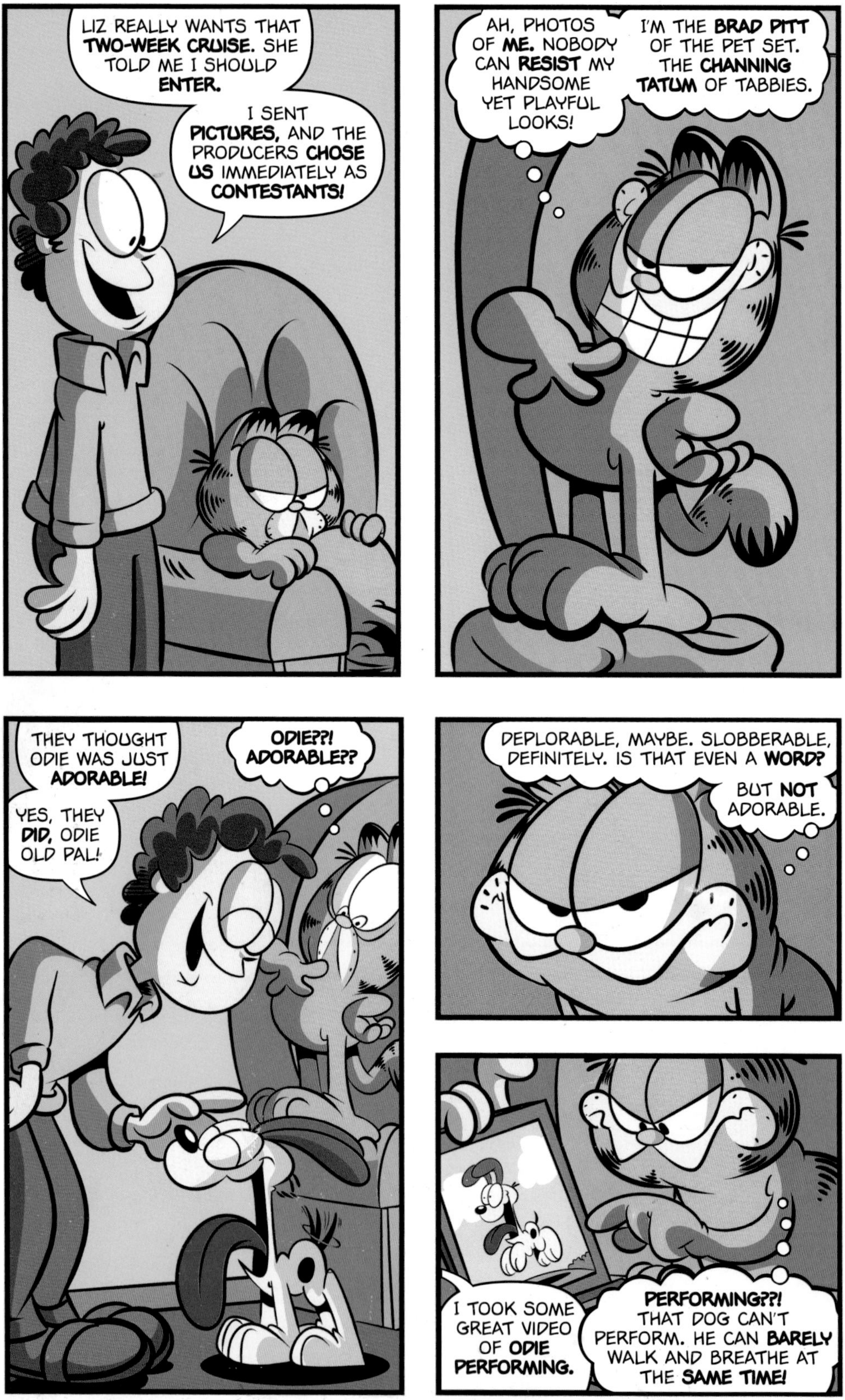
LIZ REALLY WANTS THAT TWO-WEEK CRUISE. SHE TOLD ME I SHOULD ENTER.
I SENT PICTURES, AND THE PRODUCERS CHOSE US IMMEDIATELY AS CONTESTANTS!
AH, PHOTOS OF ME. NOBODY CAN RESIST MY HANDSOME YET PLAYFUL LOOKS!
I'M THE BRAD PITT OF THE PET SET. THE CHANNING TATUM OF TABBIES.
THEY THOUGHT ODIE WAS JUST ADORABLE!
ODIE??! ADORABLE??
YES, THEY DID, ODIE OLD PAL!
DEPLORABLE, MAYBE. SLOBBERABLE, DEFINITELY. IS THAT EVEN A WORD?
BUT NOT ADORABLE.
I TOOK SOME GREAT VIDEO OF ODIE PERFORMING.
PERFORMING??! THAT DOG CAN'T PERFORM. HE CAN BARELY WALK AND BREATHE AT THE SAME TIME!

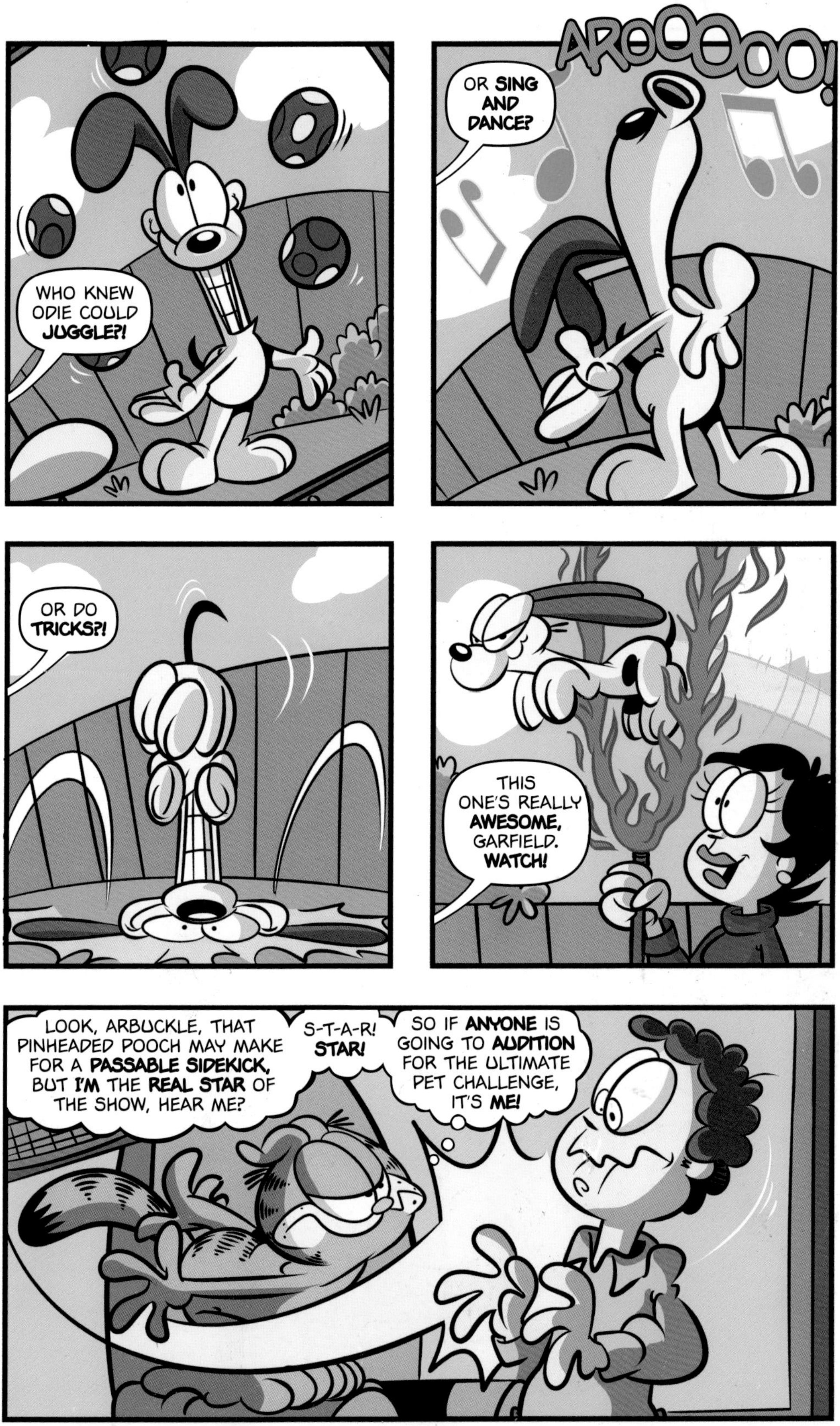
WHO KNEW ODIE COULD JUGGLE?!
OR SING AND DANCE?
AROOOOOO!
OR DO TRICKS?!
THIS ONE'S REALLY AWESOME, GARFIELD. WATCH!
LOOK, ARBUCKLE, THAT PINHEADED POOCH MAY MAKE FOR A PASSABLE SIDEKICK, BUT I'M THE REAL STAR OF THE SHOW, HEAR ME?
S-T-A-R! STAR!
SO IF ANYONE IS GOING TO AUDITION FOR THE ULTIMATE PET CHALLENGE, IT'S ME!

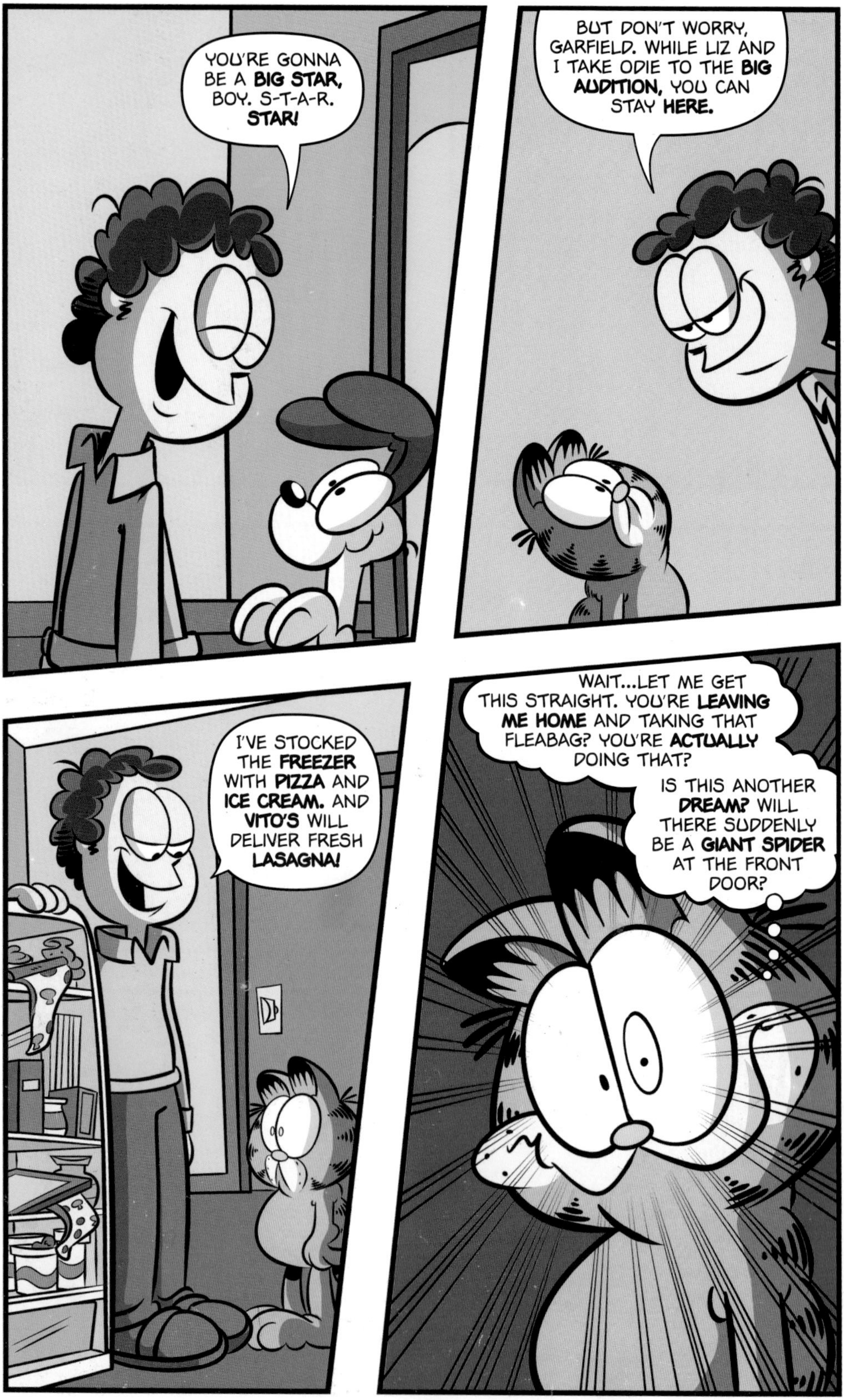
YOU'RE GONNA BE A **BIG STAR,** BOY. S-T-A-R. **STAR!**
BUT DON'T WORRY, GARFIELD. WHILE LIZ AND I TAKE ODIE TO THE **BIG AUDITION,** YOU CAN STAY **HERE.**
I'VE STOCKED THE **FREEZER** WITH **PIZZA** AND **ICE CREAM.** AND **VITO'S** WILL DELIVER FRESH **LASAGNA!**
WAIT...LET ME GET THIS STRAIGHT. YOU'RE **LEAVING ME HOME** AND TAKING THAT FLEABAG? YOU'RE **ACTUALLY** DOING THAT?
IS THIS ANOTHER **DREAM?** WILL THERE SUDDENLY BE A **GIANT SPIDER** AT THE FRONT DOOR?

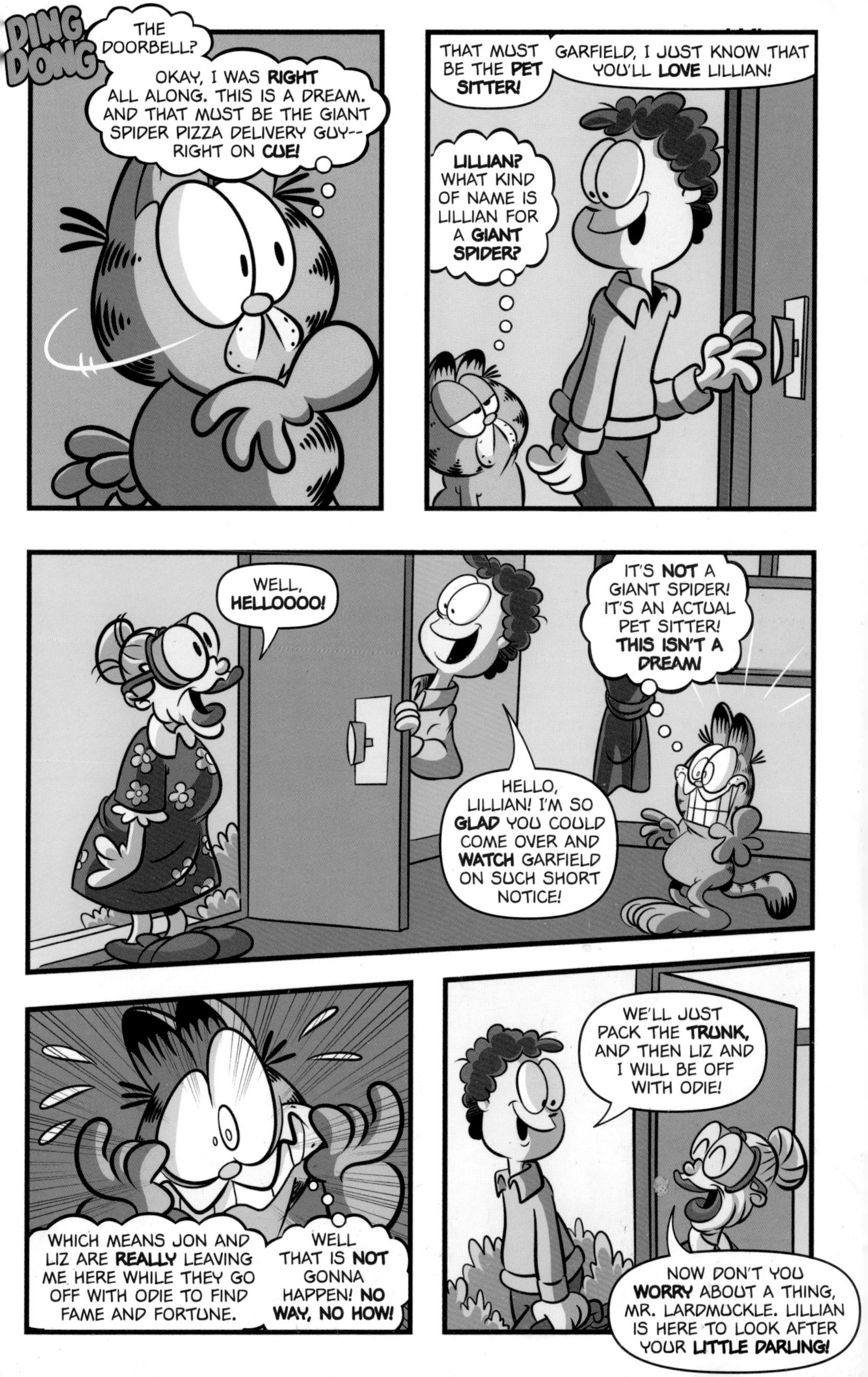
DING DONG
THE DOORBELL?
OKAY, I WAS RIGHT ALL ALONG. THIS IS A DREAM. AND THAT MUST BE THE GIANT SPIDER PIZZA DELIVERY GUY-- RIGHT ON CUE!
THAT MUST BE THE PET SITTER!
GARFIELD, I JUST KNOW THAT YOU'LL LOVE LILLIAN!
LILLIAN? WHAT KIND OF NAME IS LILLIAN FOR A GIANT SPIDER?
WELL, HELLOOOO!
HELLO, LILLIAN! I'M SO GLAD YOU COULD COME OVER AND WATCH GARFIELD ON SUCH SHORT NOTICE!
IT'S NOT A GIANT SPIDER! IT'S AN ACTUAL PET SITTER! THIS ISN'T A DREAM!
WHICH MEANS JON AND LIZ ARE REALLY LEAVING ME HERE WHILE THEY GO OFF WITH ODIE TO FIND FAME AND FORTUNE.
WELL THAT IS NOT GONNA HAPPEN! NO WAY, NO HOW!
WE'LL JUST PACK THE TRUNK, AND THEN LIZ AND I WILL BE OFF WITH ODIE!
NOW DON'T YOU WORRY ABOUT A THING, MR. LARDMUCKLE. LILLIAN IS HERE TO LOOK AFTER YOUR LITTLE DARLING!

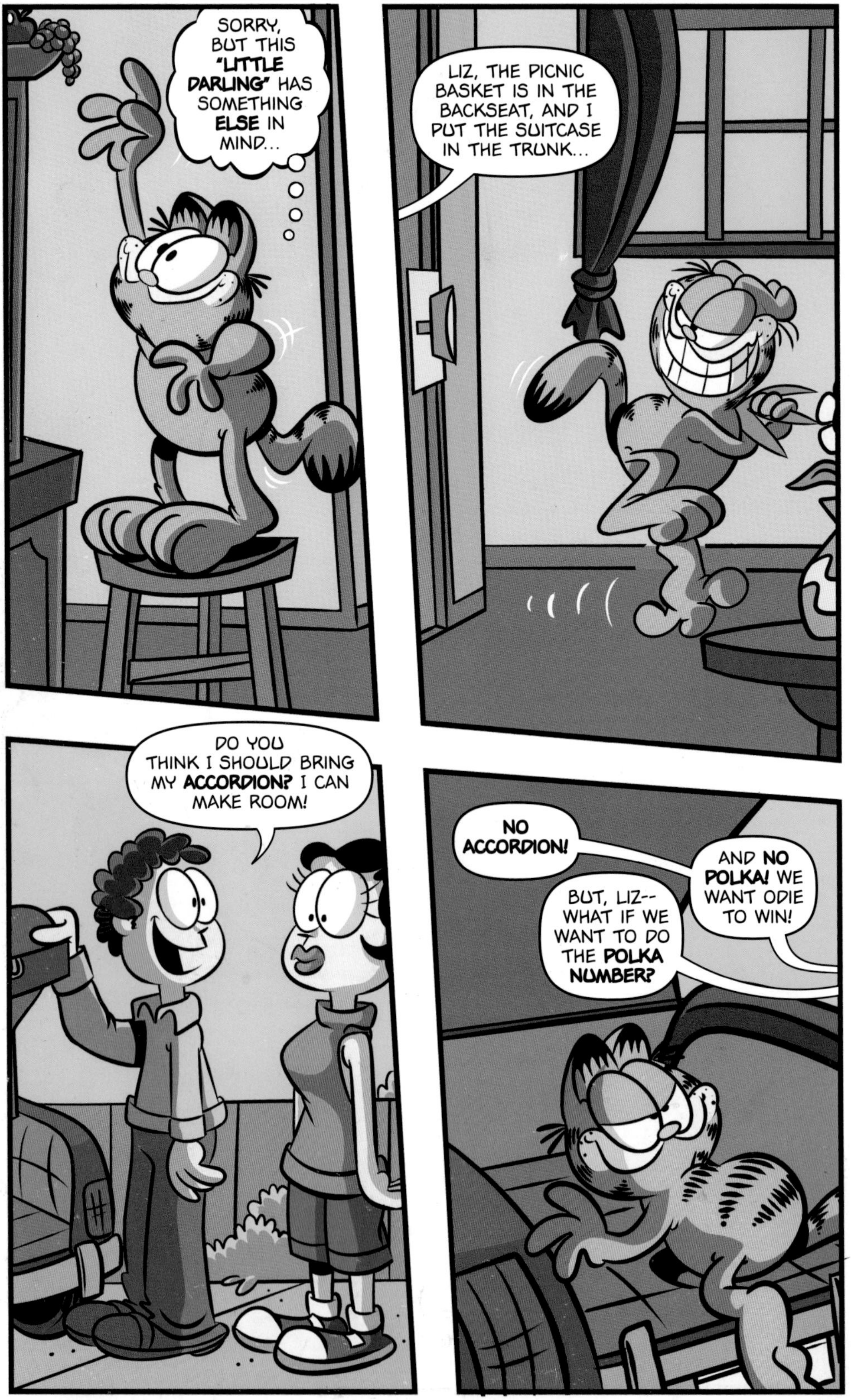
SORRY, BUT THIS "LITTLE DARLING" HAS SOMETHING ELSE IN MIND...
LIZ, THE PICNIC BASKET IS IN THE BACKSEAT, AND I PUT THE SUITCASE IN THE TRUNK...
DO YOU THINK I SHOULD BRING MY ACCORDION? I CAN MAKE ROOM!
NO ACCORDION!
BUT, LIZ-- WHAT IF WE WANT TO DO THE POLKA NUMBER?
AND NO POLKA! WE WANT ODIE TO WIN!

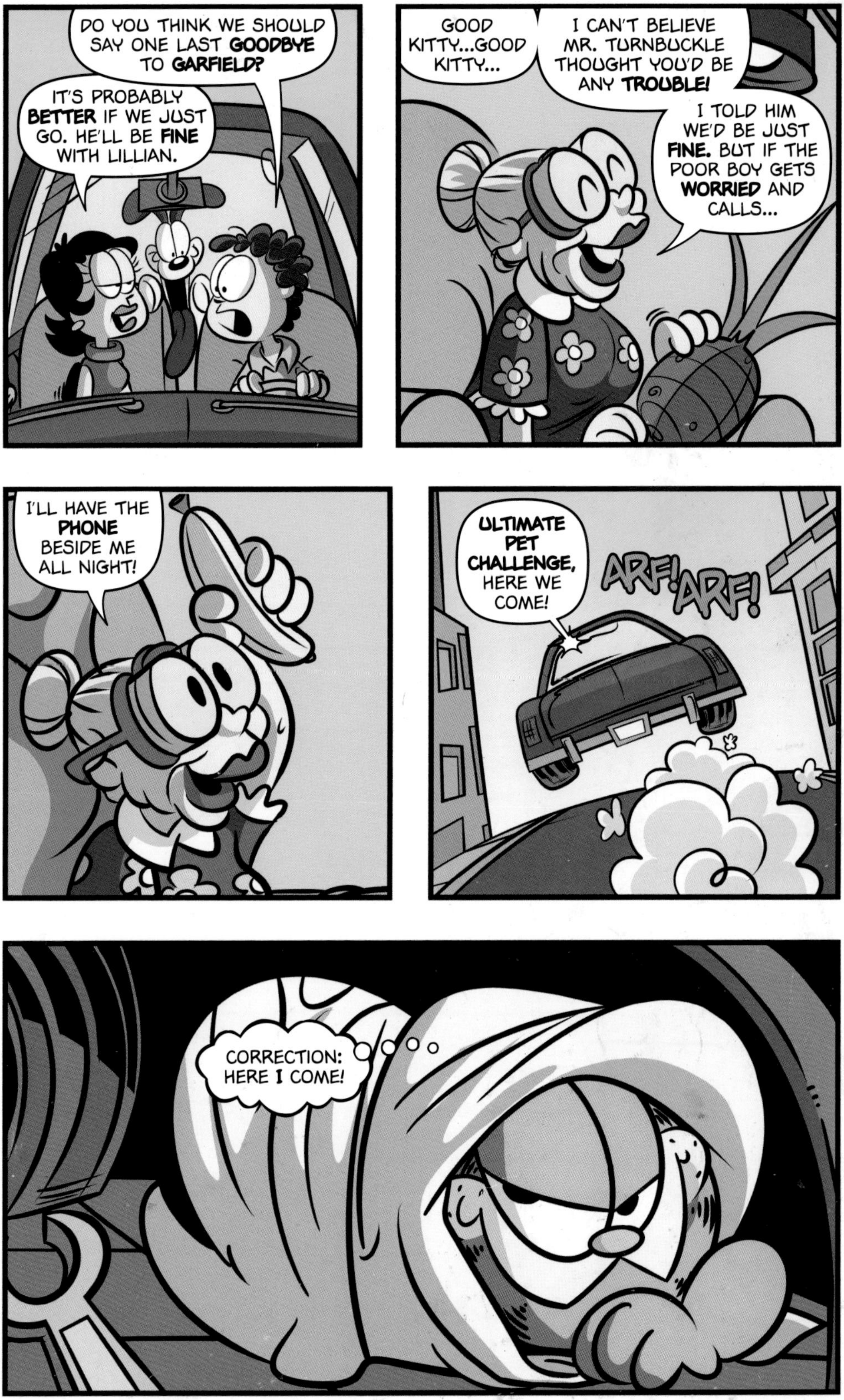
DO YOU THINK WE SHOULD SAY ONE LAST GOODBYE TO GARFIELD?
IT'S PROBABLY BETTER IF WE JUST GO. HE'LL BE FINE WITH LILLIAN.
GOOD KITTY...GOOD KITTY...
I CAN'T BELIEVE MR. TURNBUCKLE THOUGHT YOU'D BE ANY TROUBLE!
I TOLD HIM WE'D BE JUST FINE. BUT IF THE POOR BOY GETS WORRIED AND CALLS...
I'LL HAVE THE PHONE BESIDE ME ALL NIGHT!
ULTIMATE PET CHALLENGE, HERE WE COME!
ARF! ARF!
CORRECTION: HERE I COME!

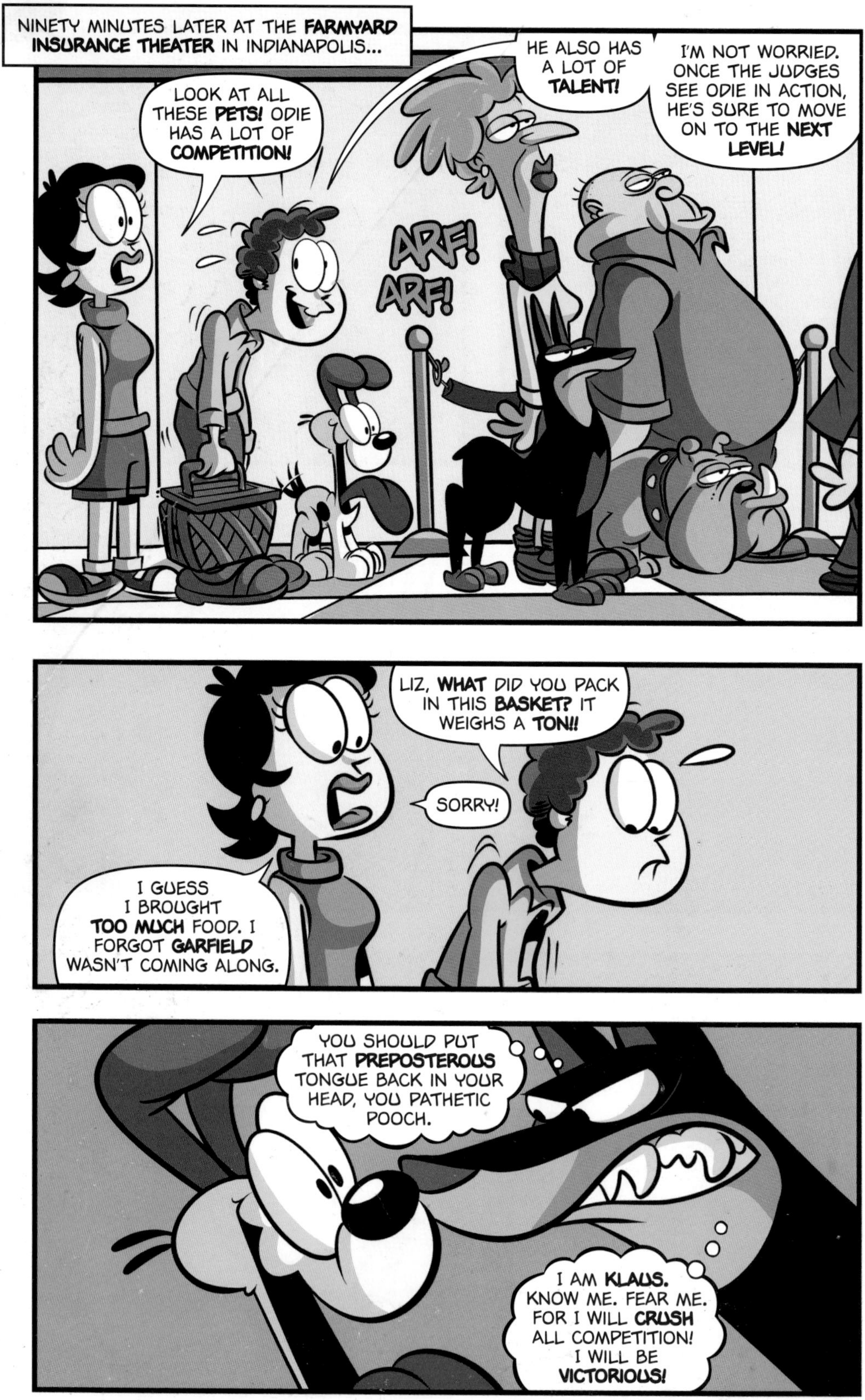
NINETY MINUTES LATER AT THE FARMYARD INSURANCE THEATER IN INDIANAPOLIS...
LOOK AT ALL THESE PETS! ODIE HAS A LOT OF COMPETITION!
HE ALSO HAS A LOT OF TALENT!
I'M NOT WORRIED. ONCE THE JUDGES SEE ODIE IN ACTION, HE'S SURE TO MOVE ON TO THE NEXT LEVEL!
ARF! ARF!
LIZ, WHAT DID YOU PACK IN THIS BASKET? IT WEIGHS A TON!!
SORRY!
I GUESS I BROUGHT TOO MUCH FOOD. I FORGOT GARFIELD WASN'T COMING ALONG.
YOU SHOULD PUT THAT PREPOSTEROUS TONGUE BACK IN YOUR HEAD, YOU PATHETIC POOCH.
I AM KLAUS. KNOW ME. FEAR ME. FOR I WILL CRUSH ALL COMPETITION! I WILL BE VICTORIOUS!

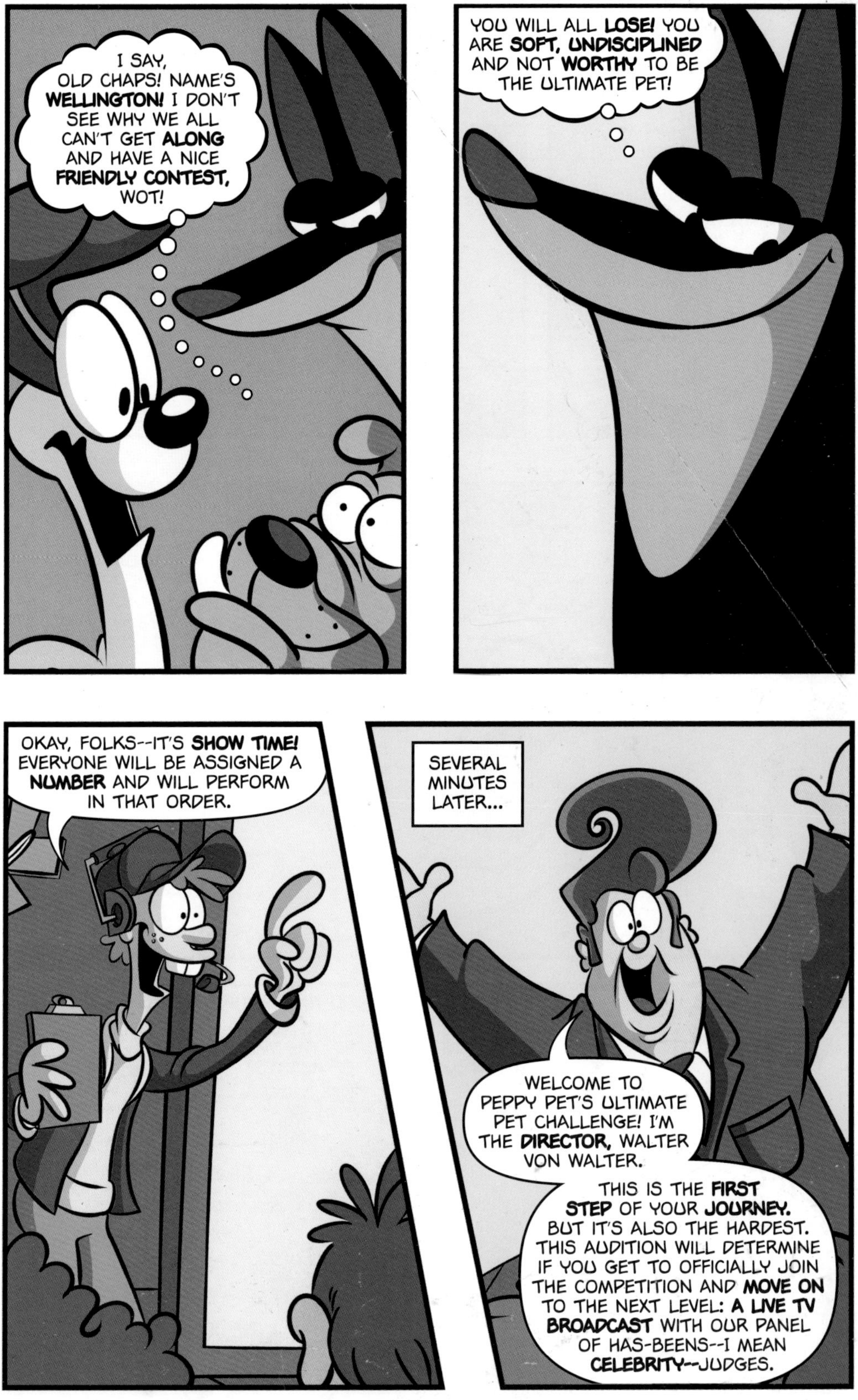
I SAY, OLD CHAPS! NAME'S **WELLINGTON!** I DON'T SEE WHY WE ALL CAN'T GET **ALONG** AND HAVE A NICE **FRIENDLY CONTEST,** WOT!
YOU WILL ALL **LOSE!** YOU ARE **SOFT, UNDISCIPLINED** AND NOT **WORTHY** TO BE THE ULTIMATE PET!
OKAY, FOLKS--IT'S **SHOW TIME!** EVERYONE WILL BE ASSIGNED A **NUMBER** AND WILL PERFORM IN THAT ORDER.
SEVERAL MINUTES LATER...
WELCOME TO PEPPY PET'S ULTIMATE PET CHALLENGE! I'M THE **DIRECTOR,** WALTER VON WALTER.
THIS IS THE **FIRST STEP** OF YOUR **JOURNEY.** BUT IT'S ALSO THE HARDEST. THIS AUDITION WILL DETERMINE IF YOU GET TO OFFICIALLY JOIN THE COMPETITION AND **MOVE ON** TO THE NEXT LEVEL: **A LIVE TV BROADCAST** WITH OUR PANEL OF HAS-BEENS--I MEAN **CELEBRITY**--JUDGES.

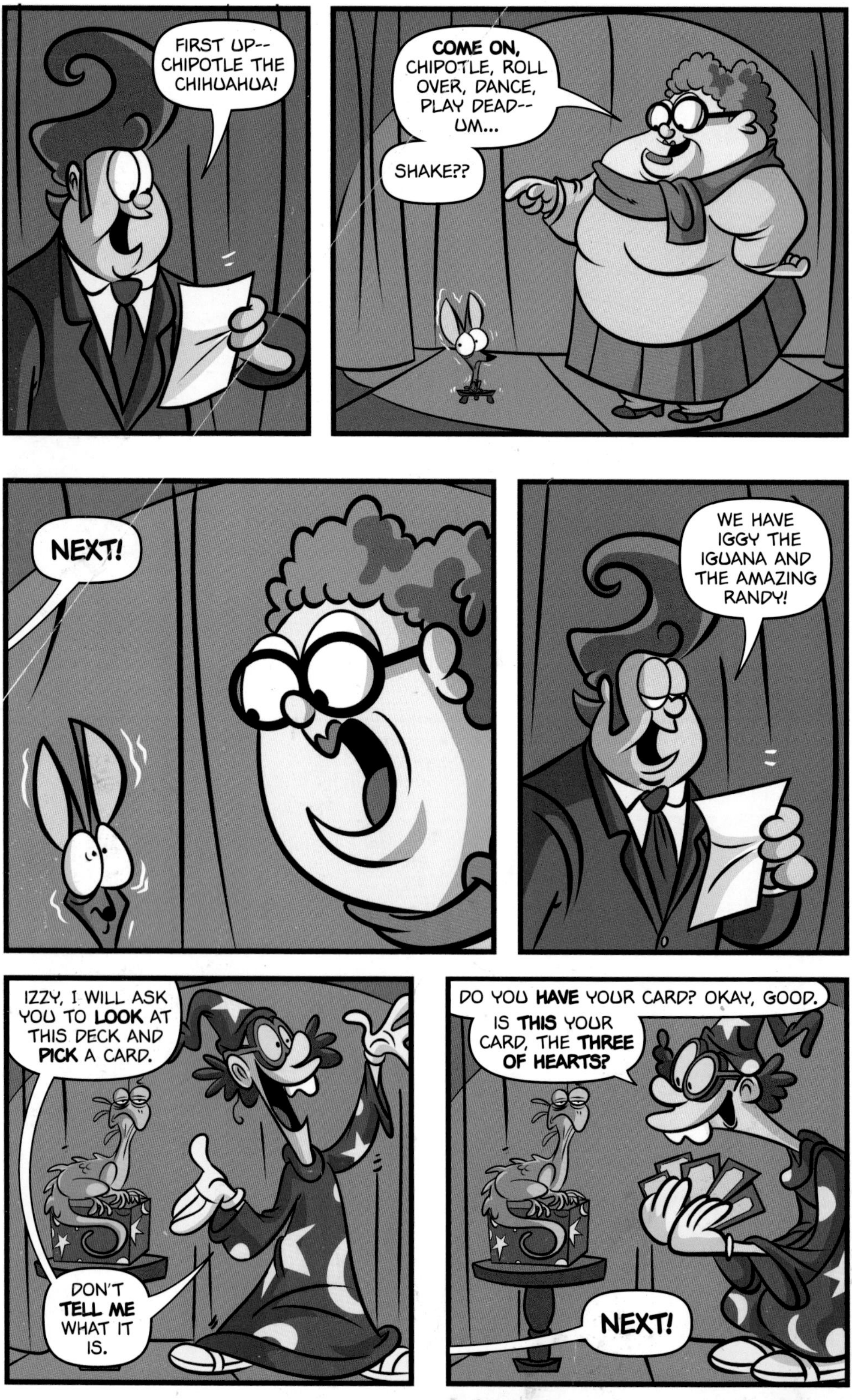
FIRST UP--
CHIPOTLE THE CHIHUAHUA!
COME ON, CHIPOTLE, ROLL OVER, DANCE, PLAY DEAD-- UM...
SHAKE??
NEXT!
WE HAVE IGGY THE IGUANA AND THE AMAZING RANDY!
IZZY, I WILL ASK YOU TO LOOK AT THIS DECK AND PICK A CARD.
DON'T TELL ME WHAT IT IS.
DO YOU HAVE YOUR CARD? OKAY, GOOD.
IS THIS YOUR CARD, THE THREE OF HEARTS?
NEXT!

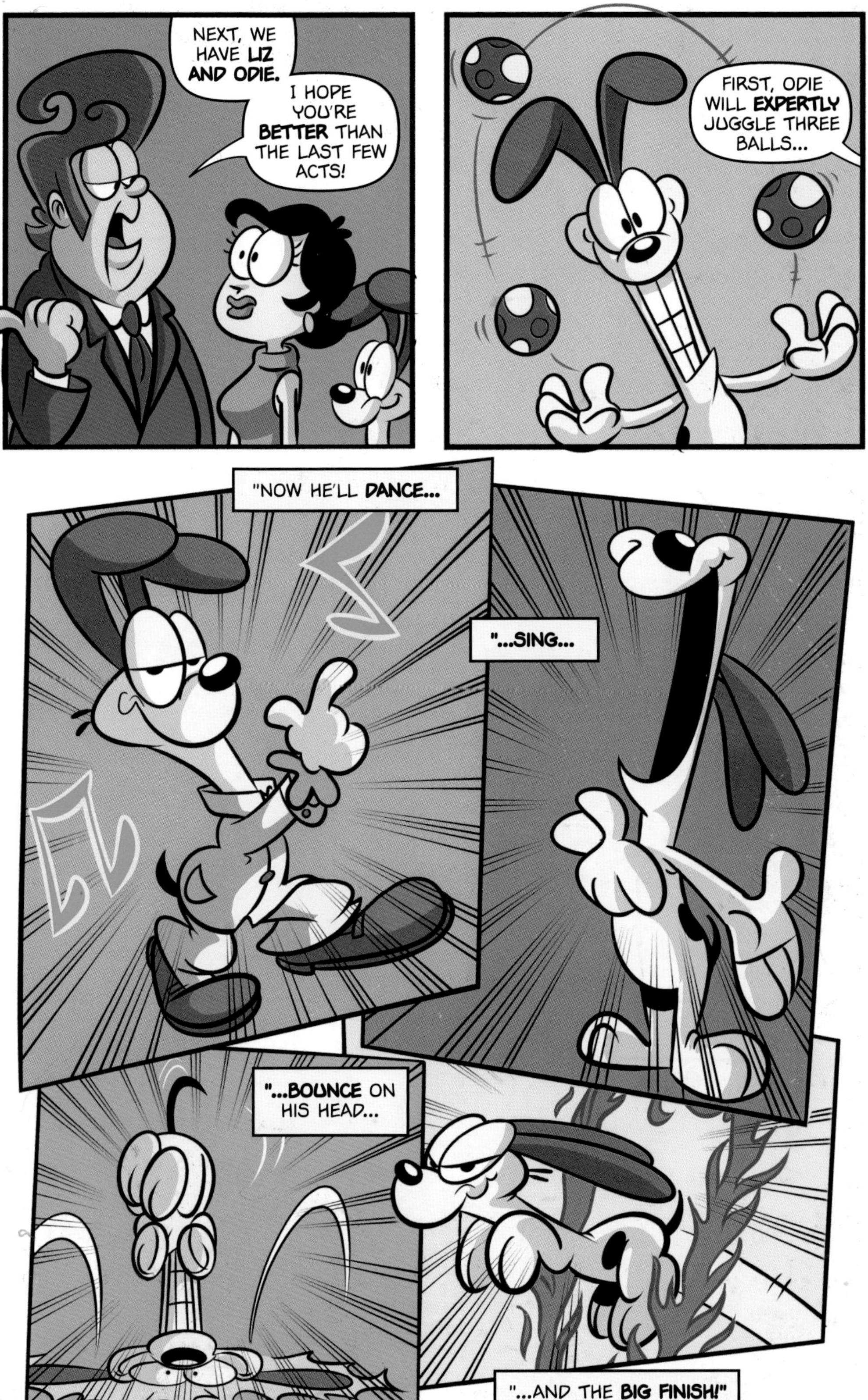
NEXT, WE HAVE LIZ AND ODIE.
I HOPE YOU'RE BETTER THAN THE LAST FEW ACTS!
FIRST, ODIE WILL EXPERTLY JUGGLE THREE BALLS...
"NOW HE'LL DANCE...
"...SING...
"...BOUNCE ON HIS HEAD...
"...AND THE BIG FINISH!"

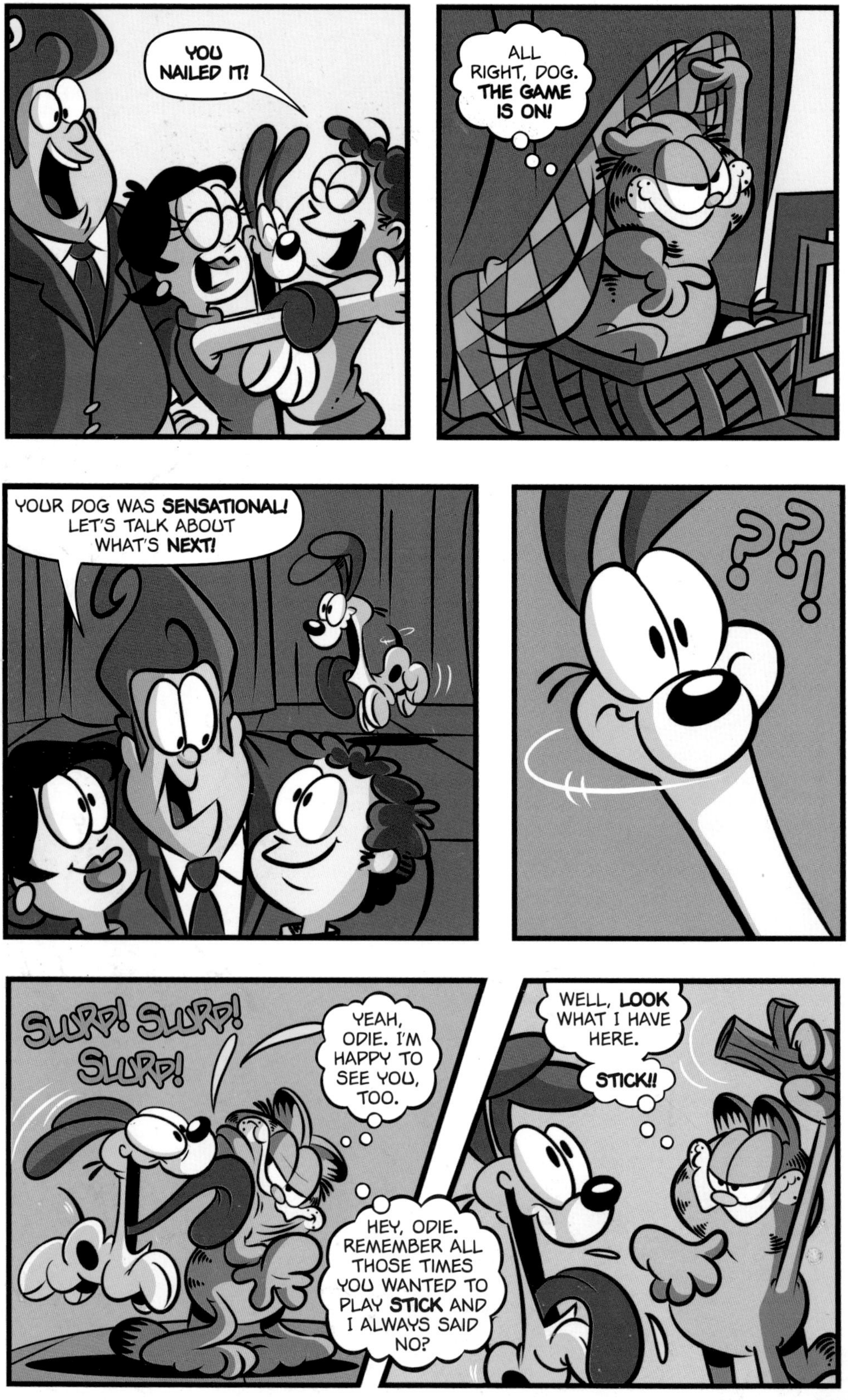
YOU NAILED IT!
ALL RIGHT, DOG. THE GAME IS ON!
YOUR DOG WAS SENSATIONAL! LET'S TALK ABOUT WHAT'S NEXT!
??!
SLURP! SLURP! SLURP!
YEAH, ODIE. I'M HAPPY TO SEE YOU, TOO.
HEY, ODIE. REMEMBER ALL THOSE TIMES YOU WANTED TO PLAY STICK AND I ALWAYS SAID NO?
WELL, LOOK WHAT I HAVE HERE.
STICK!!

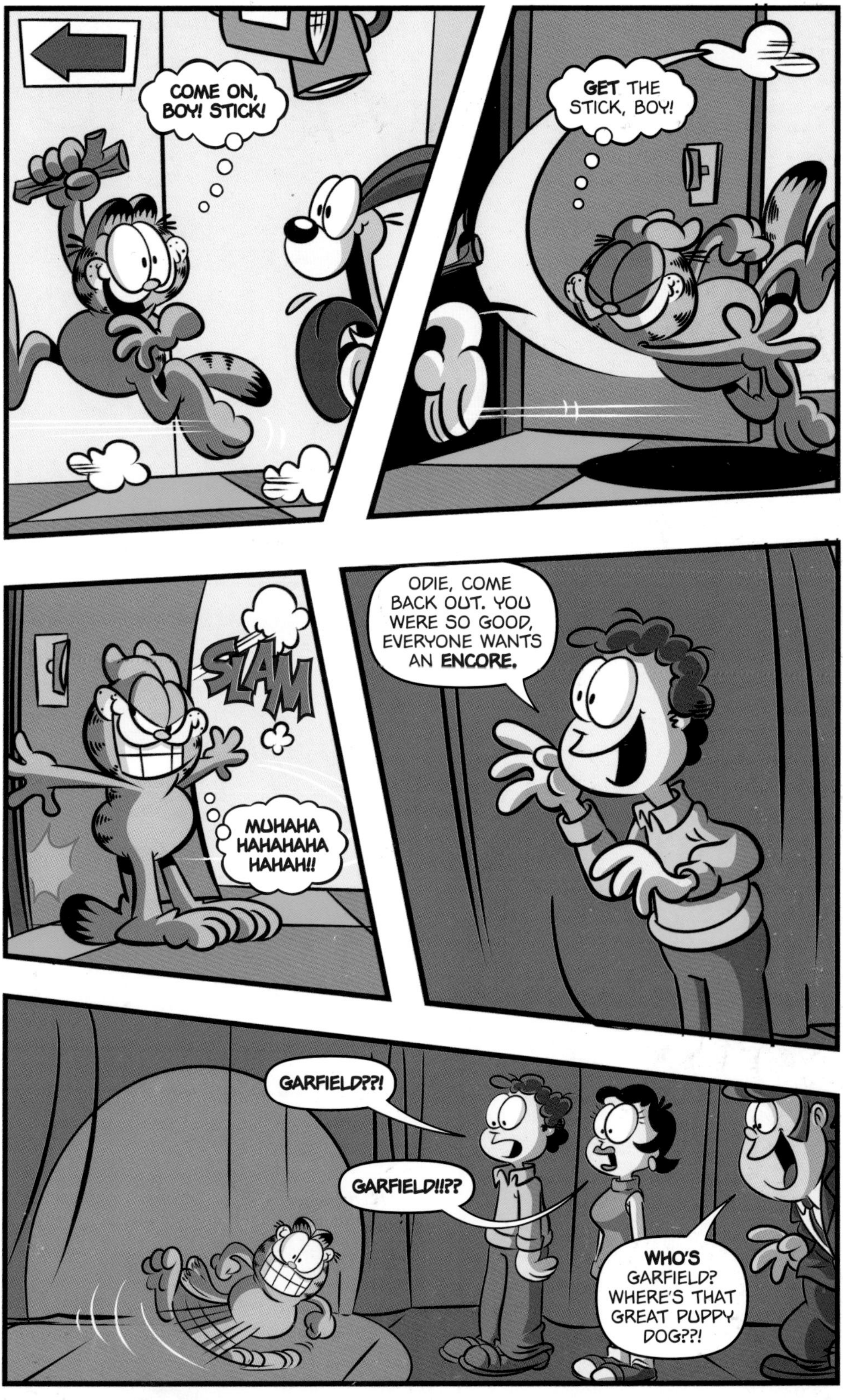
COME ON, BOY! STICK!
GET THE STICK, BOY!
SLAM
MUHAHA HAHAHAHA HAHAH!!
ODIE, COME BACK OUT. YOU WERE SO GOOD, EVERYONE WANTS AN ENCORE.
GARFIELD??!
GARFIELD!!??
WHO'S GARFIELD? WHERE'S THAT GREAT PUPPY DOG??!

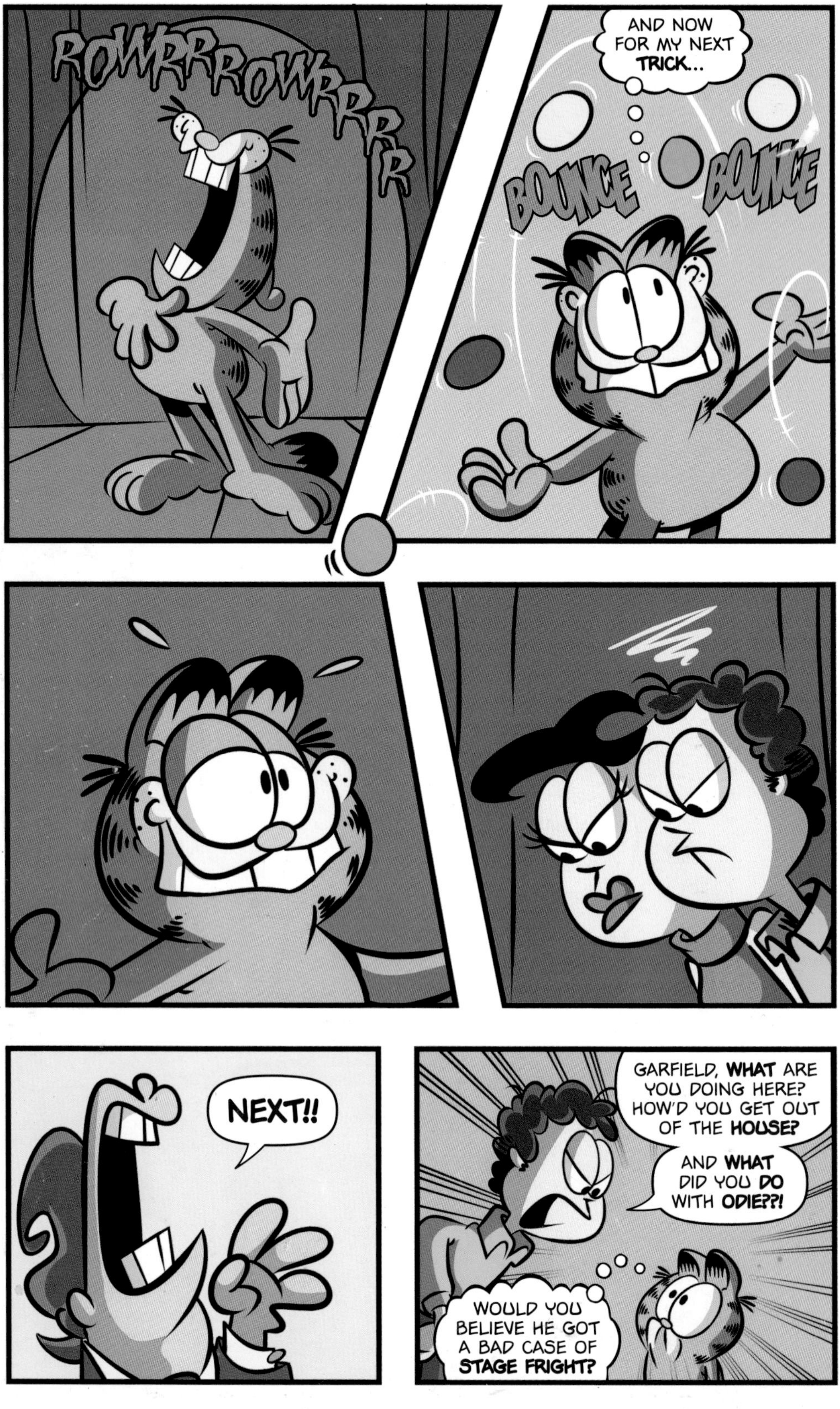
ROWRRROWRRRRR
AND NOW FOR MY NEXT TRICK...
BOUNCE
BOUNCE
NEXT!!
GARFIELD, WHAT ARE YOU DOING HERE? HOW'D YOU GET OUT OF THE HOUSE?
AND WHAT DID YOU DO WITH ODIE??!
WOULD YOU BELIEVE HE GOT A BAD CASE OF STAGE FRIGHT?

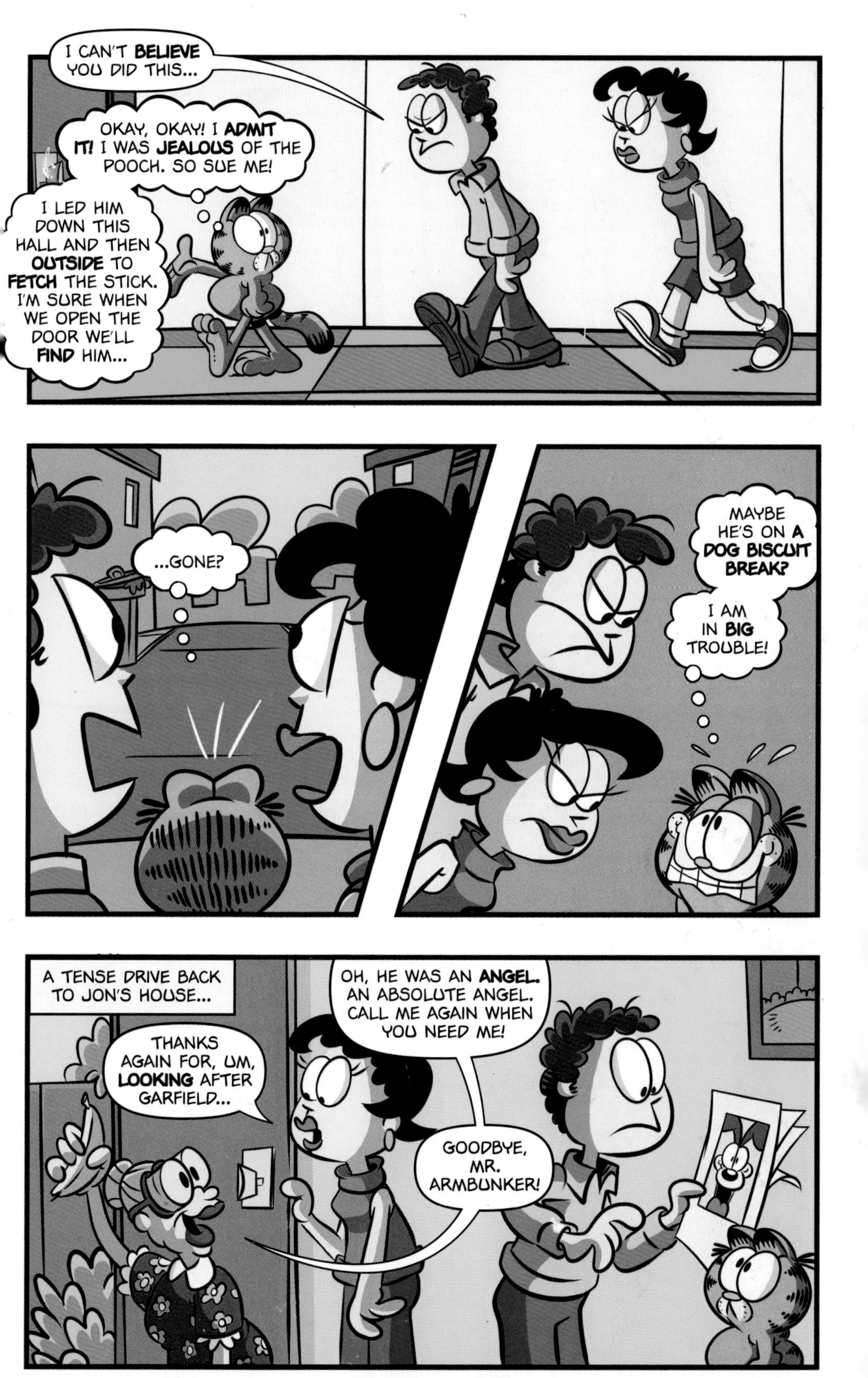
I CAN'T **BELIEVE** YOU DID THIS...
OKAY, OKAY! I **ADMIT IT!** I WAS **JEALOUS** OF THE POOCH. SO SUE ME!
I LED HIM DOWN THIS HALL AND THEN **OUTSIDE** TO **FETCH** THE STICK. I'M SURE WHEN WE OPEN THE DOOR WE'LL **FIND** HIM...
...GONE?
MAYBE HE'S ON **A DOG BISCUIT BREAK?**
I AM IN **BIG** TROUBLE!
A TENSE DRIVE BACK TO JON'S HOUSE...
THANKS AGAIN FOR, UM, **LOOKING** AFTER GARFIELD...
OH, HE WAS AN **ANGEL.** AN ABSOLUTE ANGEL. CALL ME AGAIN WHEN YOU NEED ME!
GOODBYE, MR. ARMBUNKER!

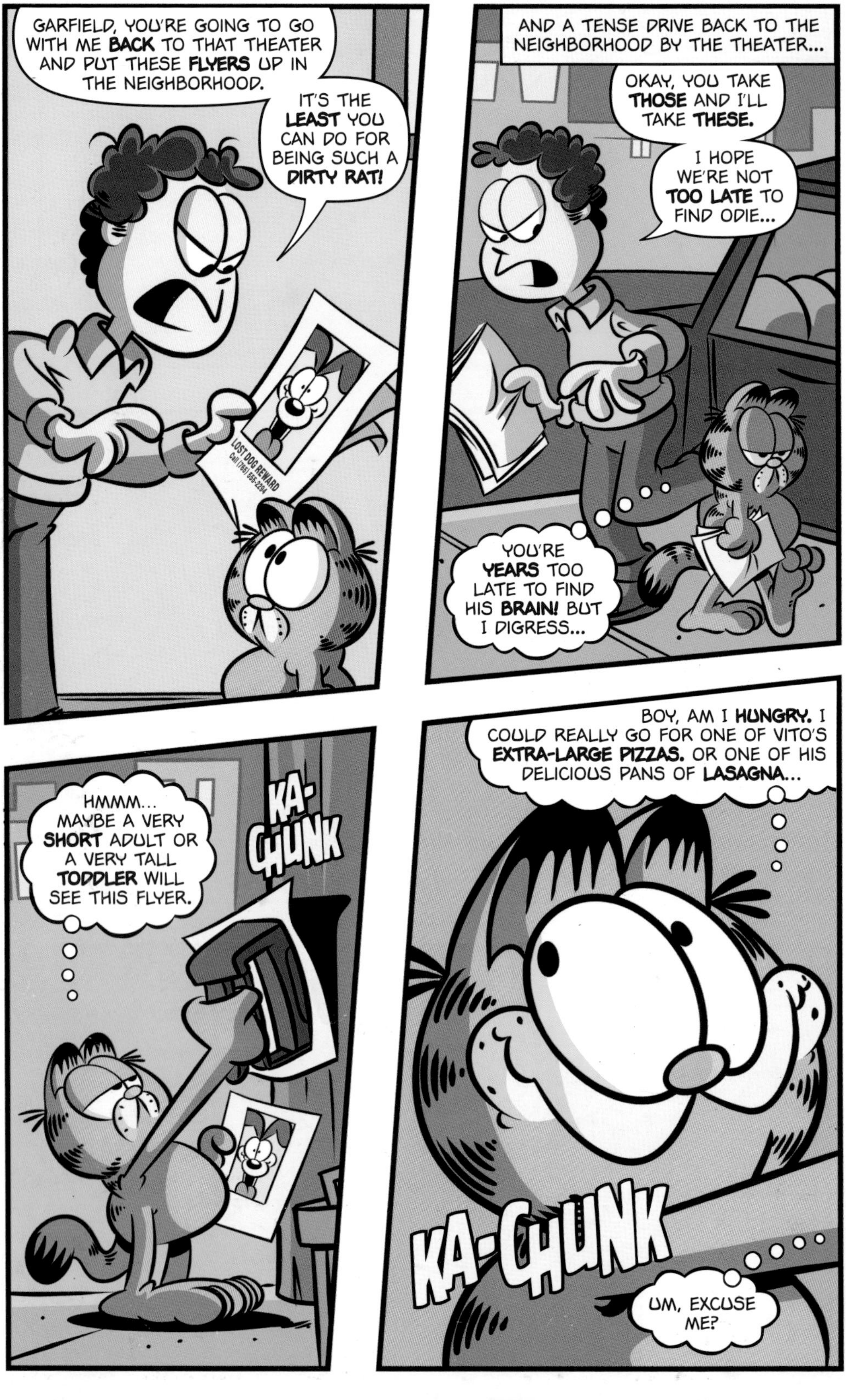

GARFIELD, YOU'RE GOING TO GO WITH ME BACK TO THAT THEATER AND PUT THESE FLYERS UP IN THE NEIGHBORHOOD.
IT'S THE LEAST YOU CAN DO FOR BEING SUCH A DIRTY RAT!
LOST DOG REWARD
Call (765) 555-2294
AND A TENSE DRIVE BACK TO THE NEIGHBORHOOD BY THE THEATER...
OKAY, YOU TAKE THOSE AND I'LL TAKE THESE.
I HOPE WE'RE NOT TOO LATE TO FIND ODIE...
YOU'RE YEARS TOO LATE TO FIND HIS BRAIN! BUT I DIGRESS...
HMMM... MAYBE A VERY SHORT ADULT OR A VERY TALL TODDLER WILL SEE THIS FLYER.
KA-CHUNK
BOY, AM I HUNGRY. I COULD REALLY GO FOR ONE OF VITO'S EXTRA-LARGE PIZZAS. OR ONE OF HIS DELICIOUS PANS OF LASAGNA...
KA-CHUNK
UM, EXCUSE ME?

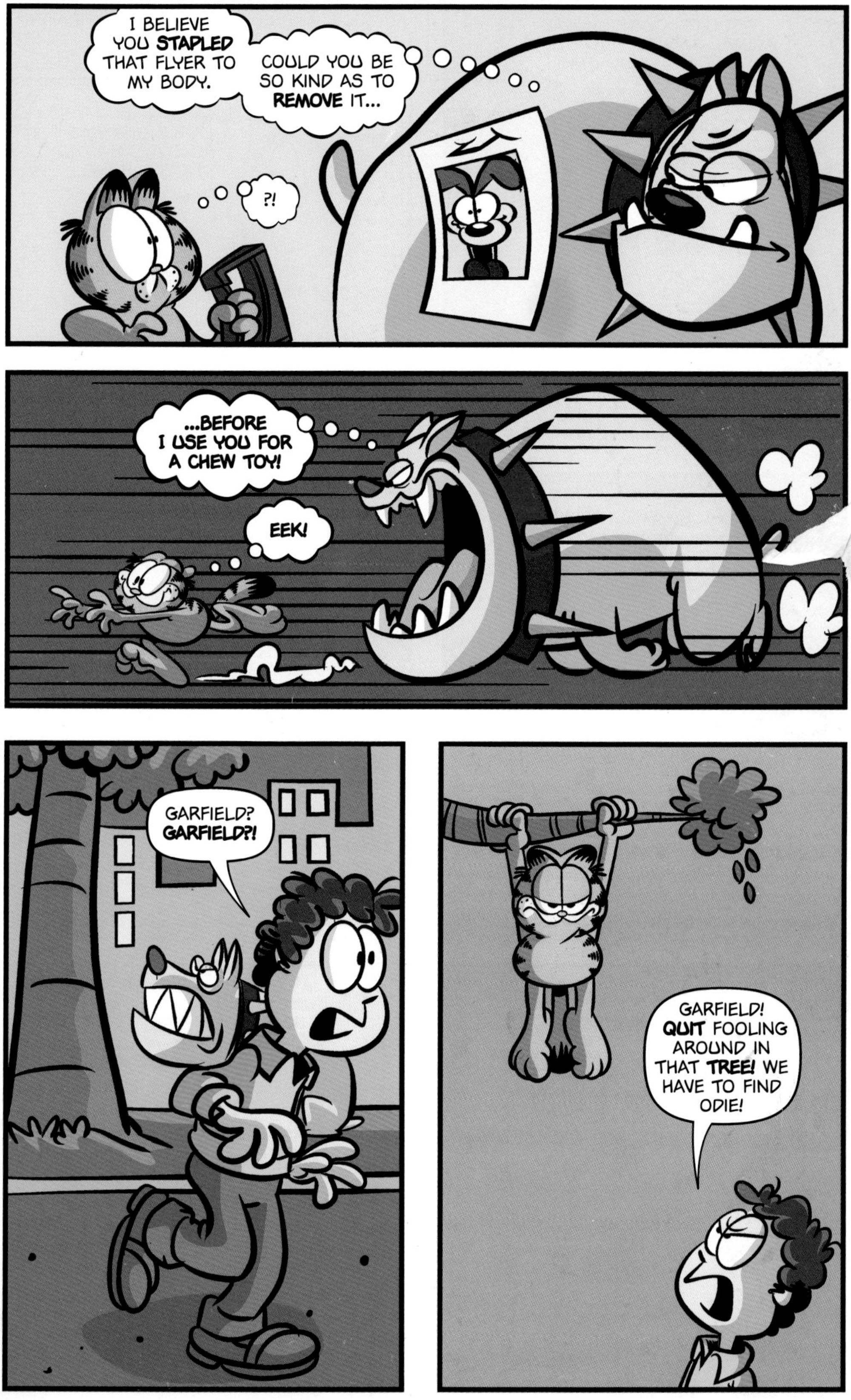
I BELIEVE YOU STAPLED THAT FLYER TO MY BODY.
COULD YOU BE SO KIND AS TO REMOVE IT...
?!
...BEFORE I USE YOU FOR A CHEW TOY!
EEK!
GARFIELD? GARFIELD?!
GARFIELD! QUIT FOOLING AROUND IN THAT TREE! WE HAVE TO FIND ODIE!

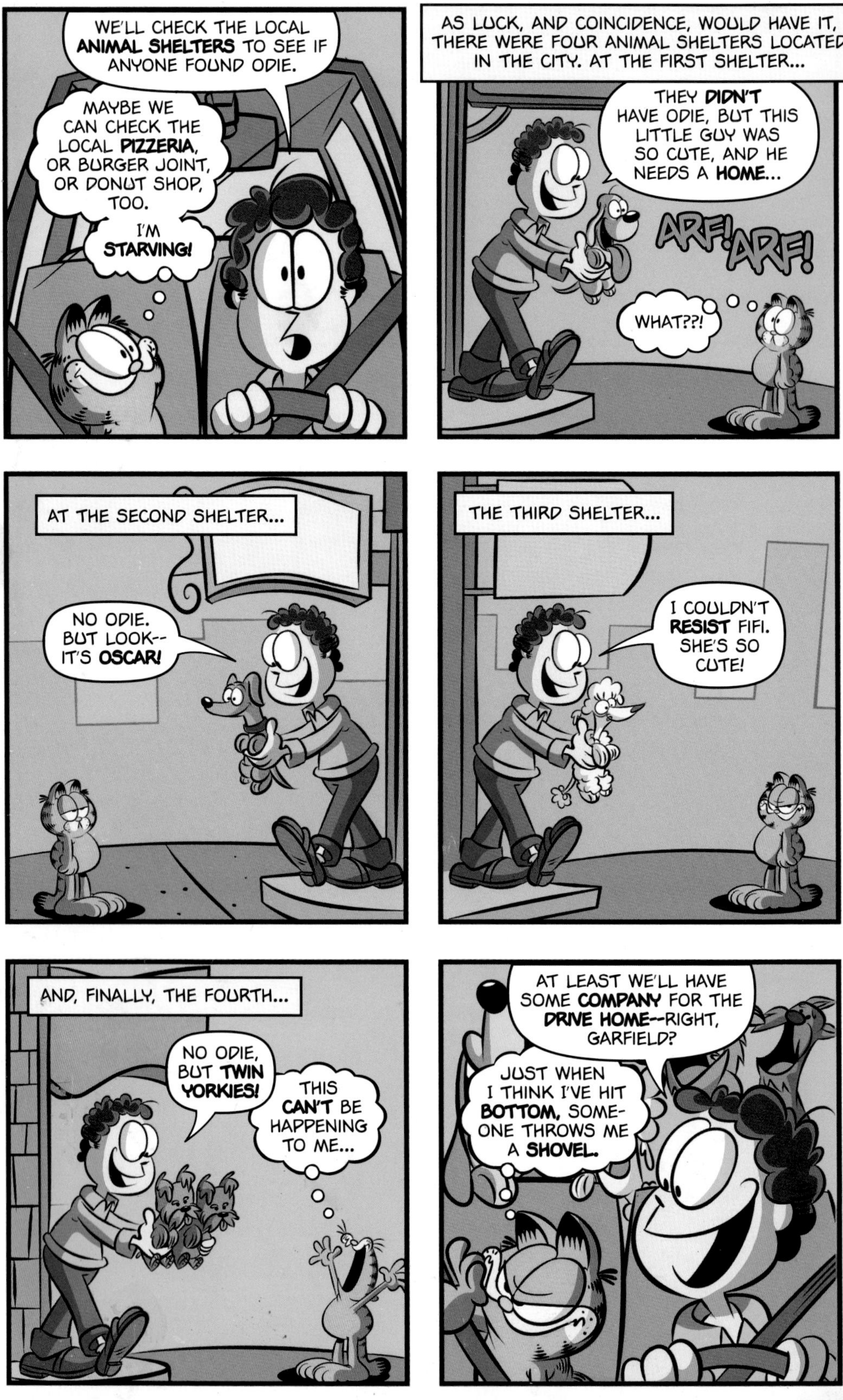
WE'LL CHECK THE LOCAL ANIMAL SHELTERS TO SEE IF ANYONE FOUND ODIE.
MAYBE WE CAN CHECK THE LOCAL PIZZERIA, OR BURGER JOINT, OR DONUT SHOP, TOO.
I'M STARVING!
AS LUCK, AND COINCIDENCE, WOULD HAVE IT, THERE WERE FOUR ANIMAL SHELTERS LOCATED IN THE CITY. AT THE FIRST SHELTER...
THEY DIDN'T HAVE ODIE, BUT THIS LITTLE GUY WAS SO CUTE, AND HE NEEDS A HOME...
ARF! ARF!
WHAT??!
AT THE SECOND SHELTER...
NO ODIE. BUT LOOK-- IT'S OSCAR!
THE THIRD SHELTER...
I COULDN'T RESIST FIFI. SHE'S SO CUTE!
AND, FINALLY, THE FOURTH...
NO ODIE, BUT TWIN YORKIES!
THIS CAN'T BE HAPPENING TO ME...
AT LEAST WE'LL HAVE SOME COMPANY FOR THE DRIVE HOME--RIGHT, GARFIELD?
JUST WHEN I THINK I'VE HIT BOTTOM, SOME-ONE THROWS ME A SHOVEL.

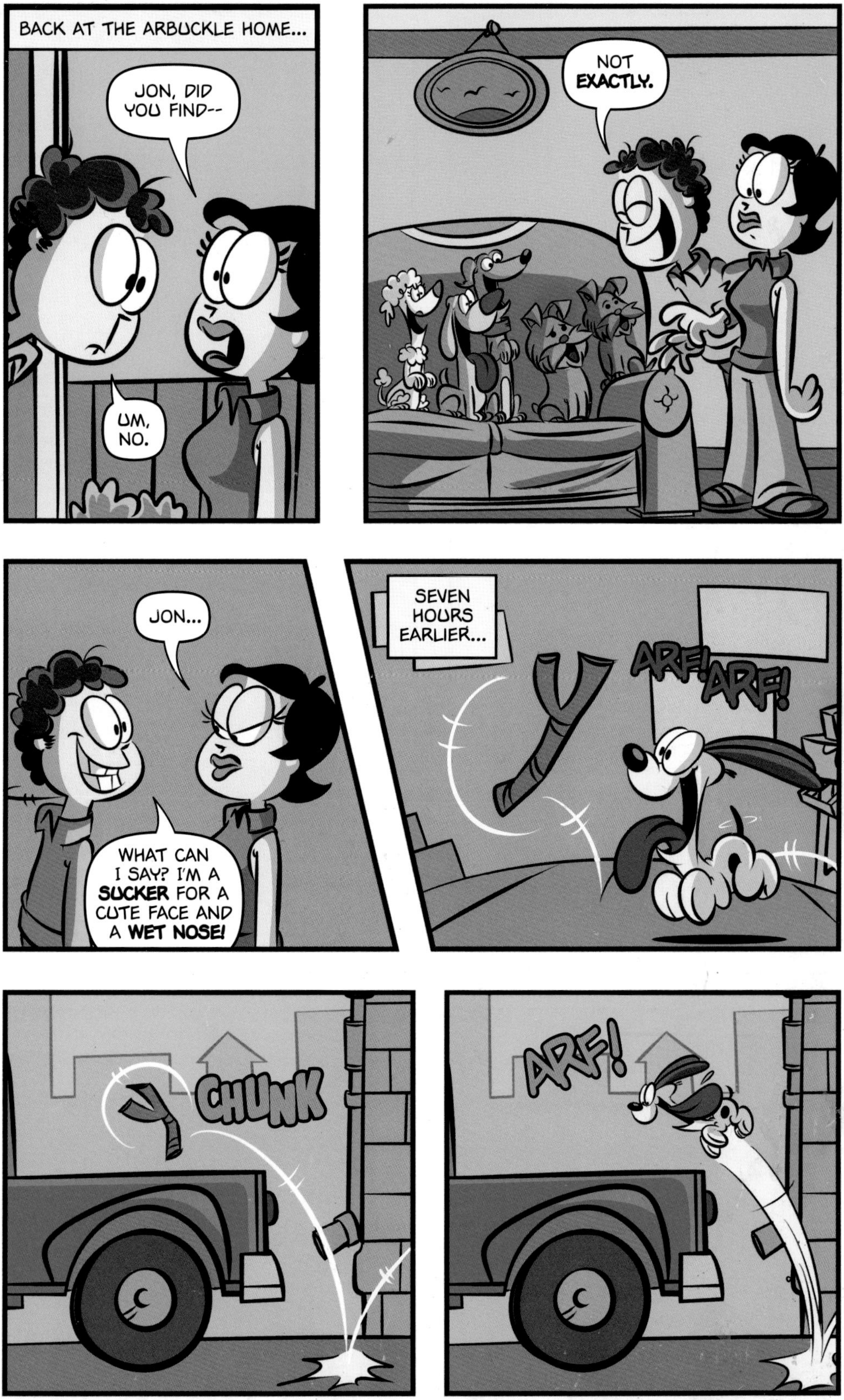
BACK AT THE ARBUCKLE HOME...
JON, DID YOU FIND--
UM, NO.
NOT **EXACTLY.**
JON...
WHAT CAN I SAY? I'M A **SUCKER** FOR A CUTE FACE AND A **WET NOSE!**
SEVEN HOURS EARLIER...
ARF! ARF!
CHUNK
ARF!

VRO'OM

HEY!

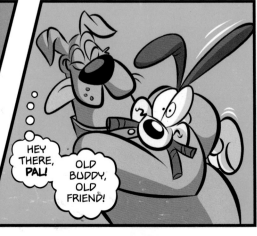

HEY THERE, PAL!

OLD BUDDY, OLD FRIEND!

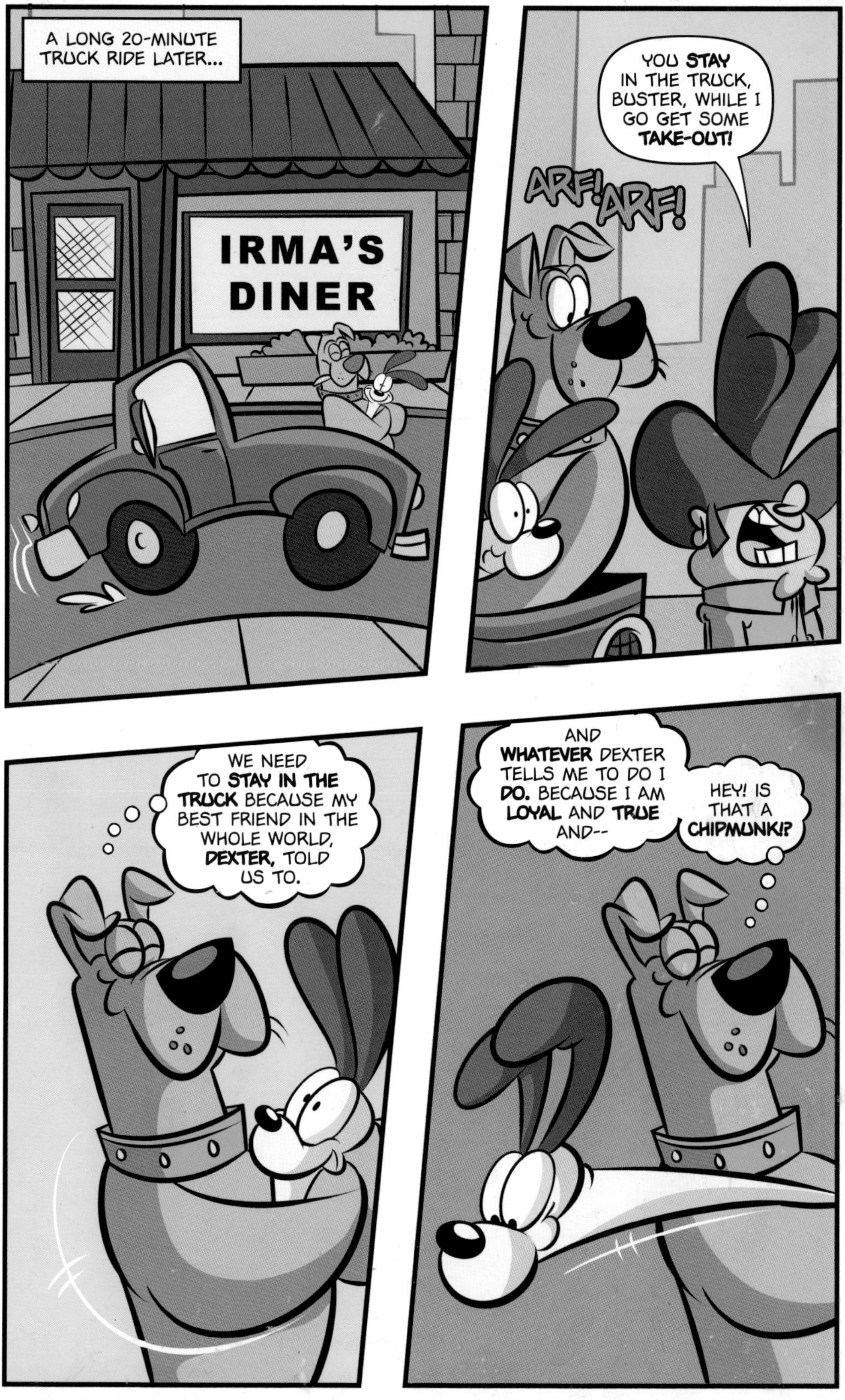
A LONG 20-MINUTE TRUCK RIDE LATER...
IRMA'S DINER
YOU STAY IN THE TRUCK, BUSTER, WHILE I GO GET SOME TAKE-OUT!
ARF! ARF!
WE NEED TO STAY IN THE TRUCK BECAUSE MY BEST FRIEND IN THE WHOLE WORLD, DEXTER, TOLD US TO.
AND WHATEVER DEXTER TELLS ME TO DO I DO. BECAUSE I AM LOYAL AND TRUE AND--
HEY! IS THAT A CHIPMUNK!?

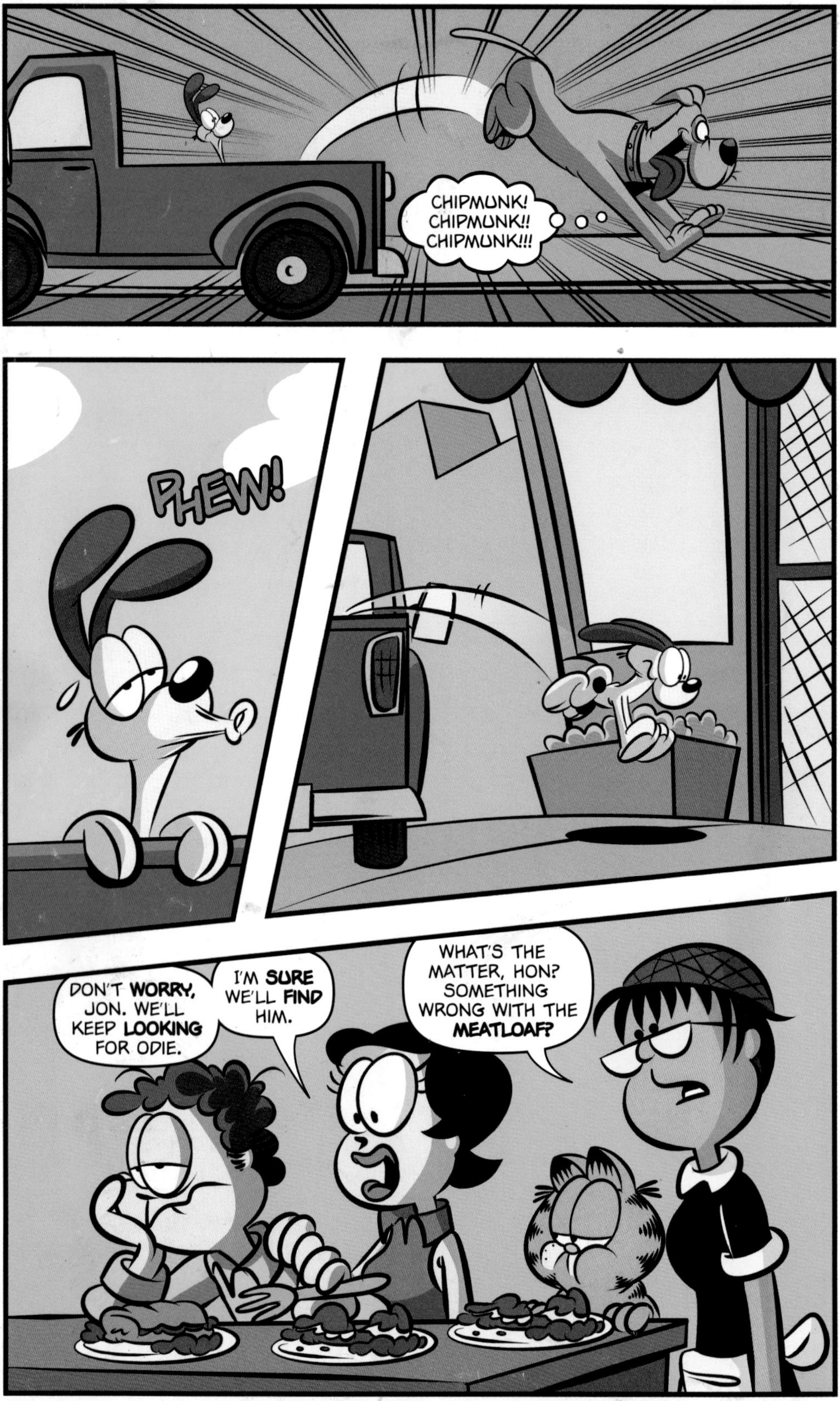
CHIPMUNK!
CHIPMUNK!!
CHIPMUNK!!!
PHEW!
DON'T WORRY, JON. WE'LL KEEP LOOKING FOR ODIE.
I'M SURE WE'LL FIND HIM.
WHAT'S THE MATTER, HON? SOMETHING WRONG WITH THE MEATLOAF?

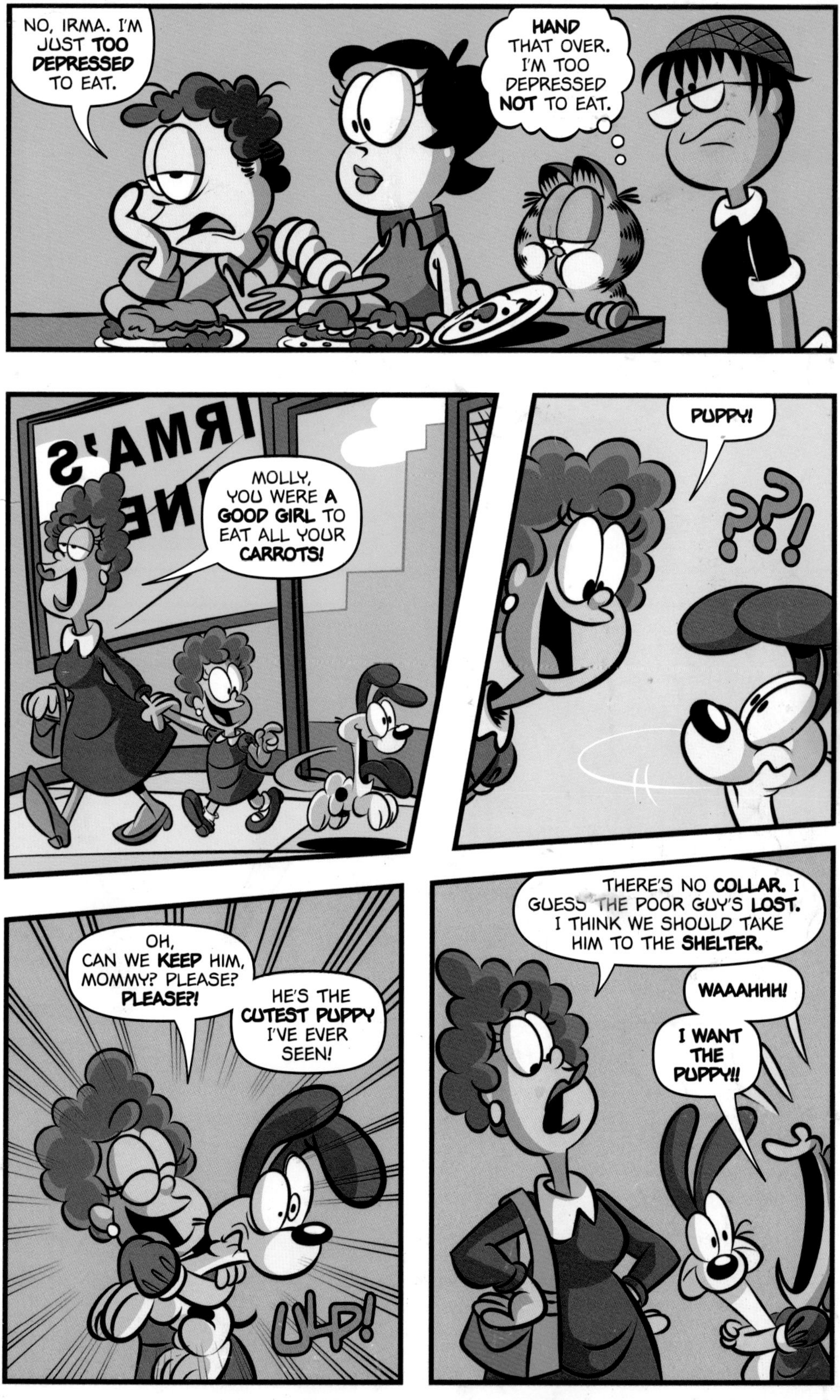

NO, IRMA. I'M JUST TOO DEPRESSED TO EAT.
HAND THAT OVER. I'M TOO DEPRESSED NOT TO EAT.
IRMA'S
MOLLY, YOU WERE A GOOD GIRL TO EAT ALL YOUR CARROTS!
PUPPY!
??!
OH, CAN WE KEEP HIM, MOMMY? PLEASE? PLEASE?!
HE'S THE CUTEST PUPPY I'VE EVER SEEN!
ULP!
THERE'S NO COLLAR. I GUESS THE POOR GUY'S LOST. I THINK WE SHOULD TAKE HIM TO THE SHELTER.
WAAAHHH!
I WANT THE PUPPY!!

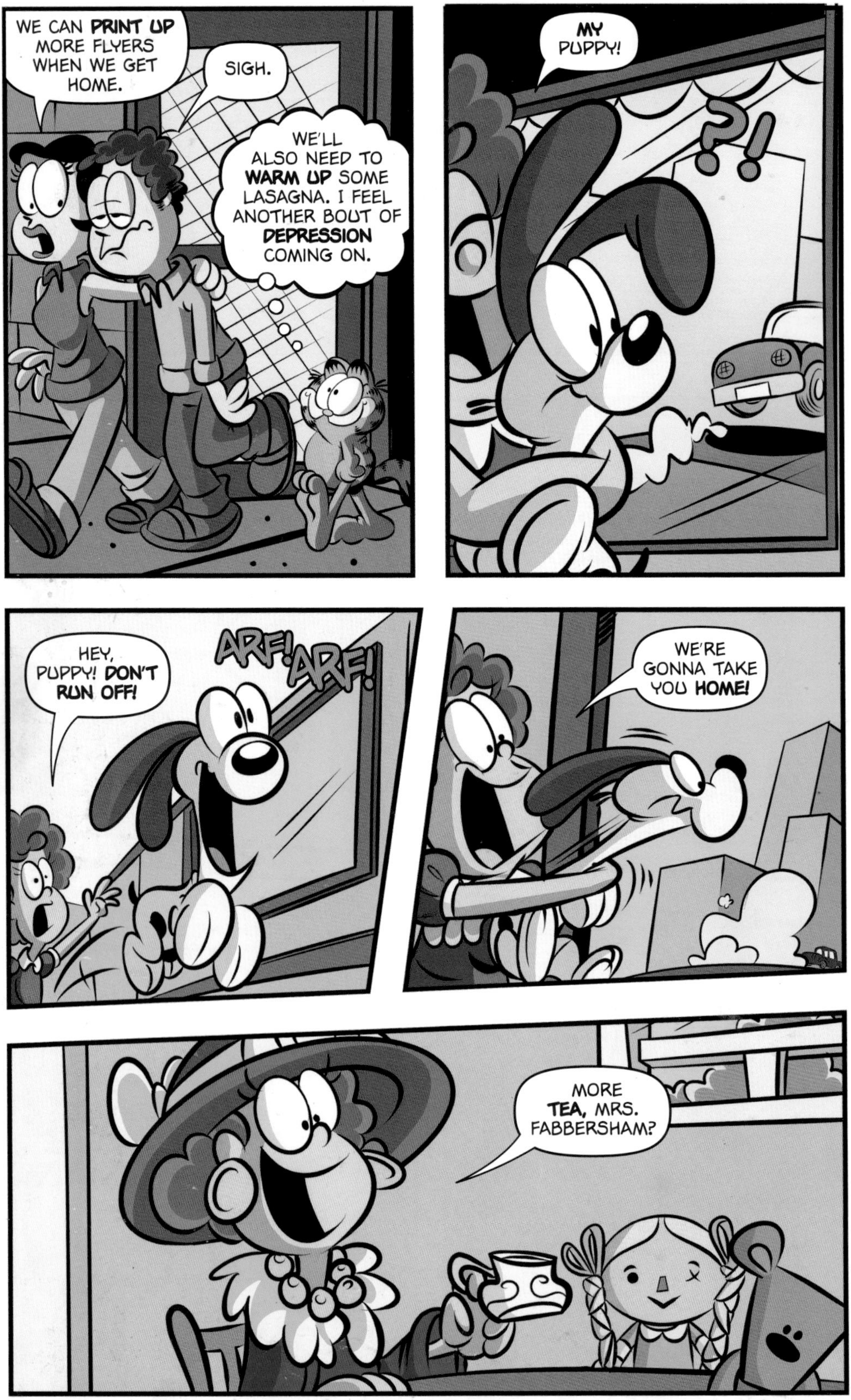

WE CAN **PRINT UP** MORE FLYERS WHEN WE GET HOME.
SIGH.
WE'LL ALSO NEED TO **WARM UP** SOME LASAGNA. I FEEL ANOTHER BOUT OF **DEPRESSION** COMING ON.
MY PUPPY!
?!
HEY, PUPPY! **DON'T RUN OFF!**
ARF! ARF!
WE'RE GONNA TAKE YOU **HOME!**
MORE **TEA,** MRS. FABBERSHAM?

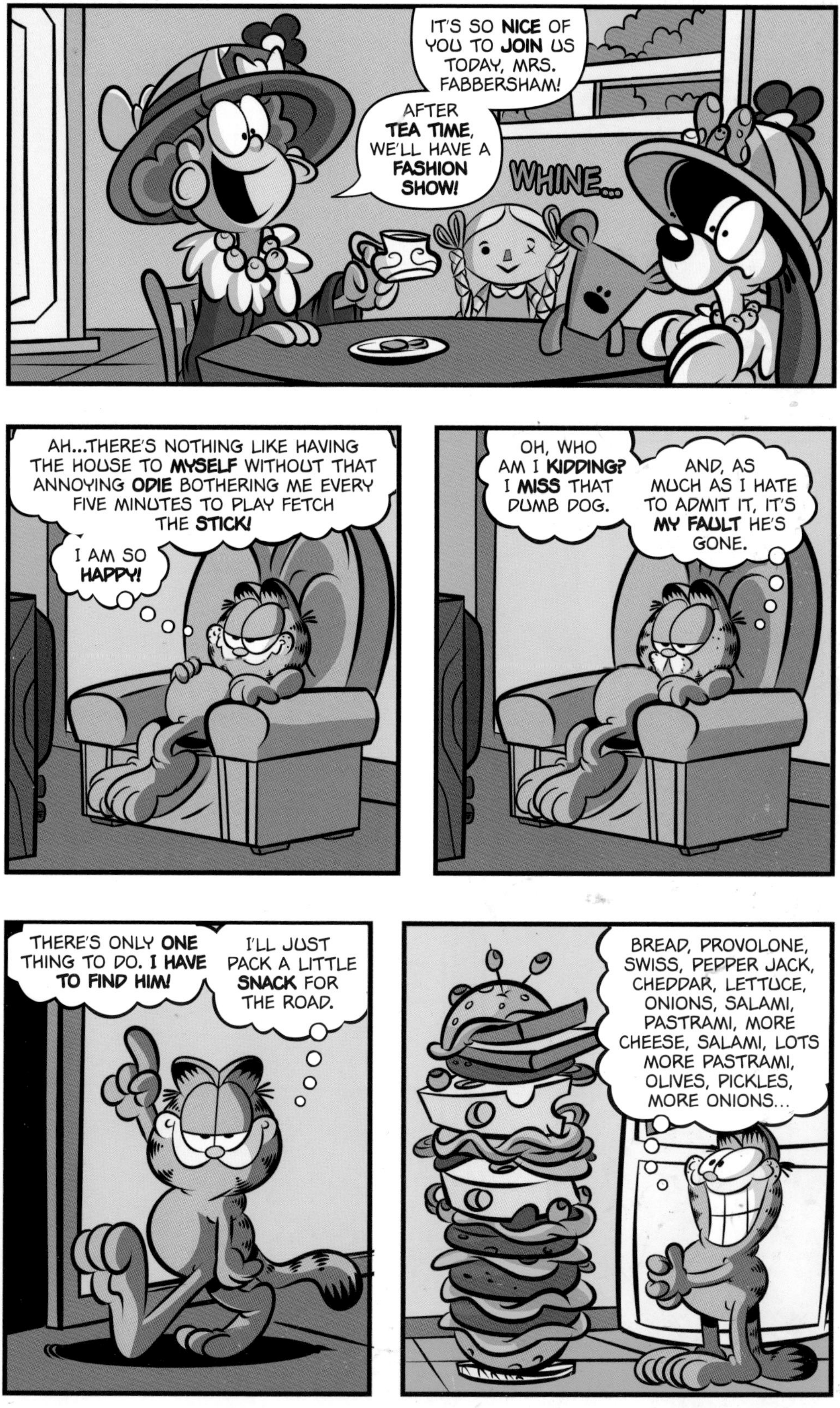
IT'S SO NICE OF YOU TO JOIN US TODAY, MRS. FABBERSHAM!
AFTER TEA TIME, WE'LL HAVE A FASHION SHOW!
WHINE...
AH...THERE'S NOTHING LIKE HAVING THE HOUSE TO MYSELF WITHOUT THAT ANNOYING ODIE BOTHERING ME EVERY FIVE MINUTES TO PLAY FETCH THE STICK!
I AM SO HAPPY!
OH, WHO AM I KIDDING? I MISS THAT DUMB DOG.
AND, AS MUCH AS I HATE TO ADMIT IT, IT'S MY FAULT HE'S GONE.
THERE'S ONLY ONE THING TO DO. I HAVE TO FIND HIM!
I'LL JUST PACK A LITTLE SNACK FOR THE ROAD.
BREAD, PROVOLONE, SWISS, PEPPER JACK, CHEDDAR, LETTUCE, ONIONS, SALAMI, PASTRAMI, MORE CHEESE, SALAMI, LOTS MORE PASTRAMI, OLIVES, PICKLES, MORE ONIONS...

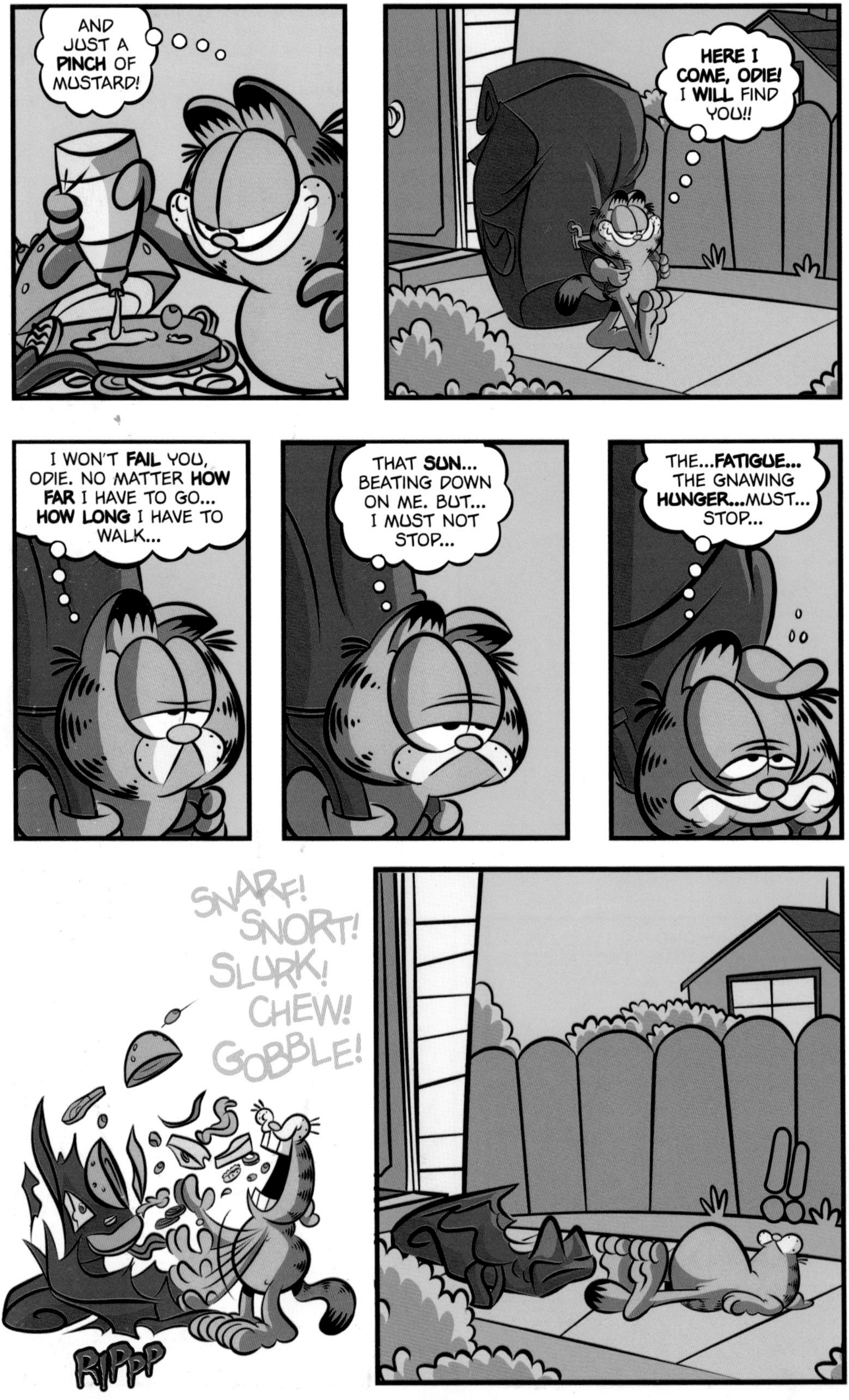
AND JUST A PINCH OF MUSTARD!
HERE I COME, ODIE! I WILL FIND YOU!!
I WON'T FAIL YOU, ODIE. NO MATTER HOW FAR I HAVE TO GO... HOW LONG I HAVE TO WALK...
THAT SUN... BEATING DOWN ON ME. BUT... I MUST NOT STOP...
THE...FATIGUE... THE GNAWING HUNGER...MUST... STOP...
SNARF! SNORT! SLURK! CHEW! GOBBLE!
RIPPP

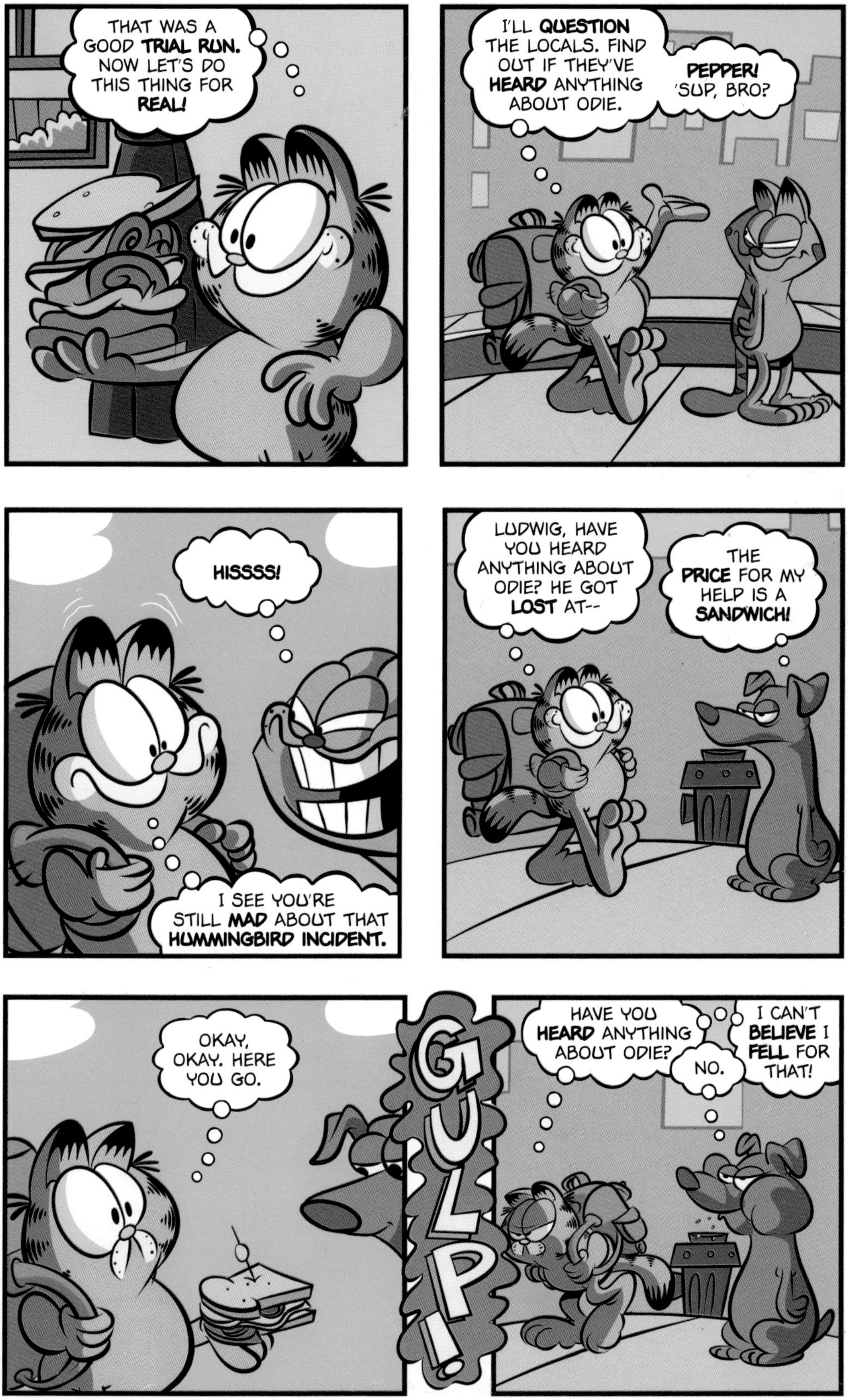
THAT WAS A GOOD TRIAL RUN. NOW LET'S DO THIS THING FOR REAL!
I'LL QUESTION THE LOCALS. FIND OUT IF THEY'VE HEARD ANYTHING ABOUT ODIE.
PEPPER! 'SUP, BRO?
HISSSS!
I SEE YOU'RE STILL MAD ABOUT THAT HUMMINGBIRD INCIDENT.
LUDWIG, HAVE YOU HEARD ANYTHING ABOUT ODIE? HE GOT LOST AT--
THE PRICE FOR MY HELP IS A SANDWICH!
OKAY, OKAY. HERE YOU GO.
GULP!
HAVE YOU HEARD ANYTHING ABOUT ODIE?
NO.
I CAN'T BELIEVE I FELL FOR THAT!

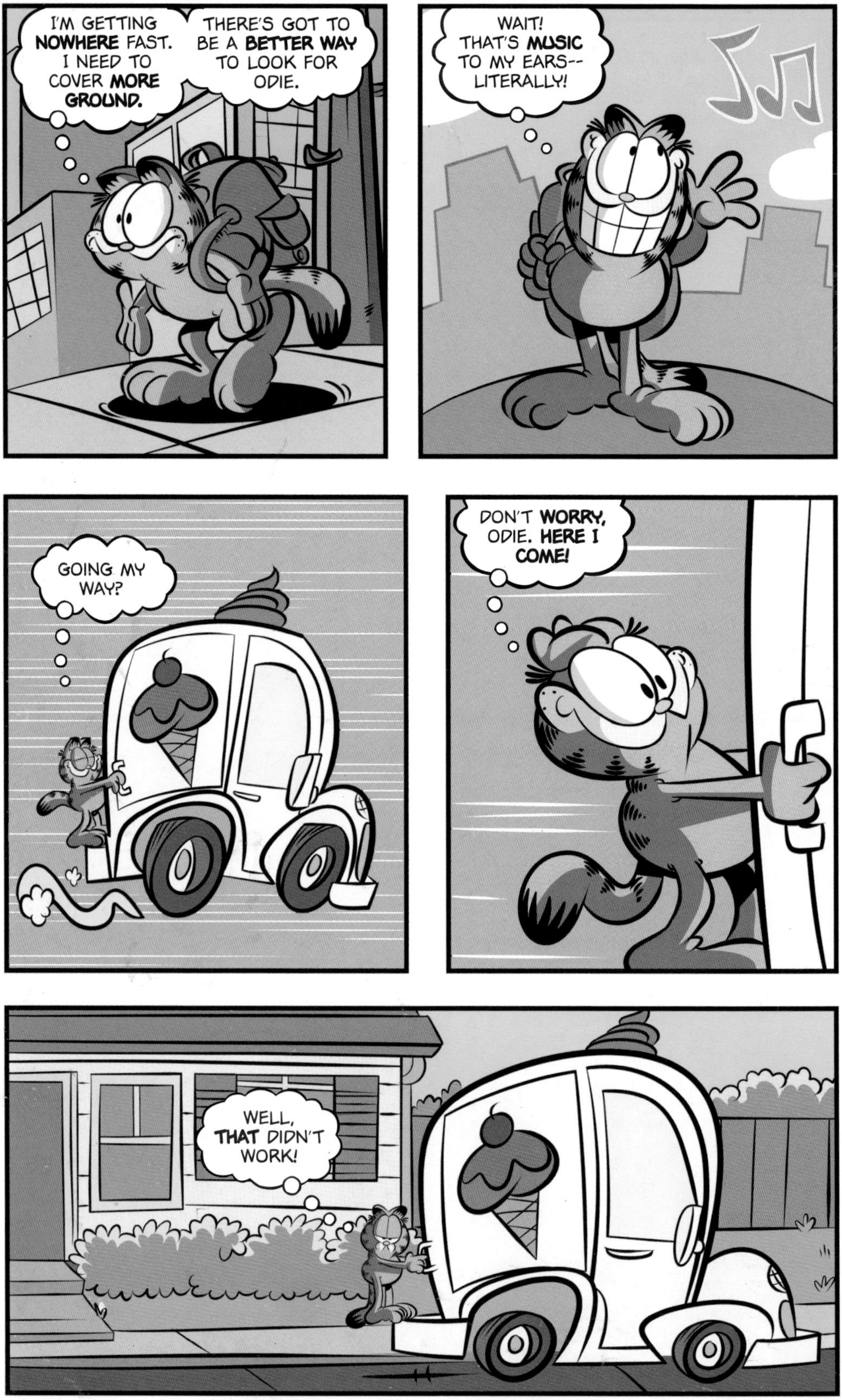
I'M GETTING NOWHERE FAST. I NEED TO COVER MORE GROUND.
THERE'S GOT TO BE A BETTER WAY TO LOOK FOR ODIE.
WAIT! THAT'S MUSIC TO MY EARS-- LITERALLY!
GOING MY WAY?
DON'T WORRY, ODIE. HERE I COME!
WELL, THAT DIDN'T WORK!

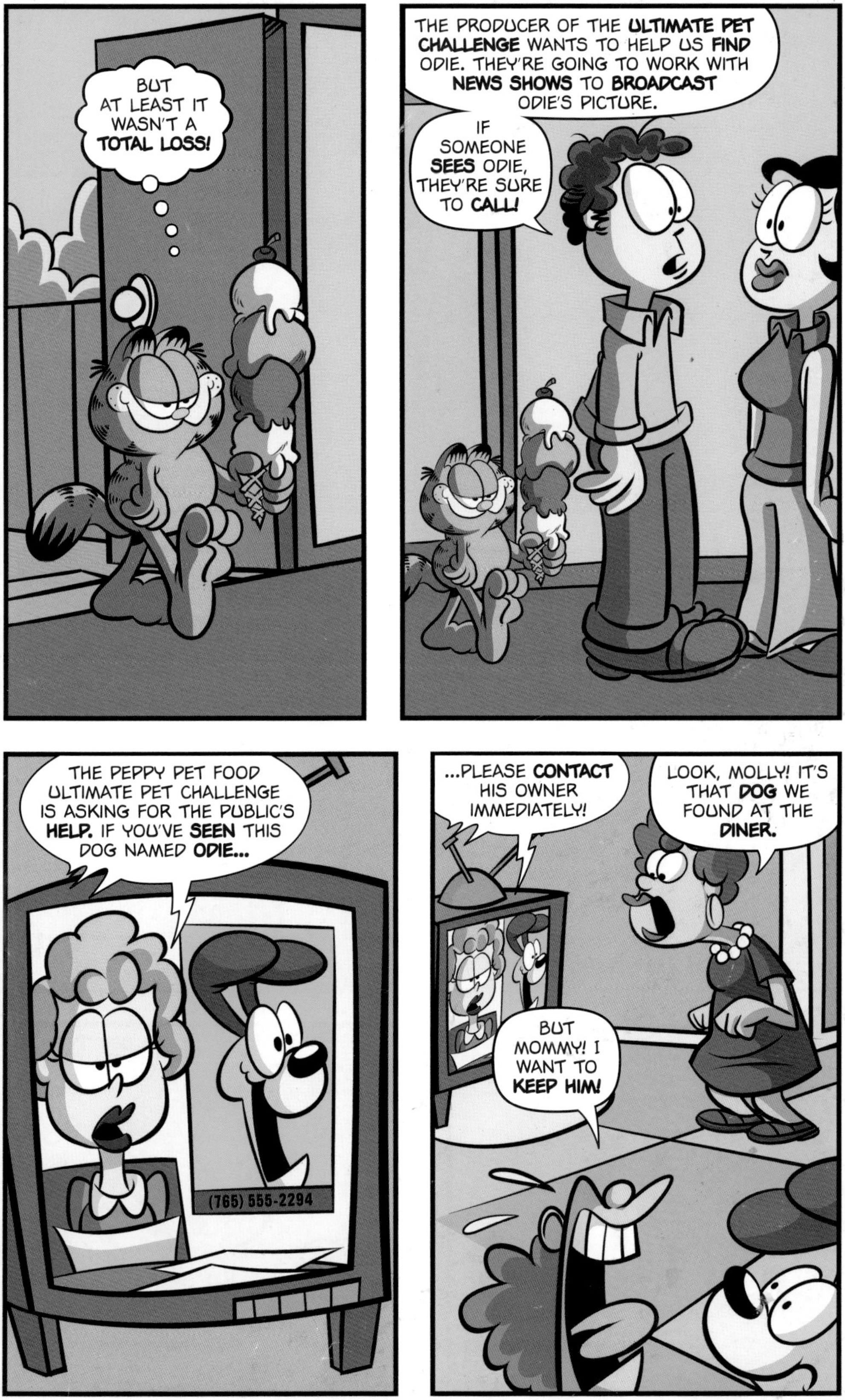
BUT AT LEAST IT WASN'T A **TOTAL LOSS!**
THE PRODUCER OF THE **ULTIMATE PET CHALLENGE** WANTS TO HELP US **FIND** ODIE. THEY'RE GOING TO WORK WITH **NEWS SHOWS** TO **BROADCAST** ODIE'S PICTURE.
IF SOMEONE **SEES** ODIE, THEY'RE SURE TO **CALL!**
THE PEPPY PET FOOD ULTIMATE PET CHALLENGE IS ASKING FOR THE PUBLIC'S **HELP.** IF YOU'VE **SEEN** THIS DOG NAMED **ODIE...**
(765) 555-2294
...PLEASE **CONTACT** HIS OWNER IMMEDIATELY!
LOOK, MOLLY! IT'S THAT **DOG** WE FOUND AT THE **DINER.**
BUT MOMMY! I WANT TO **KEEP HIM!**

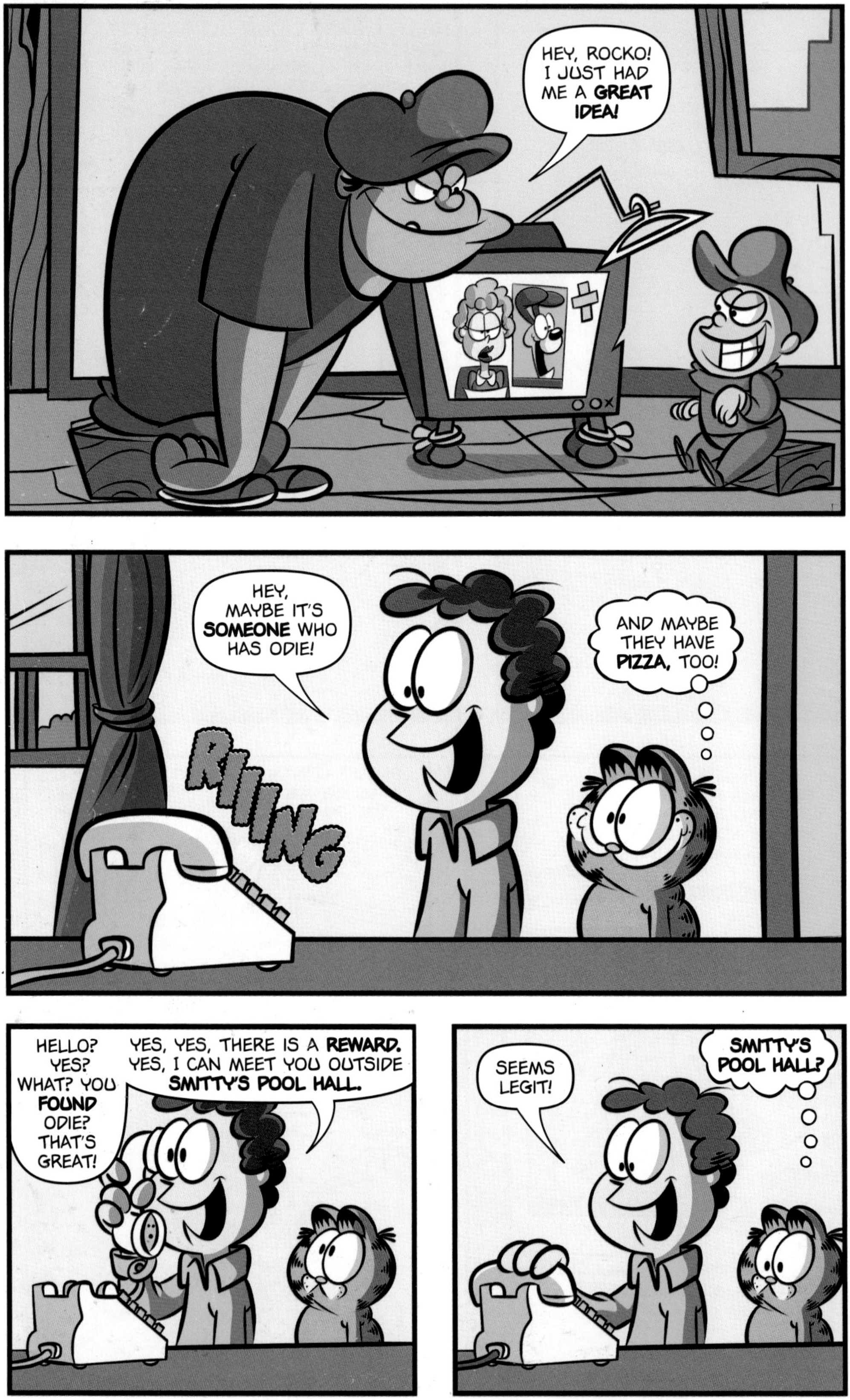
HEY, ROCKO! I JUST HAD ME A GREAT IDEA!
HEY, MAYBE IT'S SOMEONE WHO HAS ODIE!
AND MAYBE THEY HAVE PIZZA, TOO!
RIIING
HELLO? YES? WHAT? YOU FOUND ODIE? THAT'S GREAT!
YES, YES, THERE IS A REWARD. YES, I CAN MEET YOU OUTSIDE SMITTY'S POOL HALL.
SEEMS LEGIT!
SMITTY'S POOL HALL?

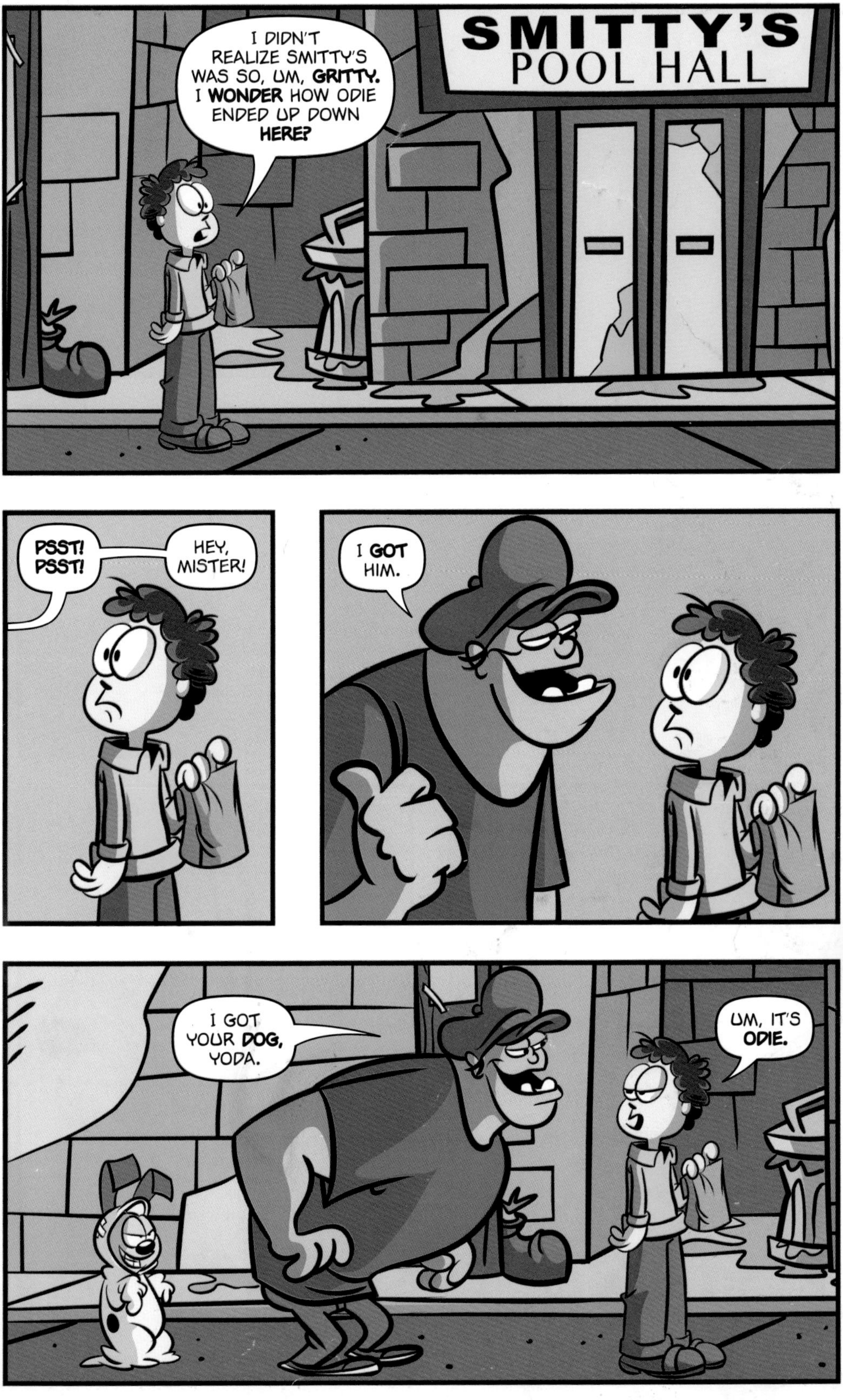
SMITTY'S POOL HALL
I DIDN'T REALIZE SMITTY'S WAS SO, UM, GRITTY. I WONDER HOW ODIE ENDED UP DOWN HERE?
PSSST! PSSST!
HEY, MISTER!
I GOT HIM.
I GOT YOUR DOG, YODA.
UM, IT'S ODIE.

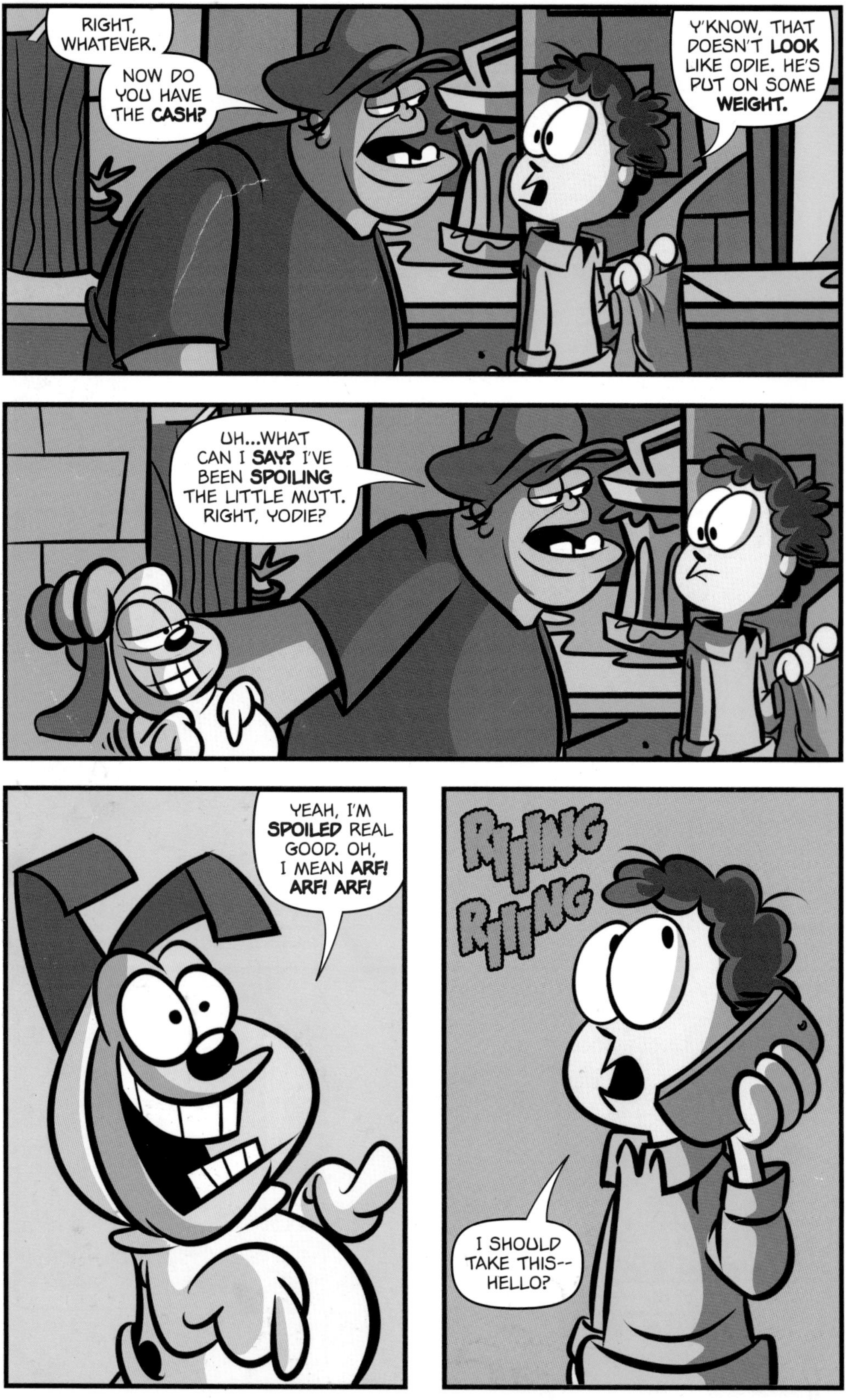
RIGHT, WHATEVER.
NOW DO YOU HAVE THE **CASH?**
Y'KNOW, THAT DOESN'T **LOOK** LIKE ODIE. HE'S PUT ON SOME **WEIGHT.**
UH...WHAT CAN I **SAY?** I'VE BEEN **SPOILING** THE LITTLE MUTT. RIGHT, YODIE?
YEAH, I'M **SPOILED** REAL GOOD. OH, I MEAN **ARF! ARF! ARF!**
RIIING
RIIING
I SHOULD TAKE THIS-- HELLO?

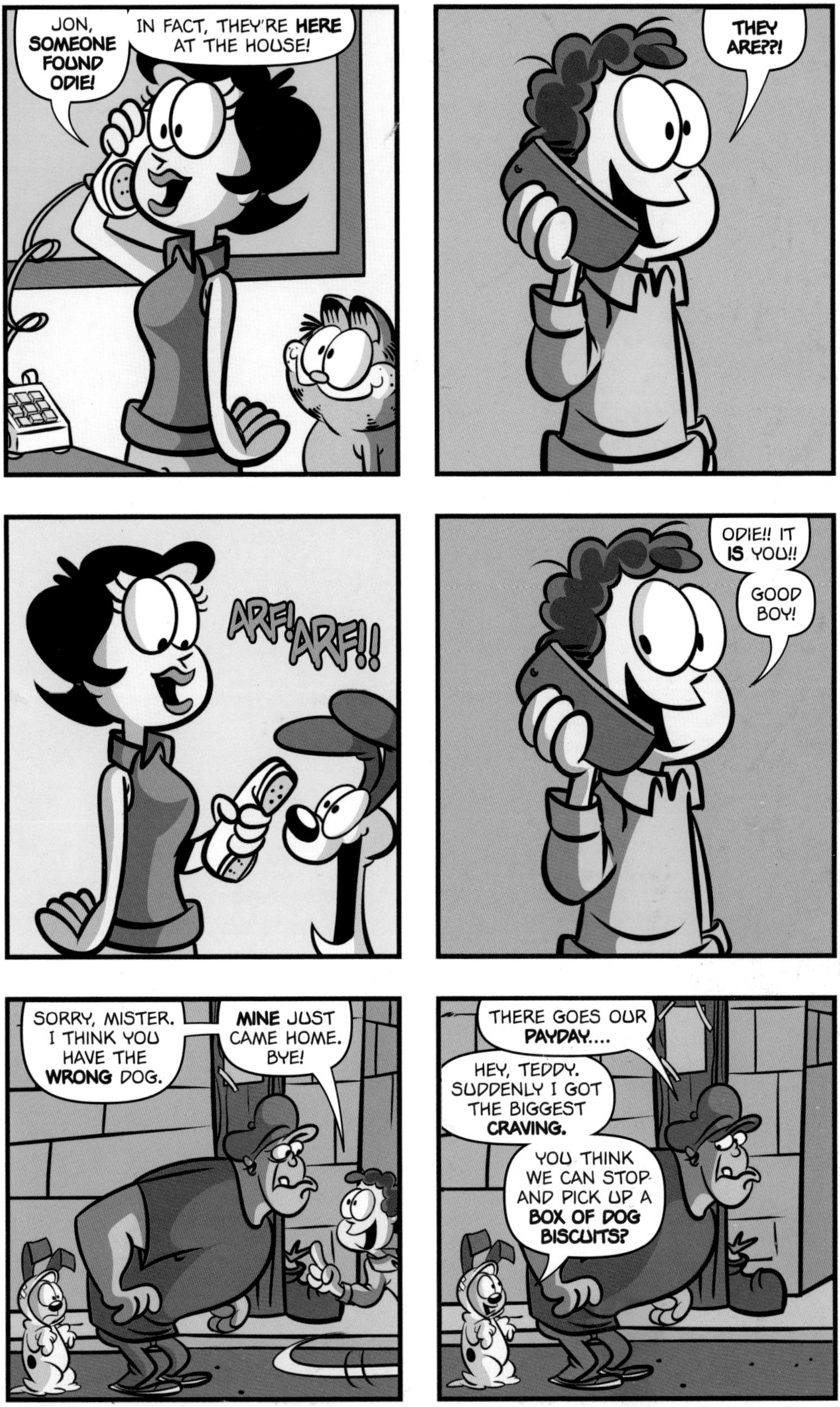
JON, SOMEONE FOUND ODIE!
IN FACT, THEY'RE HERE AT THE HOUSE!
THEY ARE??!
ARF! ARF!!
ODIE!! IT IS YOU!!
GOOD BOY!
SORRY, MISTER. I THINK YOU HAVE THE WRONG DOG.
MINE JUST CAME HOME. BYE!
THERE GOES OUR PAYDAY....
HEY, TEDDY. SUDDENLY I GOT THE BIGGEST CRAVING.
YOU THINK WE CAN STOP AND PICK UP A BOX OF DOG BISCUITS?

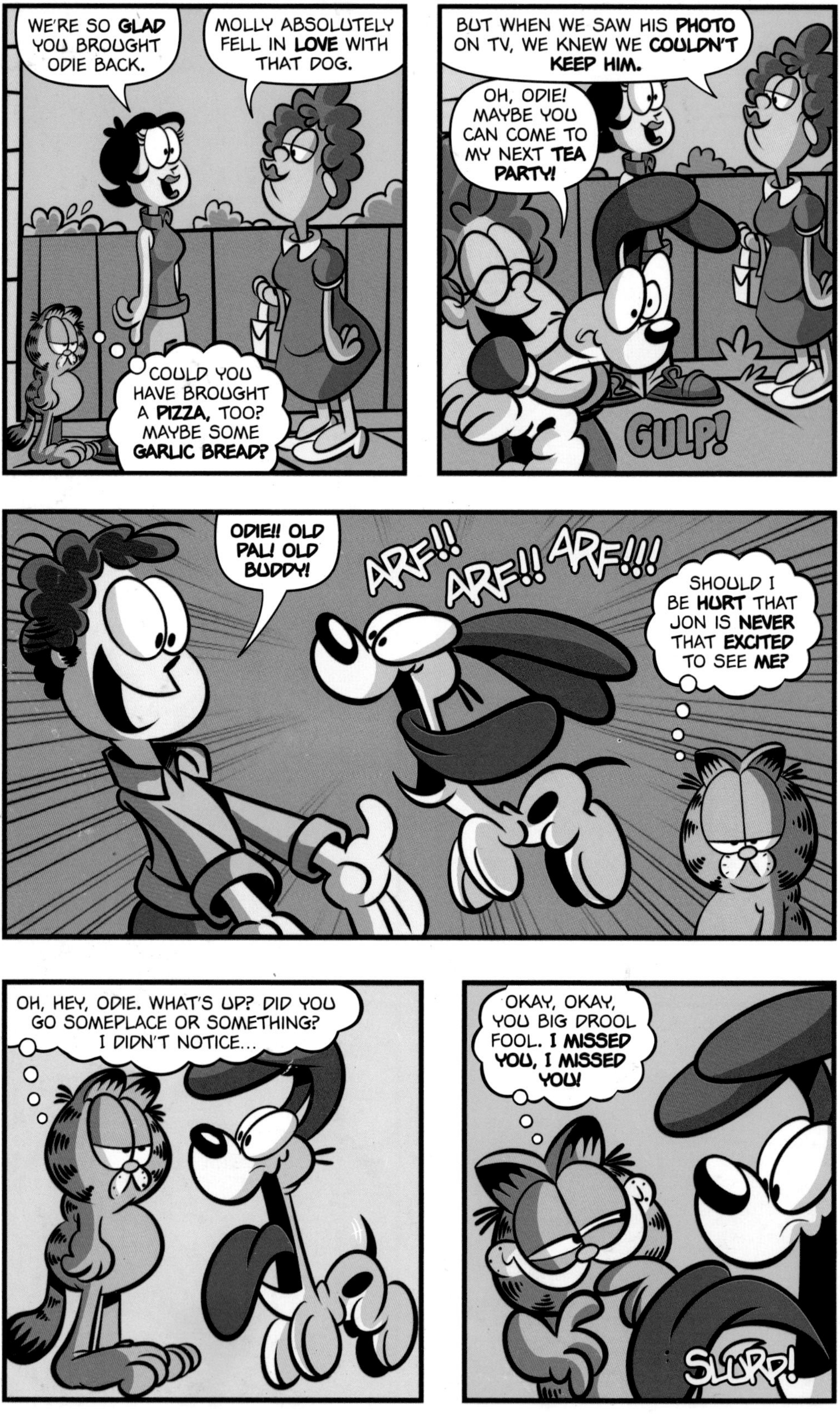
WE'RE SO **GLAD** YOU BROUGHT ODIE BACK.
MOLLY ABSOLUTELY FELL IN **LOVE** WITH THAT DOG.
COULD YOU HAVE BROUGHT A **PIZZA,** TOO? MAYBE SOME **GARLIC BREAD?**
BUT WHEN WE SAW HIS **PHOTO** ON TV, WE KNEW WE **COULDN'T KEEP HIM.**
OH, ODIE! MAYBE YOU CAN COME TO MY NEXT **TEA PARTY!**
GULP!
ODIE!! OLD PAL! OLD BUDDY!
ARF!! ARF!! ARF!!!
SHOULD I BE **HURT** THAT JON IS **NEVER** THAT **EXCITED** TO SEE **ME?**
OH, HEY, ODIE. WHAT'S UP? DID YOU GO SOMEPLACE OR SOMETHING? I DIDN'T NOTICE...
OKAY, OKAY, YOU BIG DROOL FOOL. **I MISSED YOU, I MISSED YOU!**
SLURP!

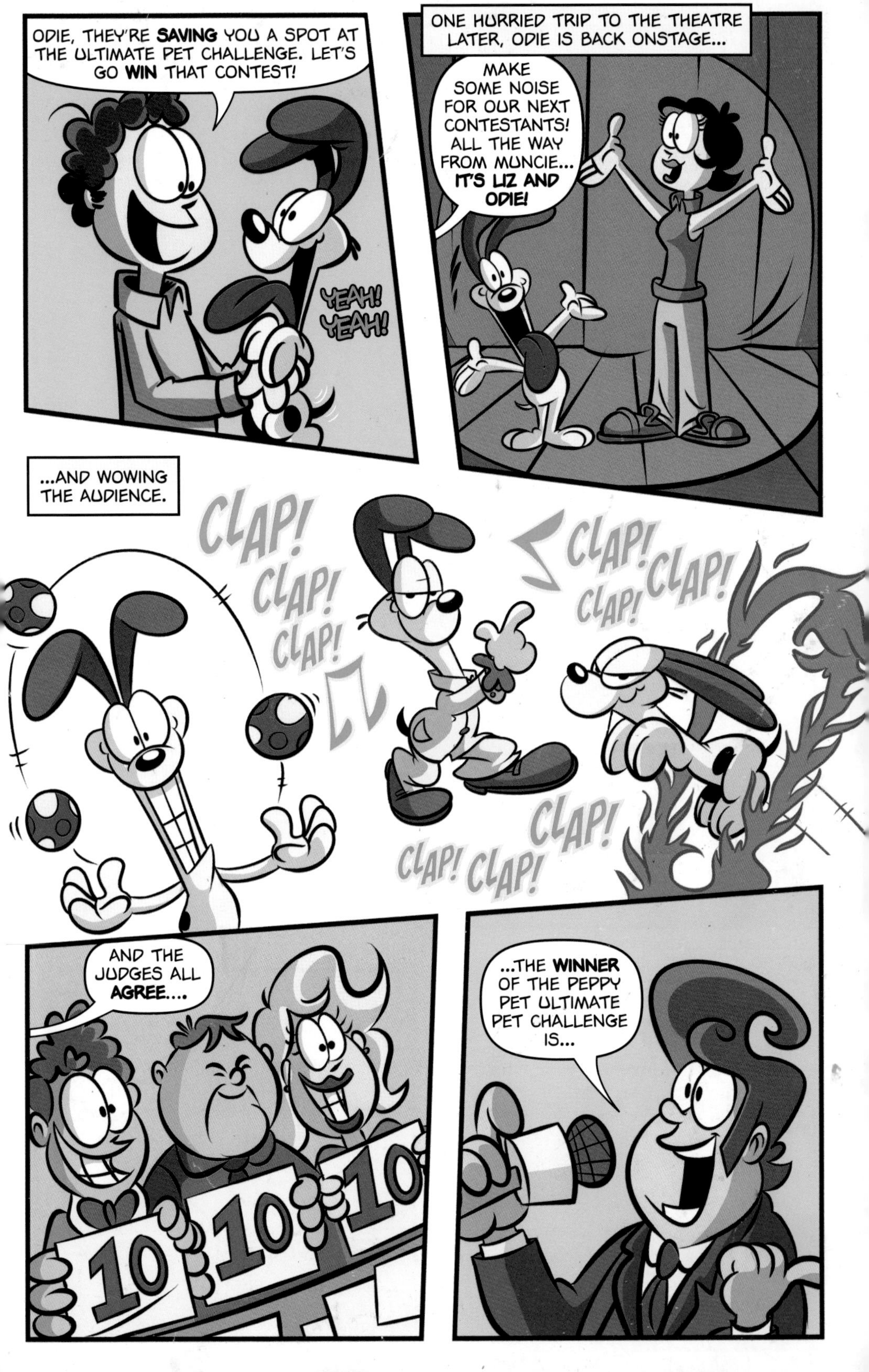
ODIE, THEY'RE SAVING YOU A SPOT AT THE ULTIMATE PET CHALLENGE. LET'S GO WIN THAT CONTEST!
YEAH! YEAH!
ONE HURRIED TRIP TO THE THEATRE LATER, ODIE IS BACK ONSTAGE...
MAKE SOME NOISE FOR OUR NEXT CONTESTANTS! ALL THE WAY FROM MUNCIE... IT'S LIZ AND ODIE!
...AND WOWING THE AUDIENCE.
CLAP! CLAP! CLAP!
CLAP! CLAP! CLAP!
CLAP! CLAP! CLAP!
AND THE JUDGES ALL AGREE....
10 10 10
...THE WINNER OF THE PEPPY PET ULTIMATE PET CHALLENGE IS...

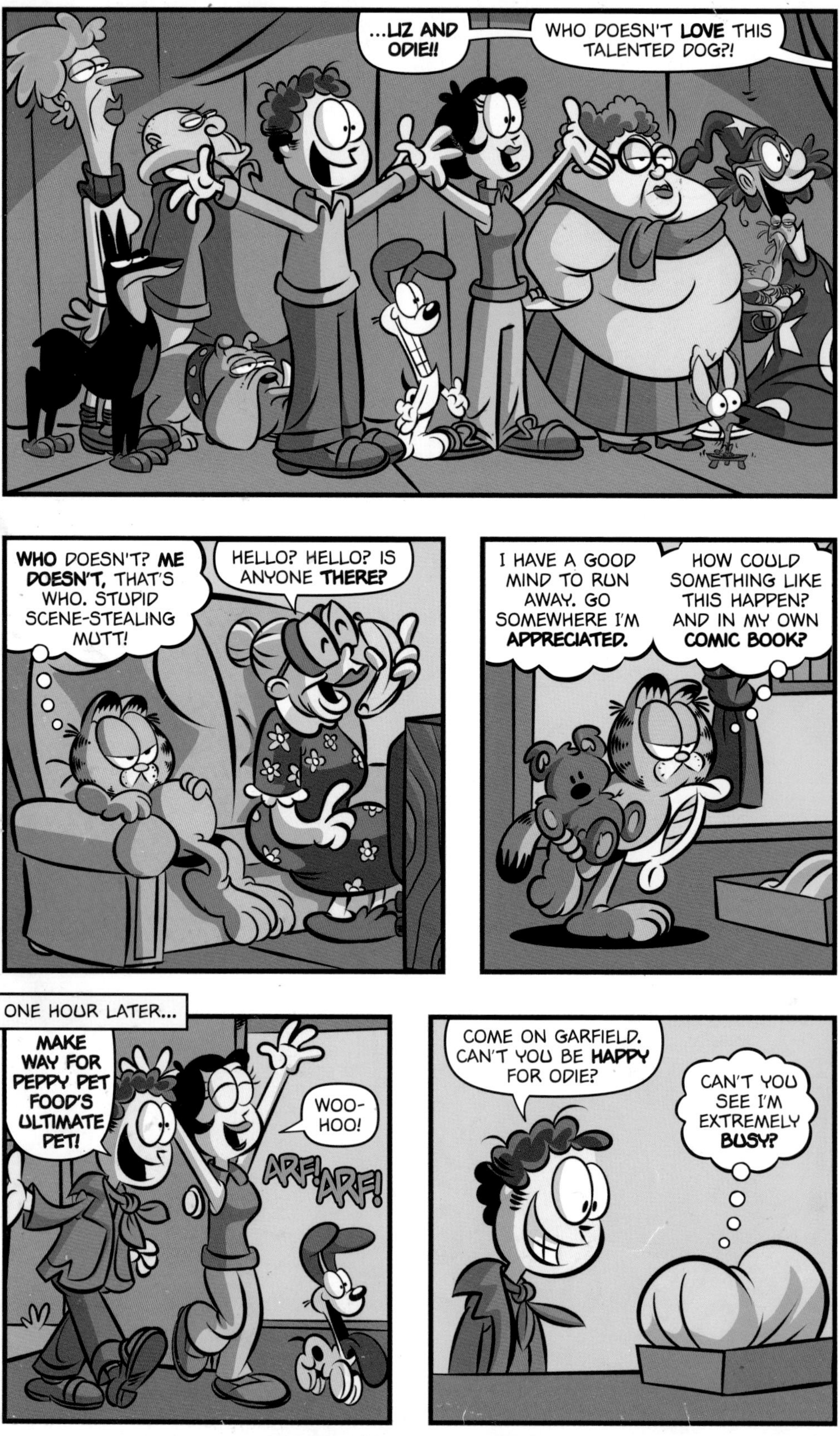
...LIZ AND ODIE!!
WHO DOESN'T LOVE THIS TALENTED DOG?!
WHO DOESN'T? ME DOESN'T, THAT'S WHO. STUPID SCENE-STEALING MUTT!
HELLO? HELLO? IS ANYONE THERE?
I HAVE A GOOD MIND TO RUN AWAY. GO SOMEWHERE I'M APPRECIATED.
HOW COULD SOMETHING LIKE THIS HAPPEN? AND IN MY OWN COMIC BOOK?
ONE HOUR LATER...
MAKE WAY FOR PEPPY PET FOOD'S ULTIMATE PET!
WOO-HOO!
ARF! ARF!
COME ON GARFIELD. CAN'T YOU BE HAPPY FOR ODIE?
CAN'T YOU SEE I'M EXTREMELY BUSY?

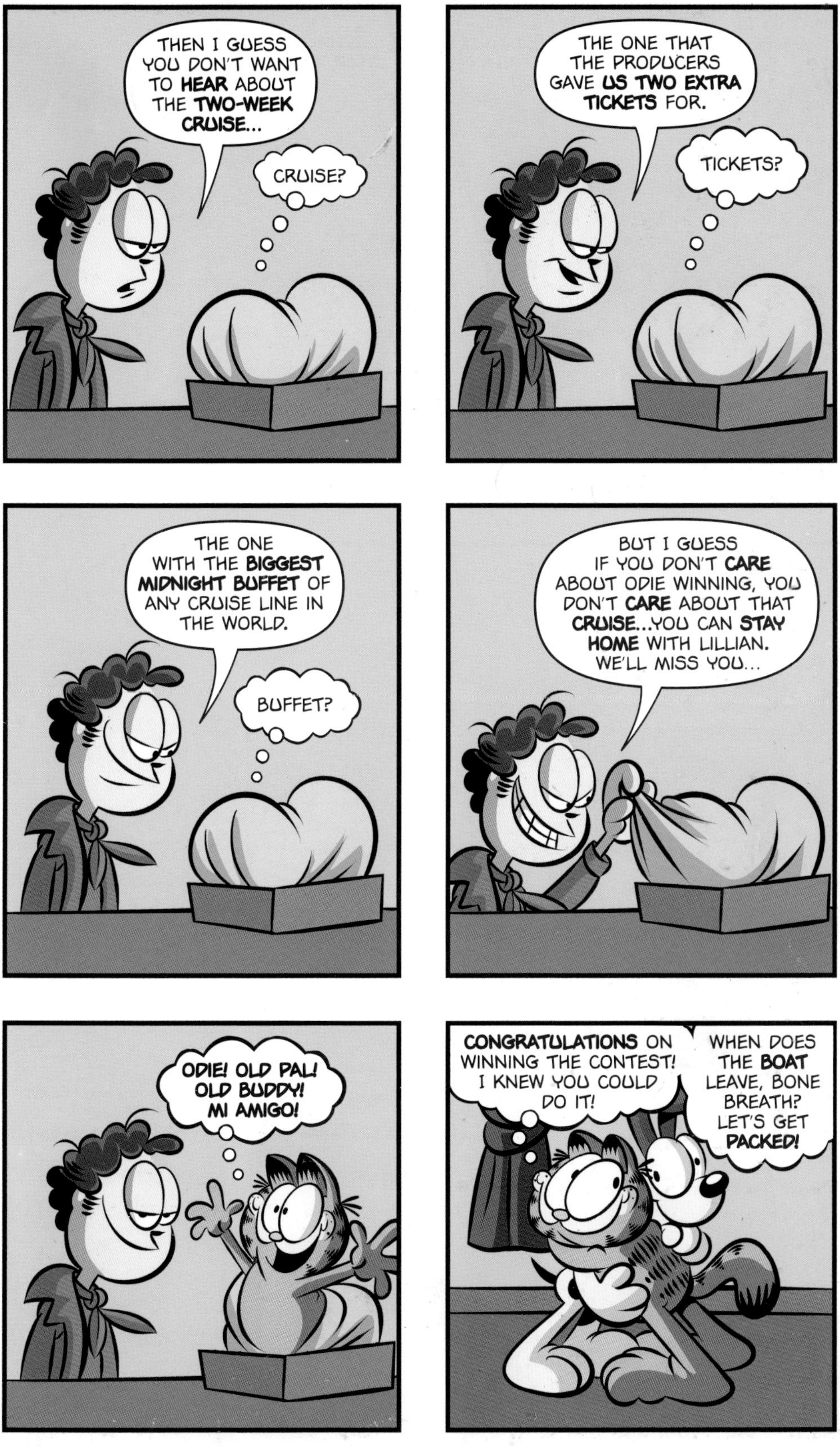
THEN I GUESS YOU DON'T WANT TO HEAR ABOUT THE TWO-WEEK CRUISE...
CRUISE?
THE ONE THAT THE PRODUCERS GAVE US TWO EXTRA TICKETS FOR.
TICKETS?
THE ONE WITH THE BIGGEST MIDNIGHT BUFFET OF ANY CRUISE LINE IN THE WORLD.
BUFFET?
BUT I GUESS IF YOU DON'T CARE ABOUT ODIE WINNING, YOU DON'T CARE ABOUT THAT CRUISE...YOU CAN STAY HOME WITH LILLIAN. WE'LL MISS YOU...
ODIE! OLD PAL! OLD BUDDY! MI AMIGO!
CONGRATULATIONS ON WINNING THE CONTEST! I KNEW YOU COULD DO IT!
WHEN DOES THE BOAT LEAVE, BONE BREATH? LET'S GET PACKED!

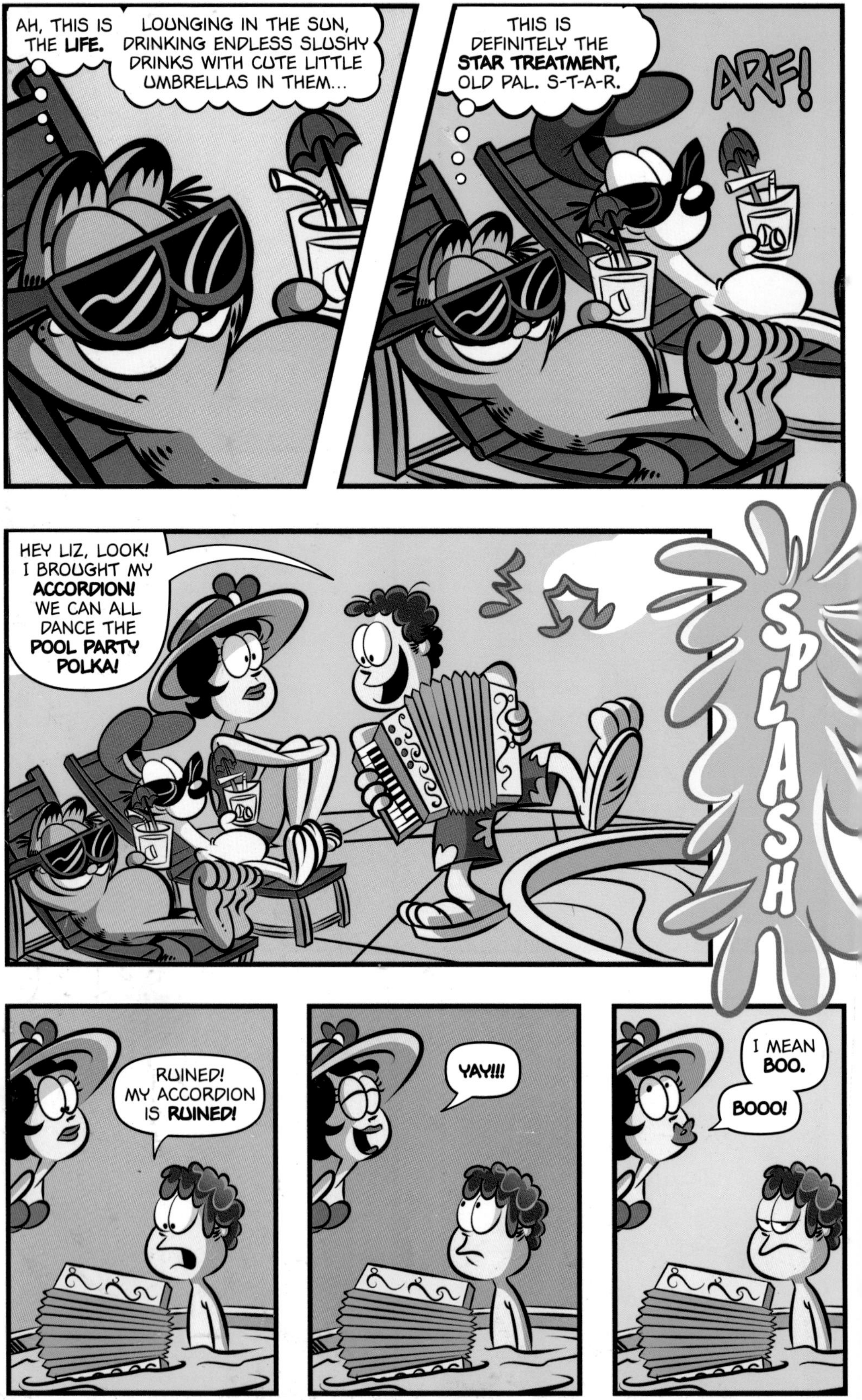

AH, THIS IS THE **LIFE.**
LOUNGING IN THE SUN, DRINKING ENDLESS SLUSHY DRINKS WITH CUTE LITTLE UMBRELLAS IN THEM...
THIS IS DEFINITELY THE **STAR TREATMENT,** OLD PAL. S-T-A-R.
ARF!
HEY LIZ, LOOK! I BROUGHT MY **ACCORDION!** WE CAN ALL DANCE THE **POOL PARTY POLKA!**
SPLASH
RUINED! MY ACCORDION IS **RUINED!**
YAY!!!
I MEAN **BOO.**
BOOO!

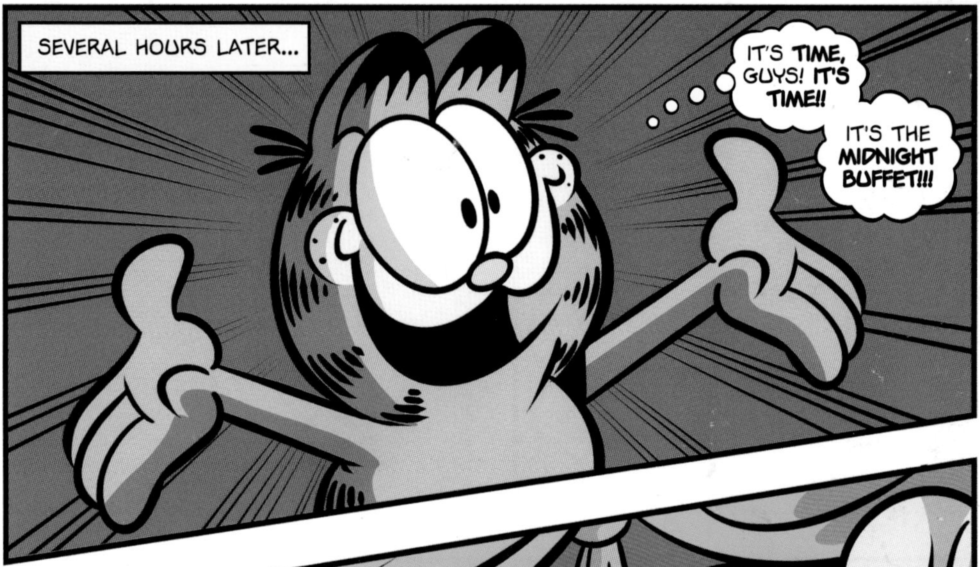
SEVERAL HOURS LATER...
IT'S TIME, GUYS! IT'S TIME!!
IT'S THE MIDNIGHT BUFFET!!!

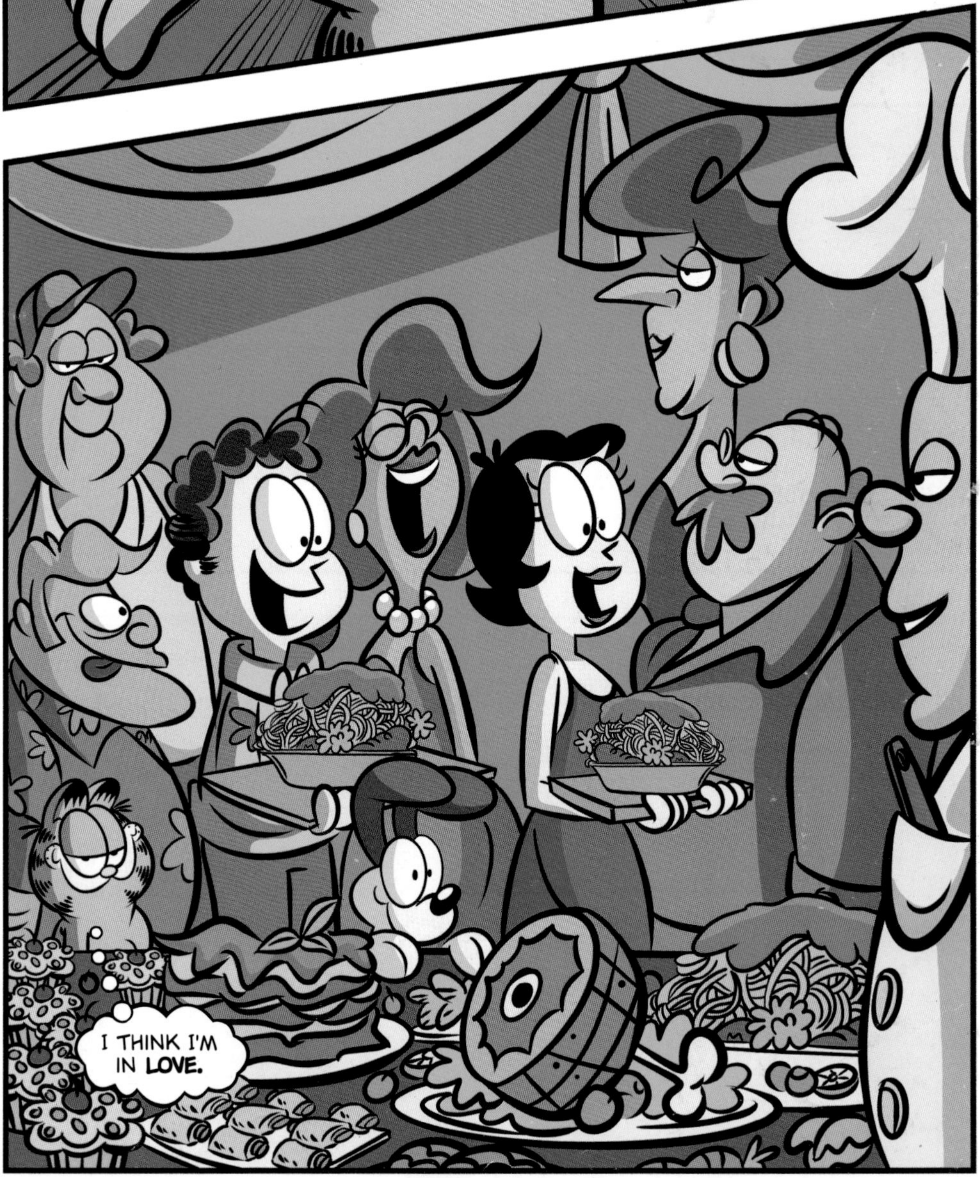
I THINK I'M IN LOVE.

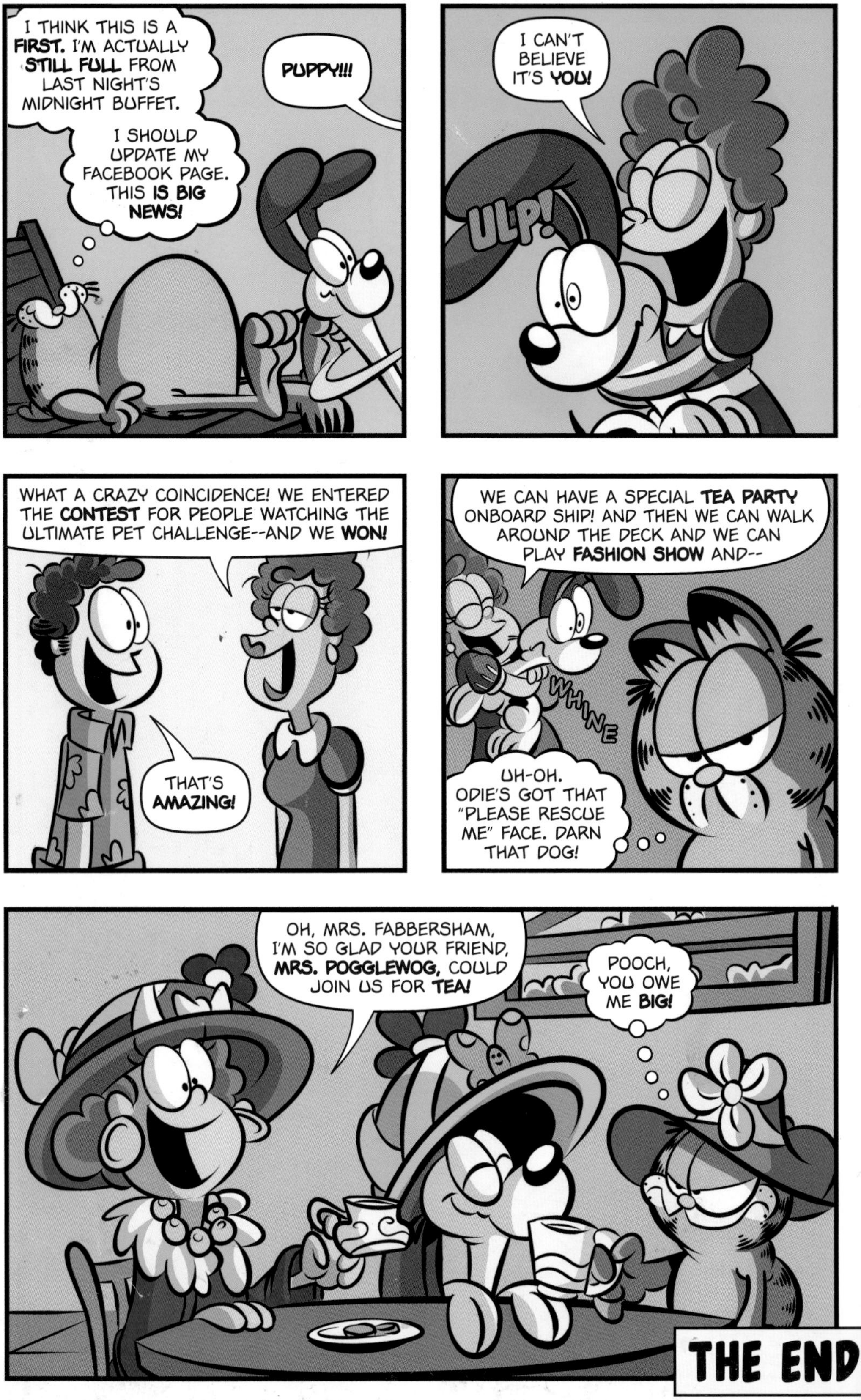

I THINK THIS IS A FIRST. I'M ACTUALLY STILL FULL FROM LAST NIGHT'S MIDNIGHT BUFFET.
I SHOULD UPDATE MY FACEBOOK PAGE. THIS IS BIG NEWS!
PUPPY!!!
I CAN'T BELIEVE IT'S YOU!
ULP!
WHAT A CRAZY COINCIDENCE! WE ENTERED THE CONTEST FOR PEOPLE WATCHING THE ULTIMATE PET CHALLENGE--AND WE WON!
THAT'S AMAZING!
WE CAN HAVE A SPECIAL TEA PARTY ONBOARD SHIP! AND THEN WE CAN WALK AROUND THE DECK AND WE CAN PLAY FASHION SHOW AND--
WHINE
UH-OH. ODIE'S GOT THAT "PLEASE RESCUE ME" FACE. DARN THAT DOG!
OH, MRS. FABBERSHAM, I'M SO GLAD YOUR FRIEND, MRS. POGGLEWOG, COULD JOIN US FOR TEA!
POOCH, YOU OWE ME BIG!
THE END

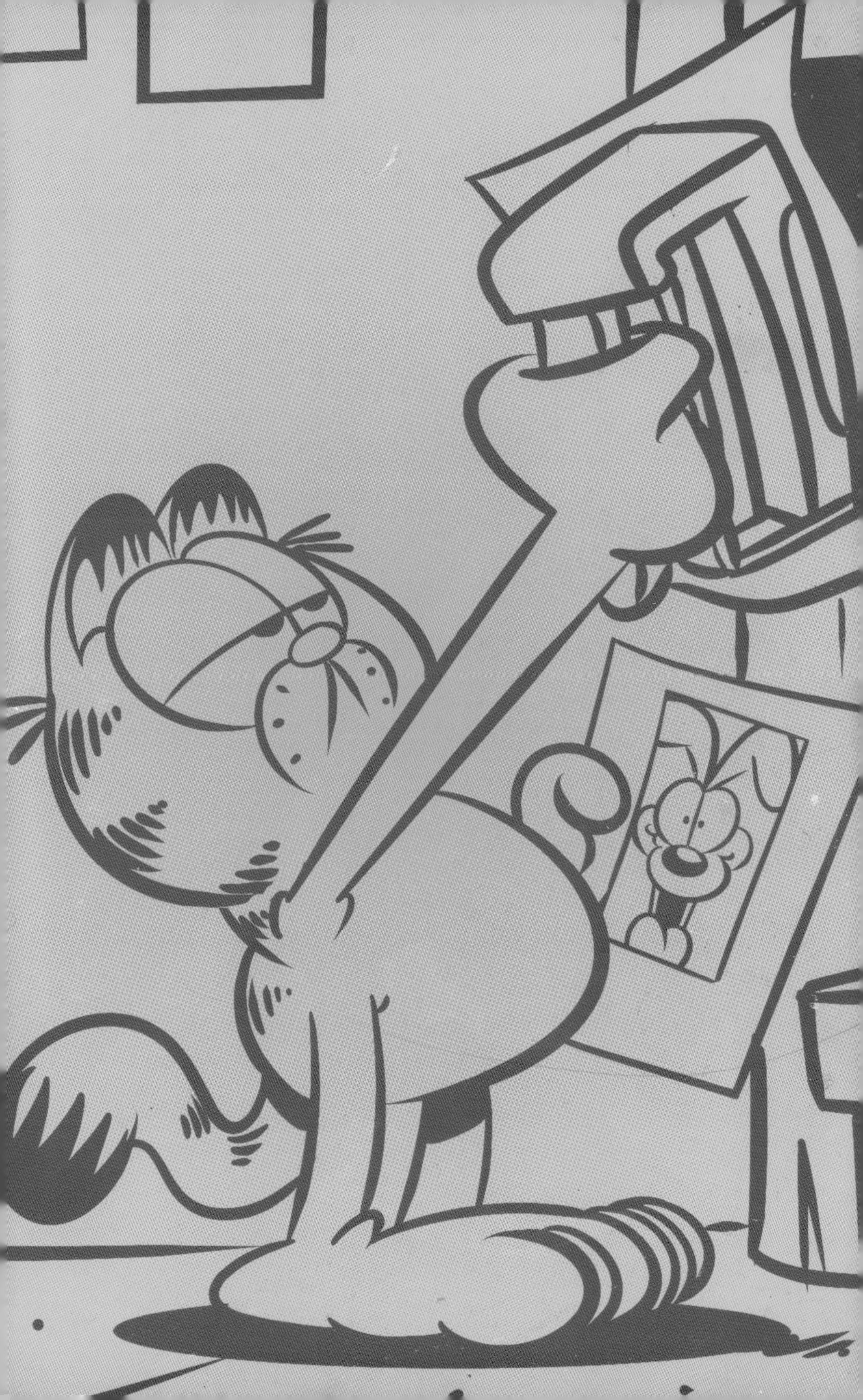

"WILFRED'S WORLD"

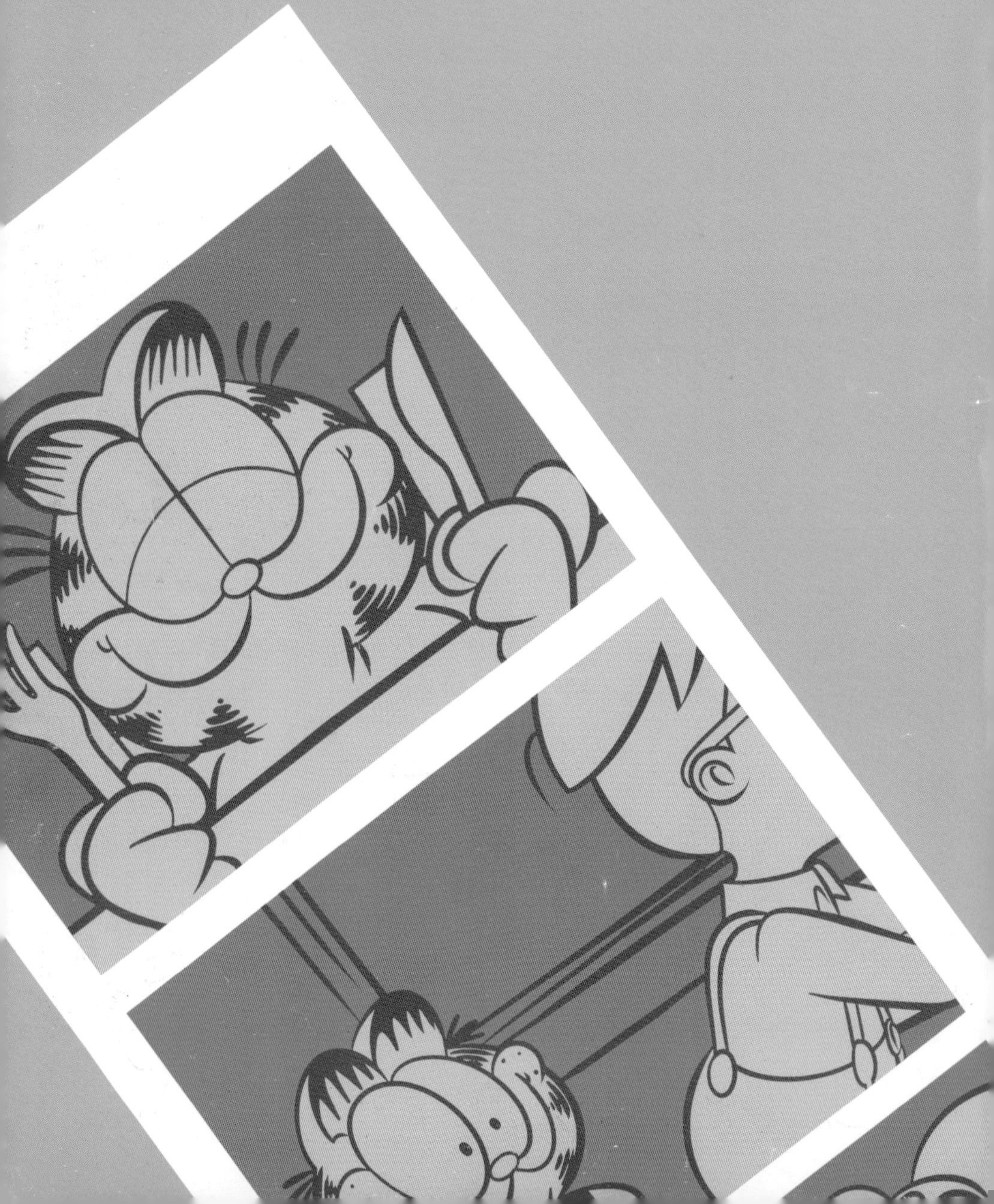

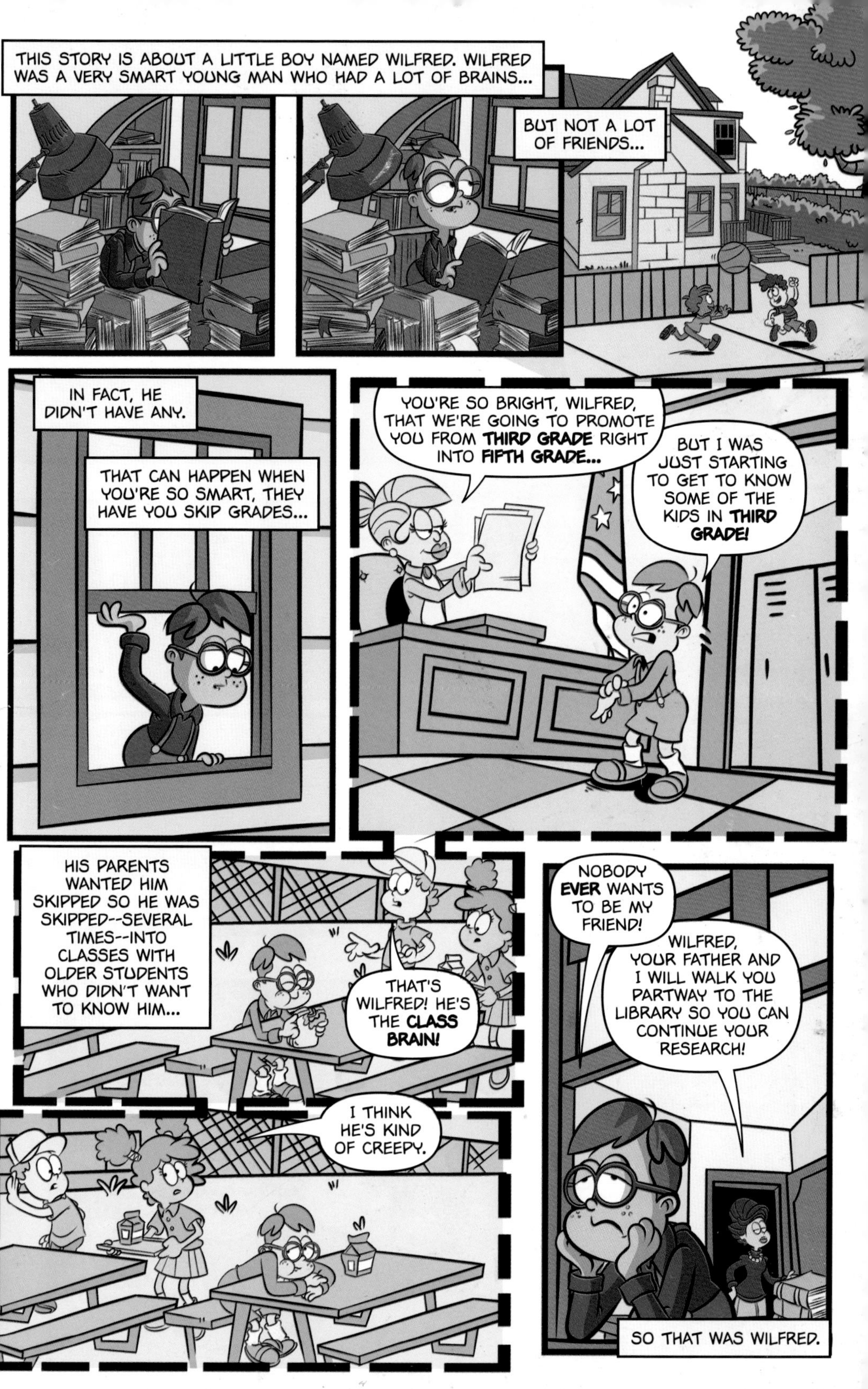
THIS STORY IS ABOUT A LITTLE BOY NAMED WILFRED. WILFRED WAS A VERY SMART YOUNG MAN WHO HAD A LOT OF BRAINS...
BUT NOT A LOT OF FRIENDS...
IN FACT, HE DIDN'T HAVE ANY.
THAT CAN HAPPEN WHEN YOU'RE SO SMART, THEY HAVE YOU SKIP GRADES...
YOU'RE SO BRIGHT, WILFRED, THAT WE'RE GOING TO PROMOTE YOU FROM **THIRD GRADE** RIGHT INTO **FIFTH GRADE...**
BUT I WAS JUST STARTING TO GET TO KNOW SOME OF THE KIDS IN **THIRD GRADE!**
HIS PARENTS WANTED HIM SKIPPED SO HE WAS SKIPPED--SEVERAL TIMES--INTO CLASSES WITH OLDER STUDENTS WHO DIDN'T WANT TO KNOW HIM...
THAT'S WILFRED! HE'S THE **CLASS BRAIN!**
I THINK HE'S KIND OF CREEPY.
NOBODY **EVER** WANTS TO BE MY FRIEND!
WILFRED, YOUR FATHER AND I WILL WALK YOU PARTWAY TO THE LIBRARY SO YOU CAN CONTINUE YOUR RESEARCH!
SO THAT WAS WILFRED.

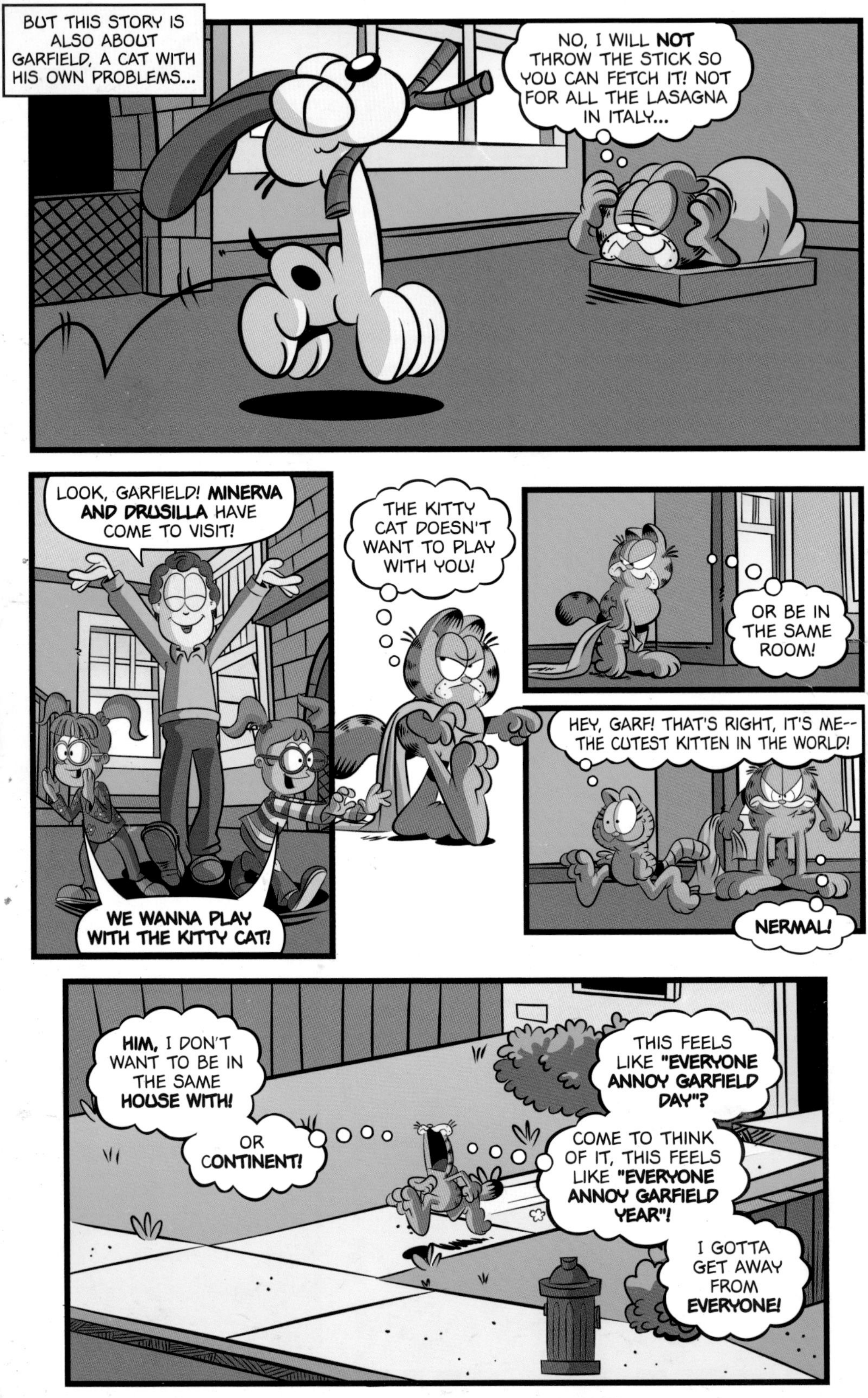
BUT THIS STORY IS ALSO ABOUT GARFIELD, A CAT WITH HIS OWN PROBLEMS...
NO, I WILL NOT THROW THE STICK SO YOU CAN FETCH IT! NOT FOR ALL THE LASAGNA IN ITALY...
LOOK, GARFIELD! MINERVA AND DRUSILLA HAVE COME TO VISIT!
WE WANNA PLAY WITH THE KITTY CAT!
THE KITTY CAT DOESN'T WANT TO PLAY WITH YOU!
OR BE IN THE SAME ROOM!
HEY, GARF! THAT'S RIGHT, IT'S ME-- THE CUTEST KITTEN IN THE WORLD!
NERMAL!
HIM, I DON'T WANT TO BE IN THE SAME HOUSE WITH!
OR CONTINENT!
THIS FEELS LIKE "EVERYONE ANNOY GARFIELD DAY"?
COME TO THINK OF IT, THIS FEELS LIKE "EVERYONE ANNOY GARFIELD YEAR"!
I GOTTA GET AWAY FROM EVERYONE!

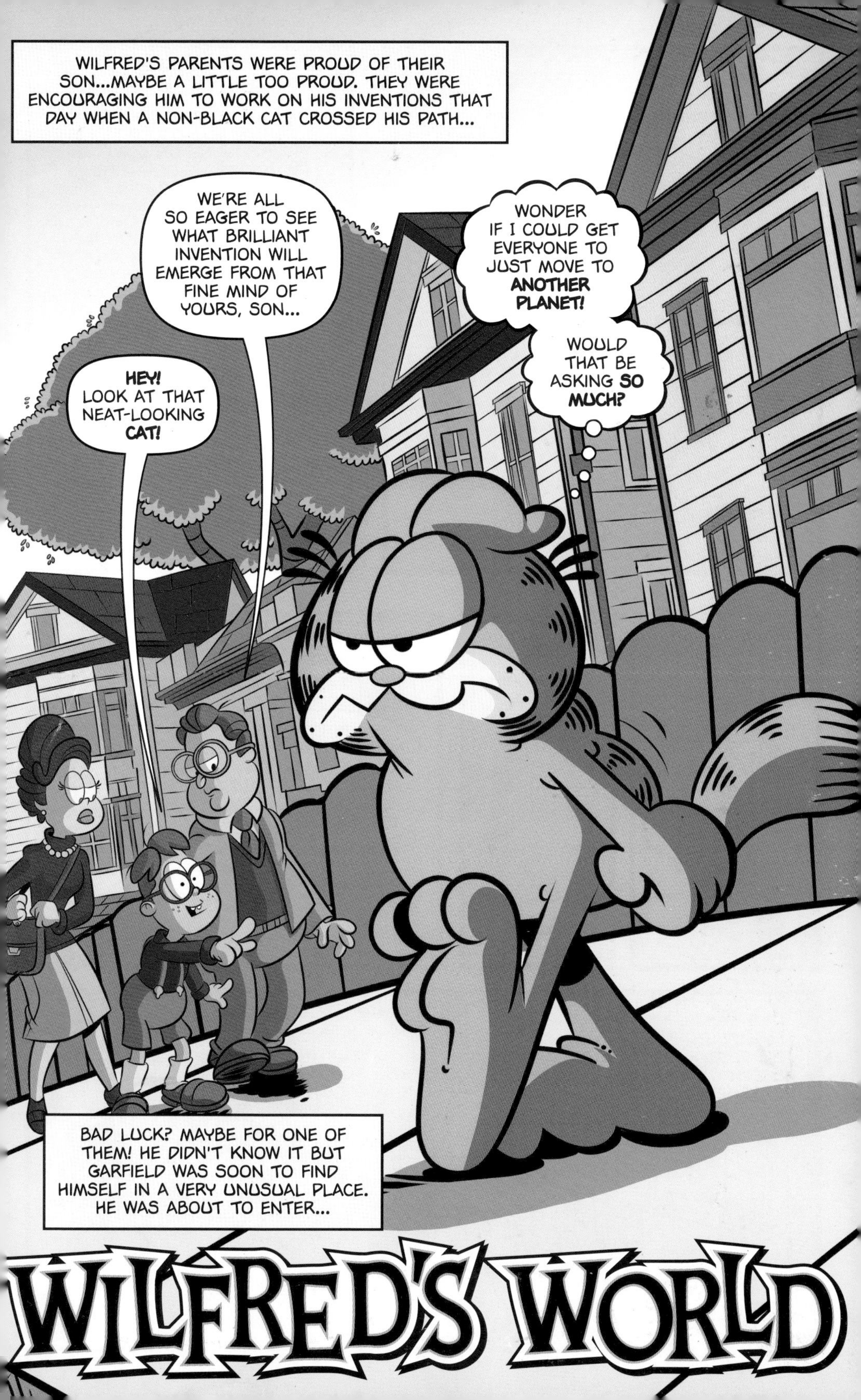
WILFRED'S PARENTS WERE PROUD OF THEIR SON...MAYBE A LITTLE TOO PROUD. THEY WERE ENCOURAGING HIM TO WORK ON HIS INVENTIONS THAT DAY WHEN A NON-BLACK CAT CROSSED HIS PATH...
WE'RE ALL SO EAGER TO SEE WHAT BRILLIANT INVENTION WILL EMERGE FROM THAT FINE MIND OF YOURS, SON...
HEY! LOOK AT THAT NEAT-LOOKING CAT!
WONDER IF I COULD GET EVERYONE TO JUST MOVE TO ANOTHER PLANET!
WOULD THAT BE ASKING SO MUCH?
BAD LUCK? MAYBE FOR ONE OF THEM! HE DIDN'T KNOW IT BUT GARFIELD WAS SOON TO FIND HIMSELF IN A VERY UNUSUAL PLACE. HE WAS ABOUT TO ENTER...
WILFRED'S WORLD

FATHER, MAY I HAVE A CAT LIKE THAT SOMEDAY?

"A CAT"!!!?

BOYS WITH YOUR INTELLECT AND POTENTIAL DO **NOT** ALLOW (ICK!) PETS TO TAKE THEM AWAY FROM IMPORTANT WORK!

BUT I WOULD **LOVE HIM** AND **TAKE CARE OF HIM** AND--

--AND WASTE TIME YOU **COULD** BE SPENDING ON SOME IMPORTANT SCIENTIFIC BREAKTHROUGH!

YOUR FATHER HAS SPOKEN, WILFRED! **THAT'S FINAL!**

YES, I SUPPOSE IT IS...

AND SO IT WAS OFF TO THE LIBRARY FOR THE LAD...

...WHERE HE CONTINUED HIS RESEARCH ON "DIMENSIONAL DISPLACEMENT"...

"IN THEORY, EACH PERSON, PLACE OR THING EXISTS IN A SPECIFIC TIME AND PLACE BUT ALSO A SPECIFIC DIMENSION...A PARTICULAR REALITY..."

INTERESTING...

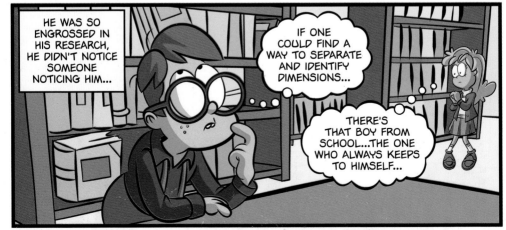

HE WAS SO ENGROSSED IN HIS RESEARCH, HE DIDN'T NOTICE SOMEONE NOTICING HIM...

IF ONE COULD FIND A WAY TO SEPARATE AND IDENTIFY DIMENSIONS...

THERE'S THAT BOY FROM SCHOOL...THE ONE WHO ALWAYS KEEPS TO HIMSELF...

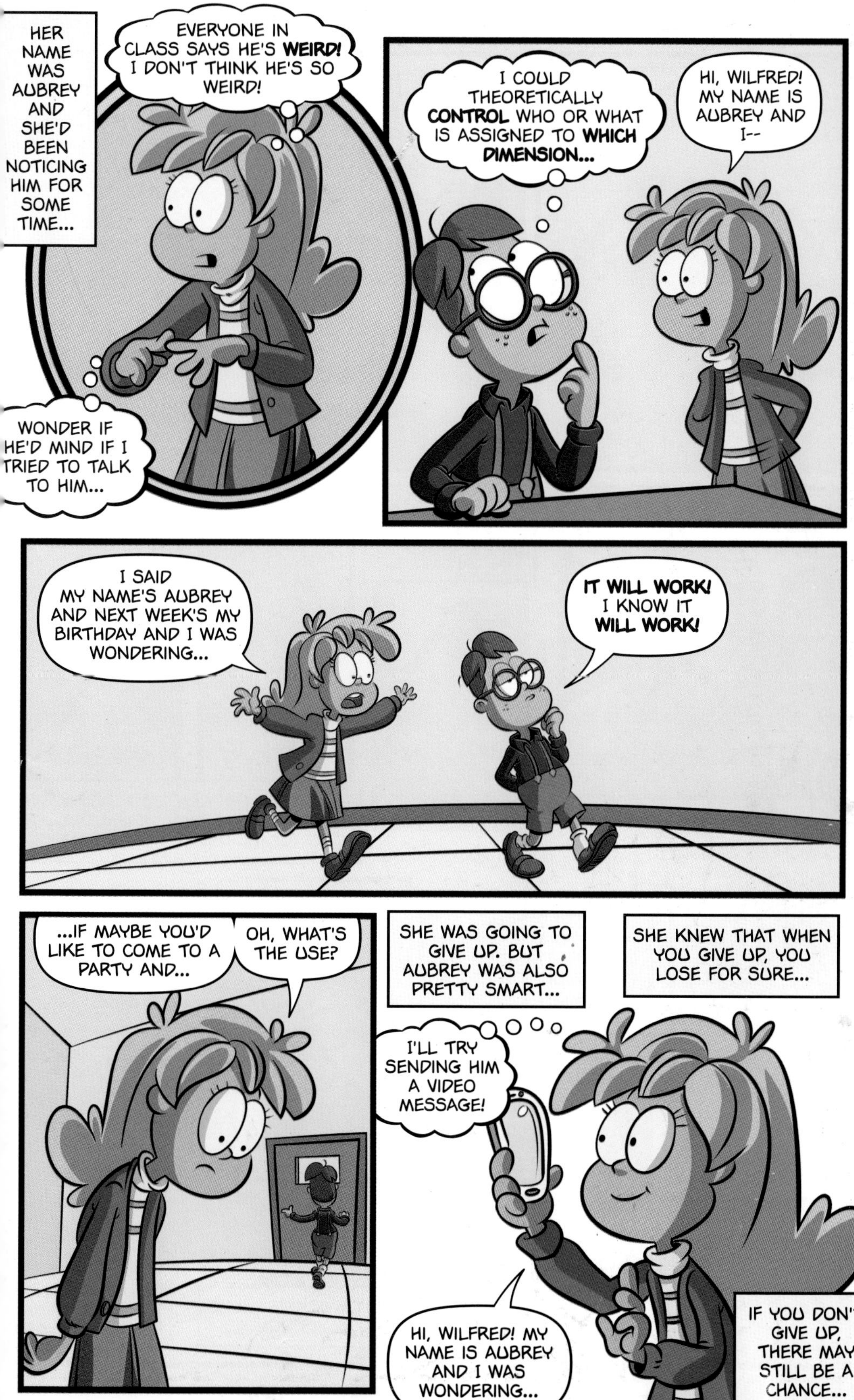

HER NAME WAS AUBREY AND SHE'D BEEN NOTICING HIM FOR SOME TIME...
EVERYONE IN CLASS SAYS HE'S **WEIRD!** I DON'T THINK HE'S SO WEIRD!
WONDER IF HE'D MIND IF I TRIED TO TALK TO HIM...
I COULD THEORETICALLY **CONTROL** WHO OR WHAT IS ASSIGNED TO **WHICH DIMENSION...**
HI, WILFRED! MY NAME IS AUBREY AND I--
I SAID MY NAME'S AUBREY AND NEXT WEEK'S MY BIRTHDAY AND I WAS WONDERING...
IT WILL WORK! I KNOW IT **WILL WORK!**
...IF MAYBE YOU'D LIKE TO COME TO A PARTY AND...
OH, WHAT'S THE USE?
SHE WAS GOING TO GIVE UP. BUT AUBREY WAS ALSO PRETTY SMART...
SHE KNEW THAT WHEN YOU GIVE UP, YOU LOSE FOR SURE...
I'LL TRY SENDING HIM A VIDEO MESSAGE!
HI, WILFRED! MY NAME IS AUBREY AND I WAS WONDERING...
IF YOU DON'T GIVE UP, THERE MAY STILL BE A CHANCE...

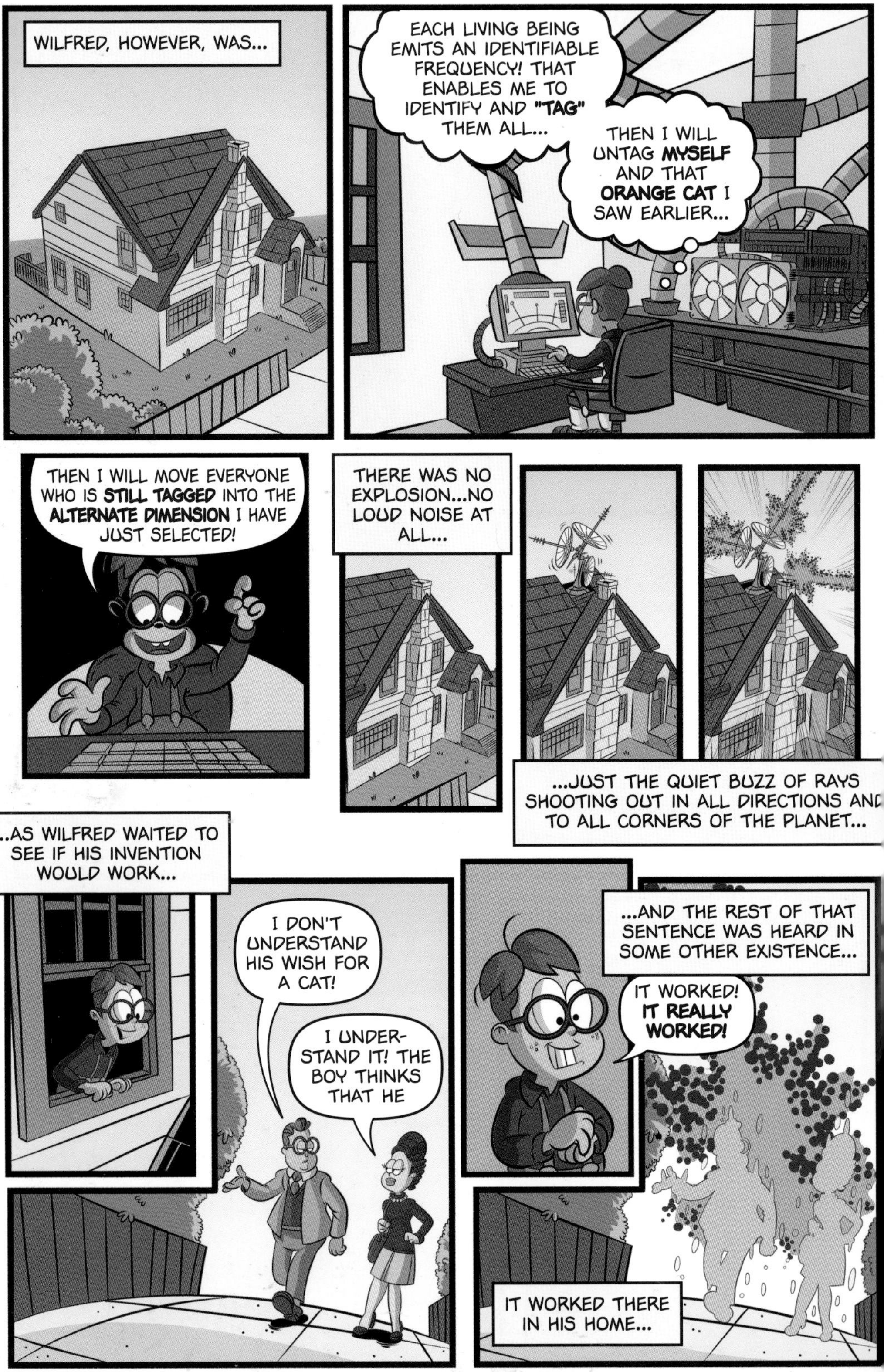
WILFRED, HOWEVER, WAS...
EACH LIVING BEING EMITS AN IDENTIFIABLE FREQUENCY! THAT ENABLES ME TO IDENTIFY AND "TAG" THEM ALL...
THEN I WILL UNTAG MYSELF AND THAT ORANGE CAT I SAW EARLIER...
THEN I WILL MOVE EVERYONE WHO IS STILL TAGGED INTO THE ALTERNATE DIMENSION I HAVE JUST SELECTED!
THERE WAS NO EXPLOSION...NO LOUD NOISE AT ALL...
...JUST THE QUIET BUZZ OF RAYS SHOOTING OUT IN ALL DIRECTIONS AND TO ALL CORNERS OF THE PLANET...
...AS WILFRED WAITED TO SEE IF HIS INVENTION WOULD WORK...
I DON'T UNDERSTAND HIS WISH FOR A CAT!
I UNDER-STAND IT! THE BOY THINKS THAT HE
...AND THE REST OF THAT SENTENCE WAS HEARD IN SOME OTHER EXISTENCE...
IT WORKED! IT REALLY WORKED!
IT WORKED THERE IN HIS HOME...

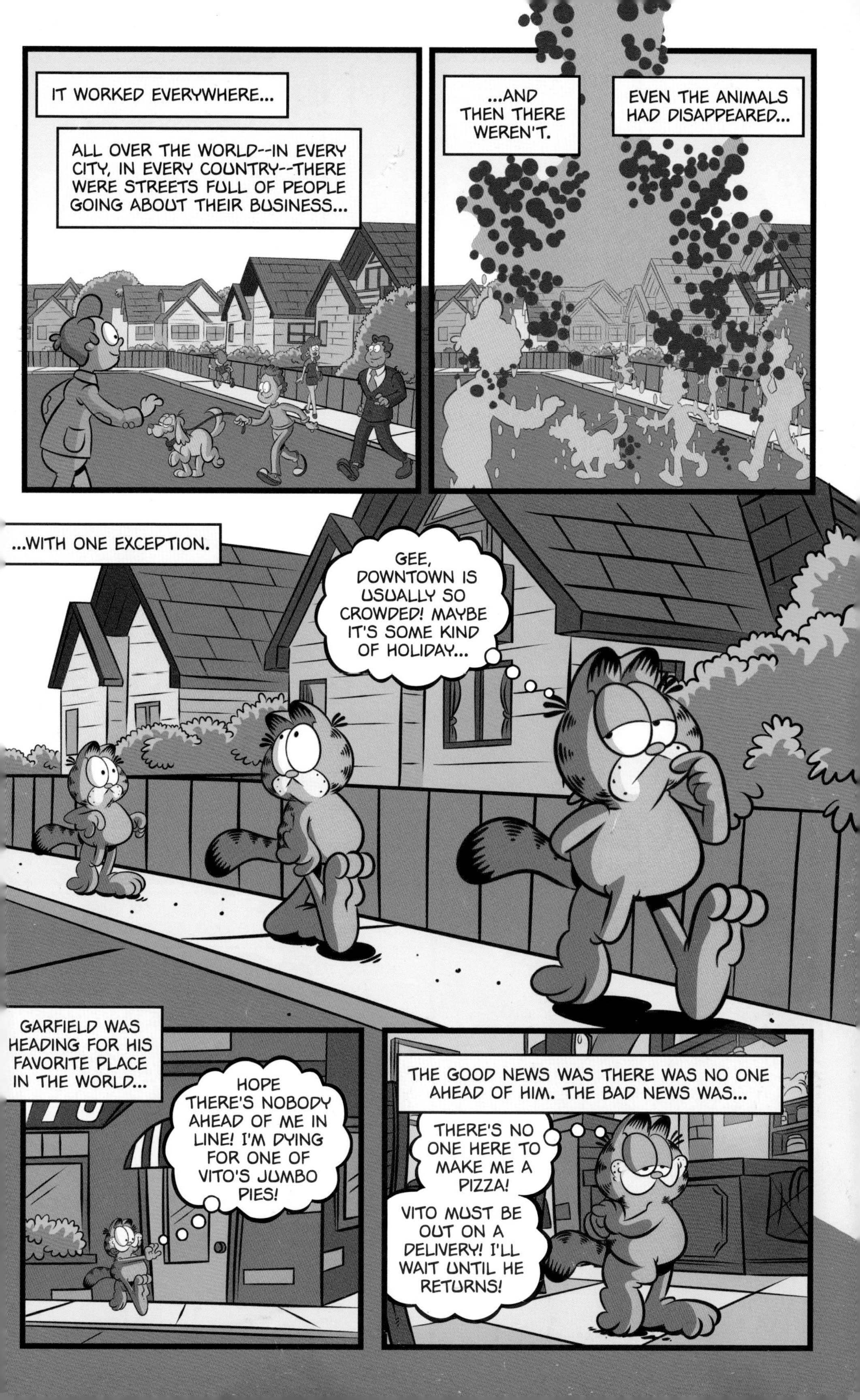
IT WORKED EVERYWHERE...
ALL OVER THE WORLD--IN EVERY CITY, IN EVERY COUNTRY--THERE WERE STREETS FULL OF PEOPLE GOING ABOUT THEIR BUSINESS...
...AND THEN THERE WEREN'T.
EVEN THE ANIMALS HAD DISAPPEARED...
...WITH ONE EXCEPTION.
GEE, DOWNTOWN IS USUALLY SO CROWDED! MAYBE IT'S SOME KIND OF HOLIDAY...
GARFIELD WAS HEADING FOR HIS FAVORITE PLACE IN THE WORLD...
HOPE THERE'S NOBODY AHEAD OF ME IN LINE! I'M DYING FOR ONE OF VITO'S JUMBO PIES!
THE GOOD NEWS WAS THERE WAS NO ONE AHEAD OF HIM. THE BAD NEWS WAS...
THERE'S NO ONE HERE TO MAKE ME A PIZZA!
VITO MUST BE OUT ON A DELIVERY! I'LL WAIT UNTIL HE RETURNS!

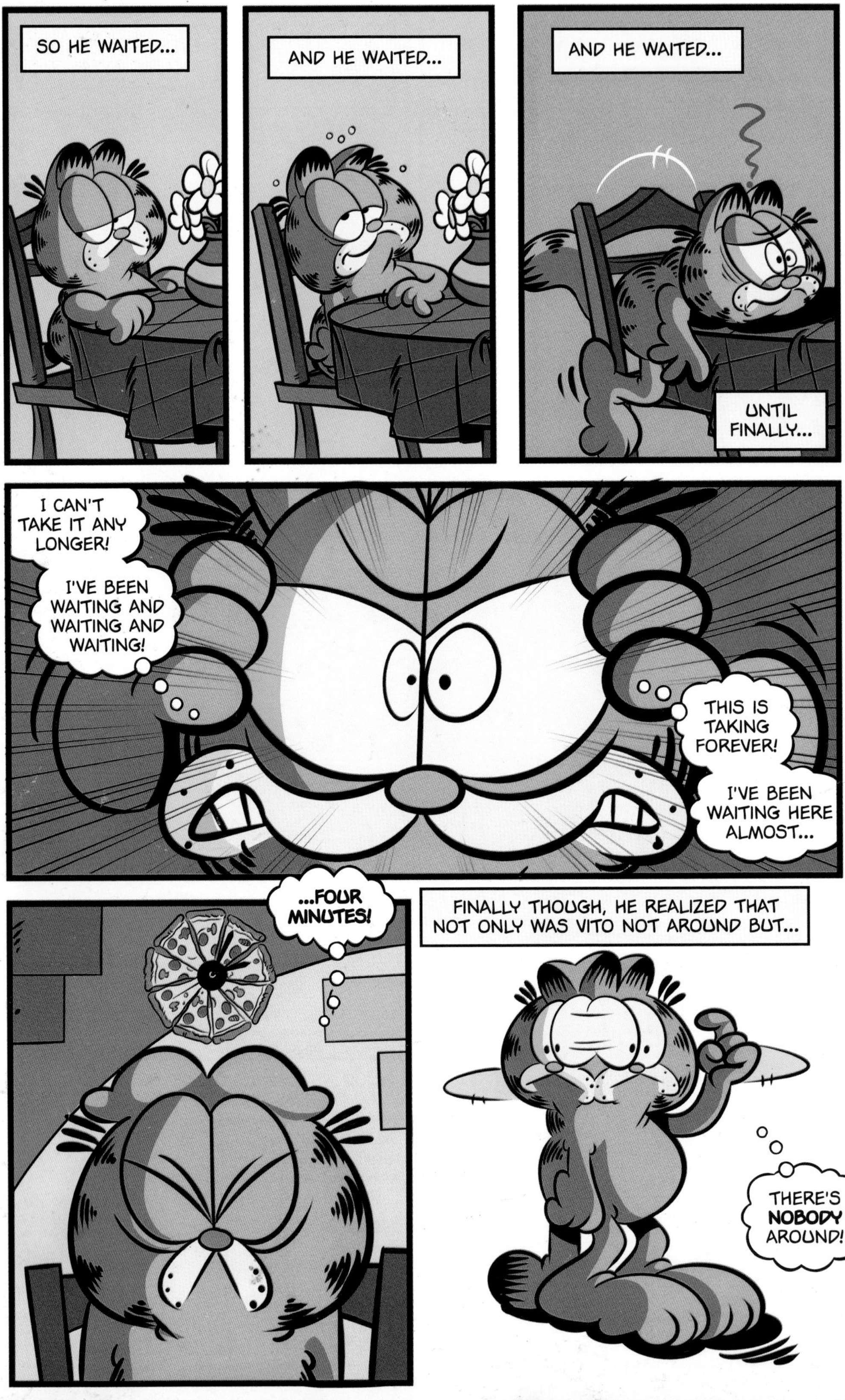
SO HE WAITED...
AND HE WAITED...
AND HE WAITED...
UNTIL FINALLY...
I CAN'T TAKE IT ANY LONGER!
I'VE BEEN WAITING AND WAITING AND WAITING!
THIS IS TAKING FOREVER!
I'VE BEEN WAITING HERE ALMOST...
...FOUR MINUTES!
FINALLY THOUGH, HE REALIZED THAT NOT ONLY WAS VITO NOT AROUND BUT...
THERE'S NOBODY AROUND!

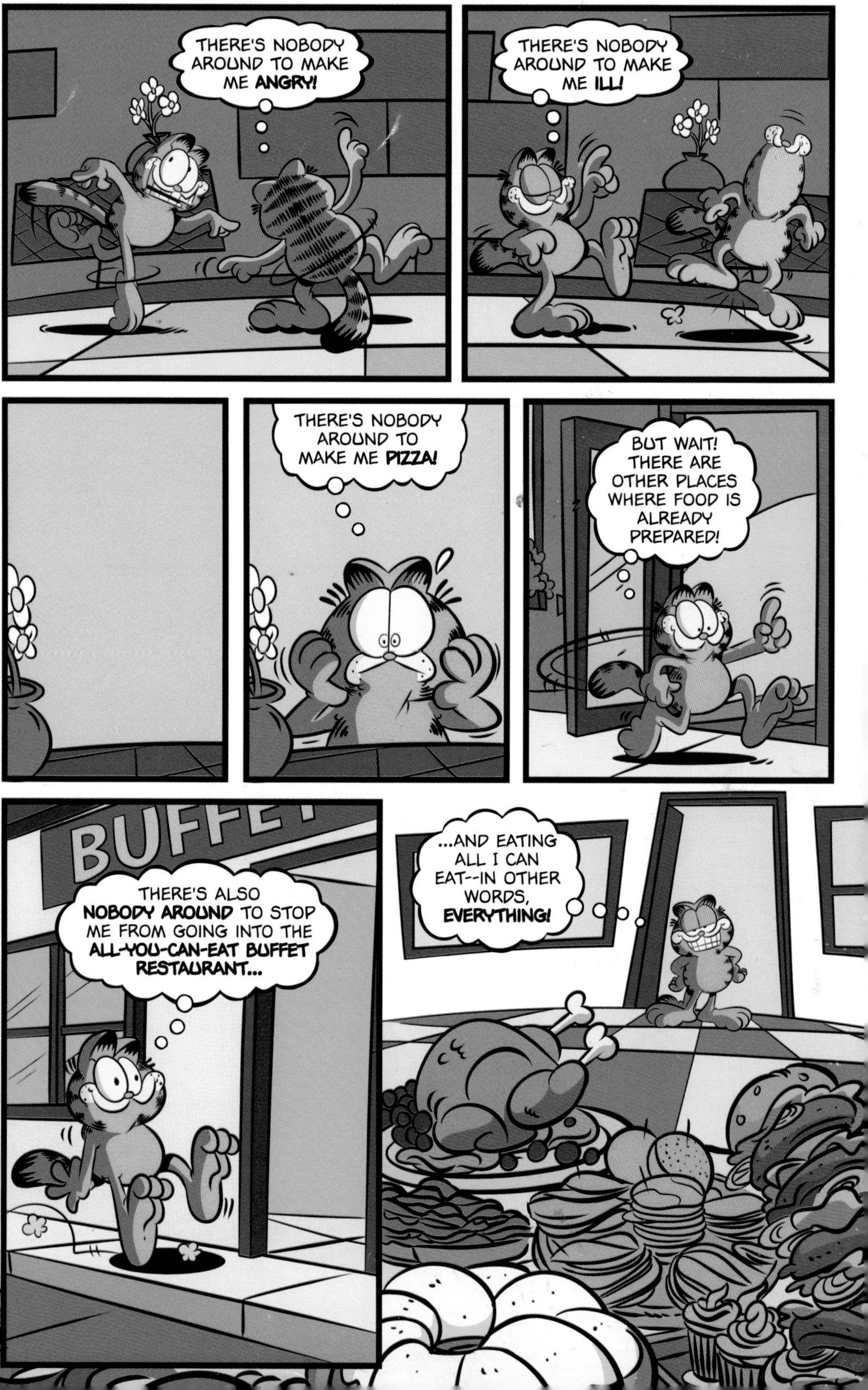
THERE'S NOBODY AROUND TO MAKE ME **ANGRY!**
THERE'S NOBODY AROUND TO MAKE ME **ILL!**
THERE'S NOBODY AROUND TO MAKE ME **PIZZA!**
BUT WAIT! THERE ARE OTHER PLACES WHERE FOOD IS ALREADY PREPARED!
BUFFE
THERE'S ALSO **NOBODY AROUND** TO STOP ME FROM GOING INTO THE **ALL-YOU-CAN-EAT BUFFET RESTAURANT...**
...AND EATING ALL I CAN EAT--IN OTHER WORDS, **EVERYTHING!**

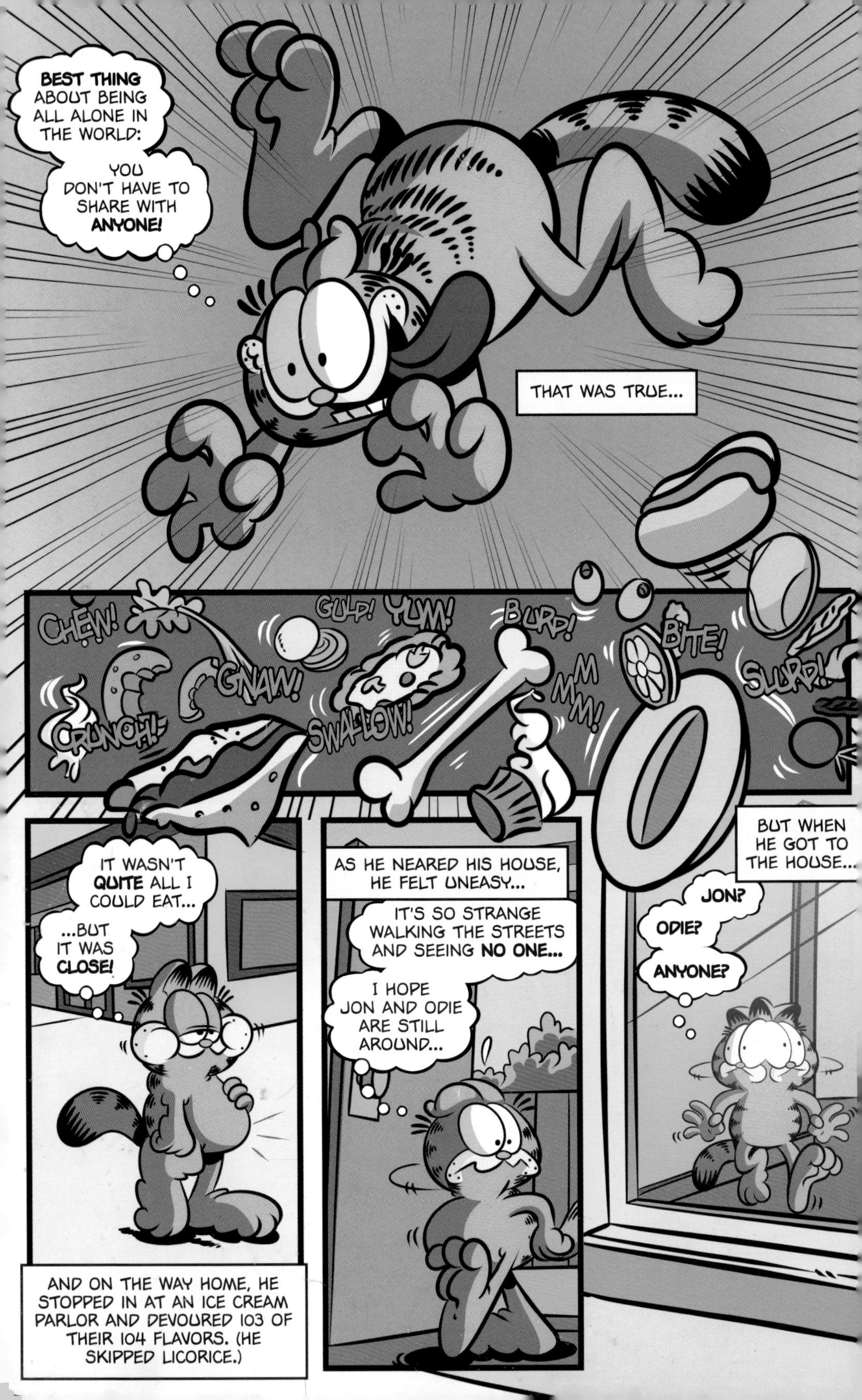
BEST THING ABOUT BEING ALL ALONE IN THE WORLD:
YOU DON'T HAVE TO SHARE WITH ANYONE!
THAT WAS TRUE...
CHEW!
CRUNCH!
GNAW!
GULP! YUM!
SWALLOW!
BURP!
MMMM!
BITE!
SLURP!
IT WASN'T QUITE ALL I COULD EAT...
...BUT IT WAS CLOSE!
AND ON THE WAY HOME, HE STOPPED IN AT AN ICE CREAM PARLOR AND DEVOURED 103 OF THEIR 104 FLAVORS. (HE SKIPPED LICORICE.)
AS HE NEARED HIS HOUSE, HE FELT UNEASY...
IT'S SO STRANGE WALKING THE STREETS AND SEEING NO ONE...
I HOPE JON AND ODIE ARE STILL AROUND...
BUT WHEN HE GOT TO THE HOUSE...
JON?
ODIE?
ANYONE?

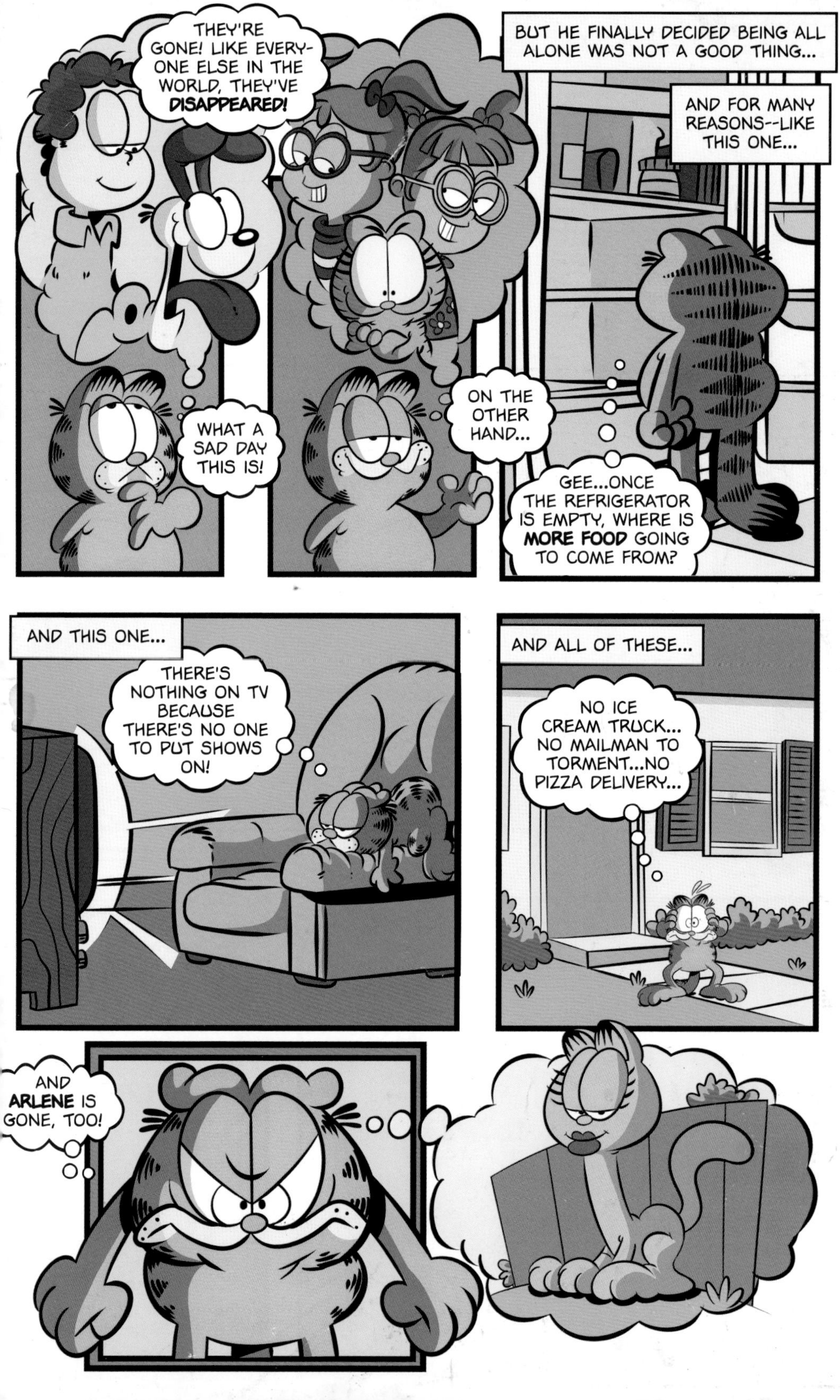
THEY'RE GONE! LIKE EVERY-ONE ELSE IN THE WORLD, THEY'VE **DISAPPEARED!**
WHAT A SAD DAY THIS IS!
ON THE OTHER HAND...
BUT HE FINALLY DECIDED BEING ALL ALONE WAS NOT A GOOD THING...
AND FOR MANY REASONS--LIKE THIS ONE...
GEE...ONCE THE REFRIGERATOR IS EMPTY, WHERE IS **MORE FOOD** GOING TO COME FROM?
AND THIS ONE...
THERE'S NOTHING ON TV BECAUSE THERE'S NO ONE TO PUT SHOWS ON!
AND ALL OF THESE...
NO ICE CREAM TRUCK... NO MAILMAN TO TORMENT...NO PIZZA DELIVERY...
AND **ARLENE** IS GONE, TOO!

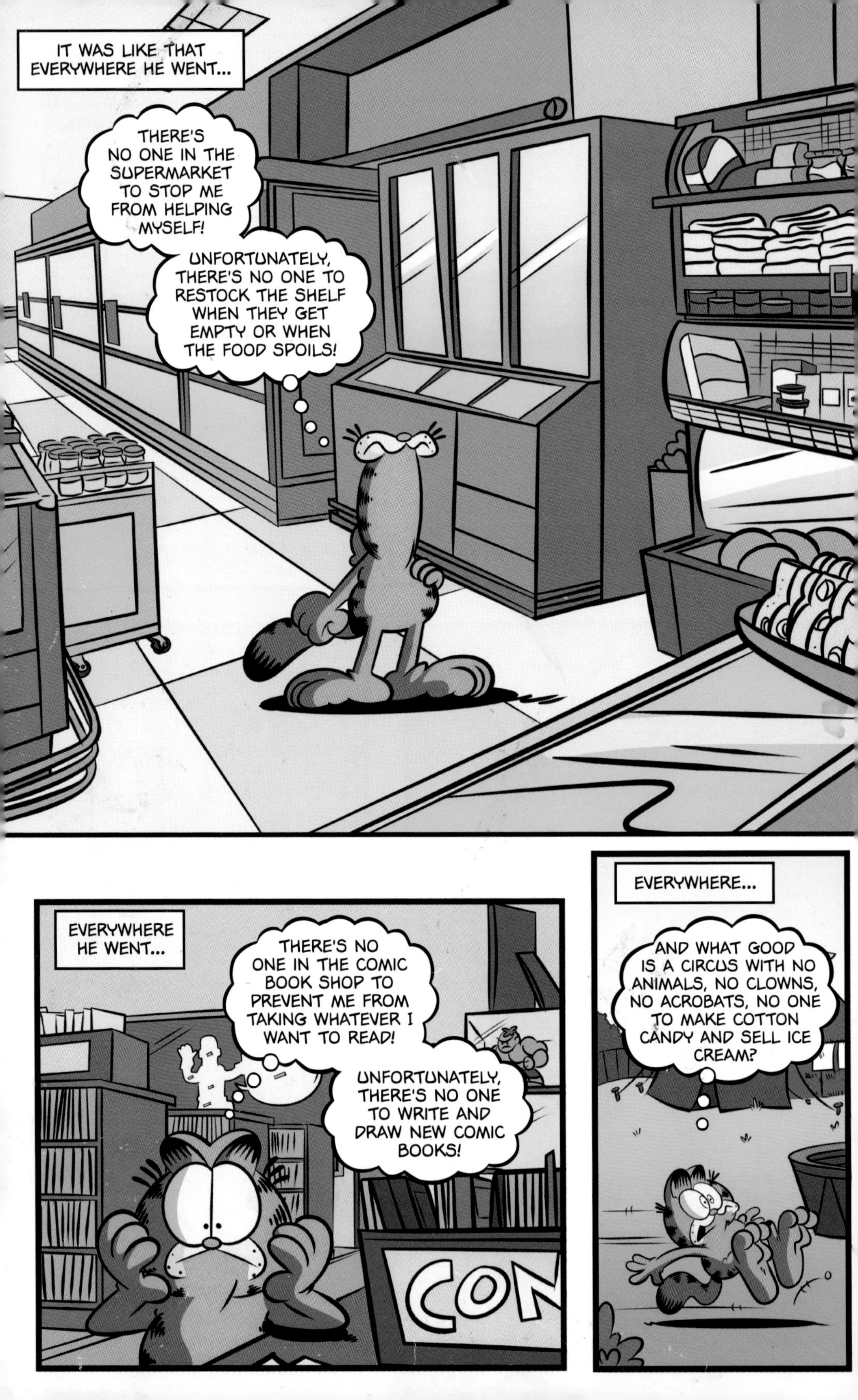
IT WAS LIKE THAT EVERYWHERE HE WENT...
THERE'S NO ONE IN THE SUPERMARKET TO STOP ME FROM HELPING MYSELF!
UNFORTUNATELY, THERE'S NO ONE TO RESTOCK THE SHELF WHEN THEY GET EMPTY OR WHEN THE FOOD SPOILS!
EVERYWHERE HE WENT...
THERE'S NO ONE IN THE COMIC BOOK SHOP TO PREVENT ME FROM TAKING WHATEVER I WANT TO READ!
UNFORTUNATELY, THERE'S NO ONE TO WRITE AND DRAW NEW COMIC BOOKS!
CON
EVERYWHERE...
AND WHAT GOOD IS A CIRCUS WITH NO ANIMALS, NO CLOWNS, NO ACROBATS, NO ONE TO MAKE COTTON CANDY AND SELL ICE CREAM?

WHERE DID EVERYBODY GO???

HI, KITTY CAT! YOU'RE PROBABLY WONDERING WHERE EVERYBODY WENT!

THE THOUGHT **HAD** CROSSED MY MIND!

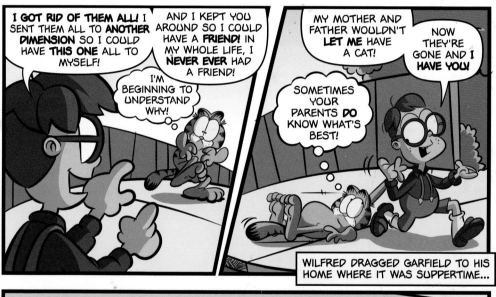

I **GOT RID OF THEM ALL!** I SENT THEM ALL TO **ANOTHER DIMENSION** SO I COULD HAVE **THIS ONE** ALL TO MYSELF!

AND I KEPT YOU AROUND SO I COULD HAVE A **FRIEND!** IN MY WHOLE LIFE, I **NEVER EVER** HAD A FRIEND!

I'M BEGINNING TO UNDERSTAND WHY!

MY MOTHER AND FATHER WOULDN'T **LET ME** HAVE A CAT!

NOW THEY'RE GONE AND I **HAVE YOU!**

SOMETIMES YOUR PARENTS **DO** KNOW WHAT'S BEST!

WILFRED DRAGGED GARFIELD TO HIS HOME WHERE IT WAS SUPPERTIME...

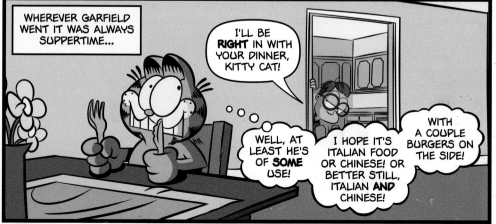

WHEREVER GARFIELD WENT IT WAS ALWAYS SUPPERTIME...

I'LL BE **RIGHT** IN WITH YOUR DINNER, KITTY CAT!

WELL, AT LEAST HE'S OF **SOME** USE!

I HOPE IT'S ITALIAN FOOD OR CHINESE! OR BETTER STILL, ITALIAN **AND** CHINESE!

WITH A COUPLE BURGERS ON THE SIDE!

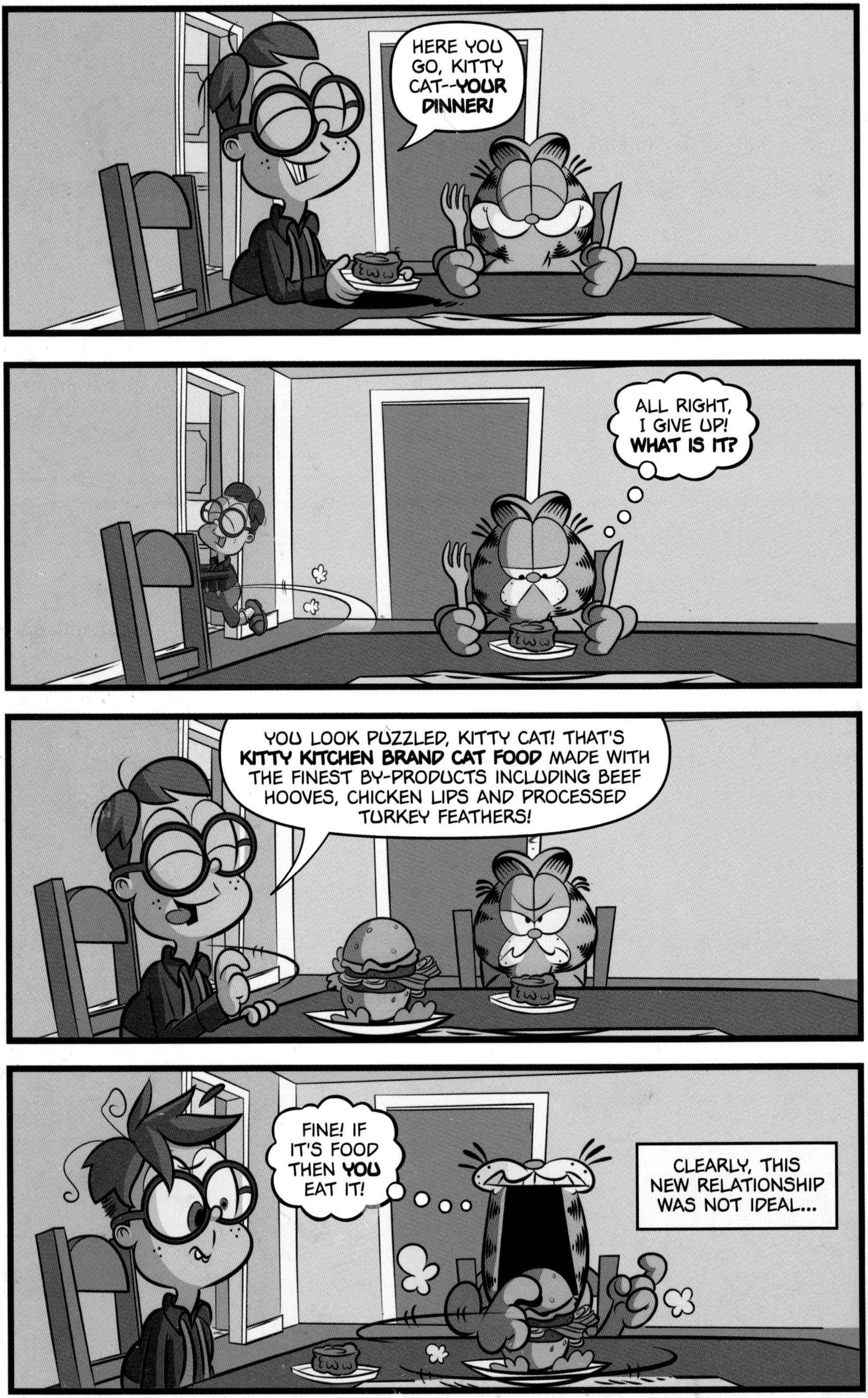
HERE YOU GO, KITTY CAT--YOUR DINNER!
ALL RIGHT, I GIVE UP! WHAT IS IT?
YOU LOOK PUZZLED, KITTY CAT! THAT'S KITTY KITCHEN BRAND CAT FOOD MADE WITH THE FINEST BY-PRODUCTS INCLUDING BEEF HOOVES, CHICKEN LIPS AND PROCESSED TURKEY FEATHERS!
FINE! IF IT'S FOOD THEN YOU EAT IT!
CLEARLY, THIS NEW RELATIONSHIP WAS NOT IDEAL...

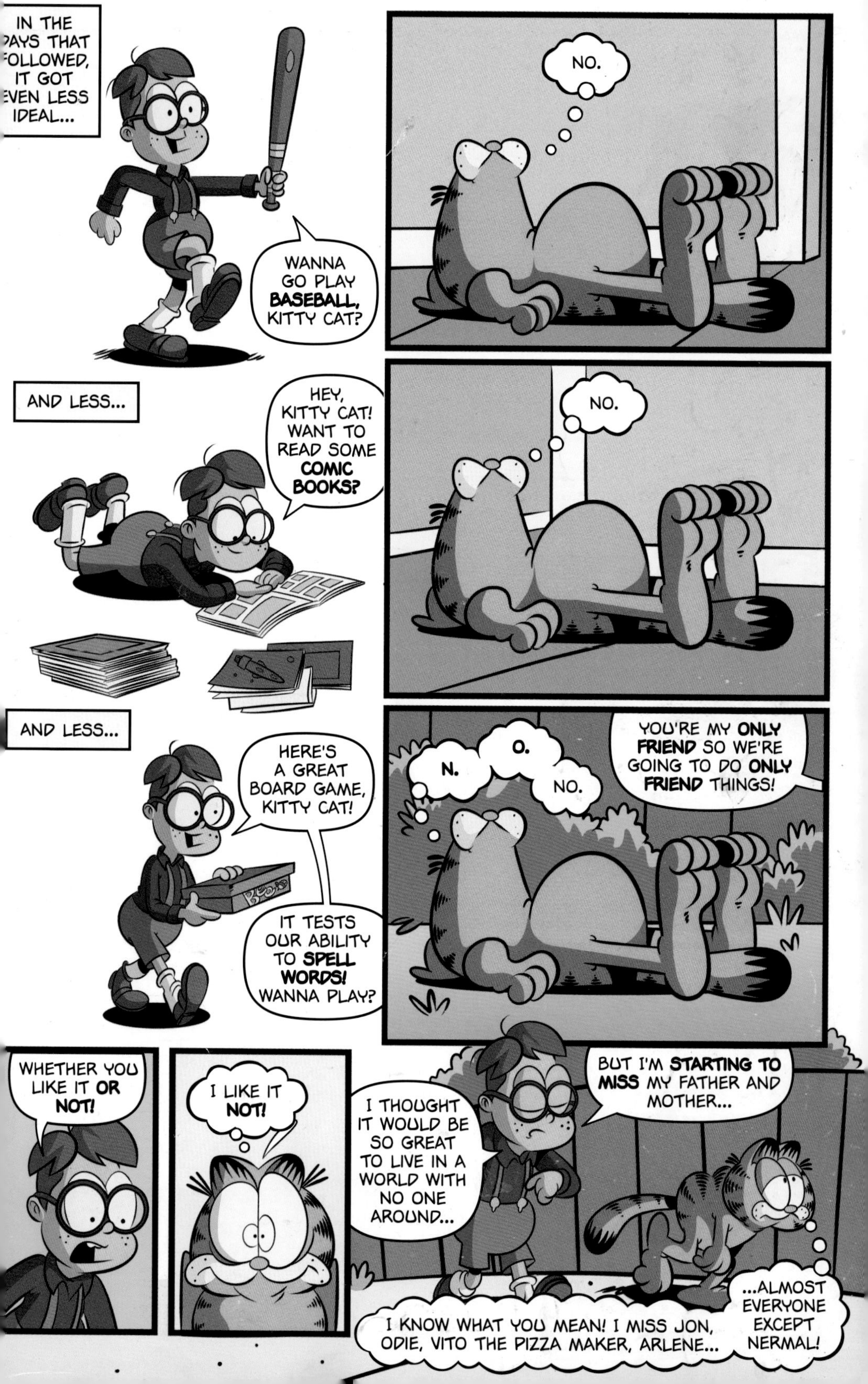

IN THE DAYS THAT FOLLOWED, IT GOT EVEN LESS IDEAL...
WANNA GO PLAY **BASEBALL,** KITTY CAT?
NO.
AND LESS...
HEY, KITTY CAT! WANT TO READ SOME **COMIC BOOKS?**
NO.
AND LESS...
HERE'S A GREAT BOARD GAME, KITTY CAT!
IT TESTS OUR ABILITY TO **SPELL WORDS!** WANNA PLAY?
N.
O.
NO.
YOU'RE MY **ONLY FRIEND** SO WE'RE GOING TO DO **ONLY FRIEND** THINGS!
WHETHER YOU LIKE IT **OR NOT!**
I LIKE IT **NOT!**
I THOUGHT IT WOULD BE SO GREAT TO LIVE IN A WORLD WITH NO ONE AROUND...
BUT I'M **STARTING TO MISS** MY FATHER AND MOTHER...
I KNOW WHAT YOU MEAN! I MISS JON, ODIE, VITO THE PIZZA MAKER, ARLENE...
...ALMOST EVERYONE EXCEPT NERMAL!

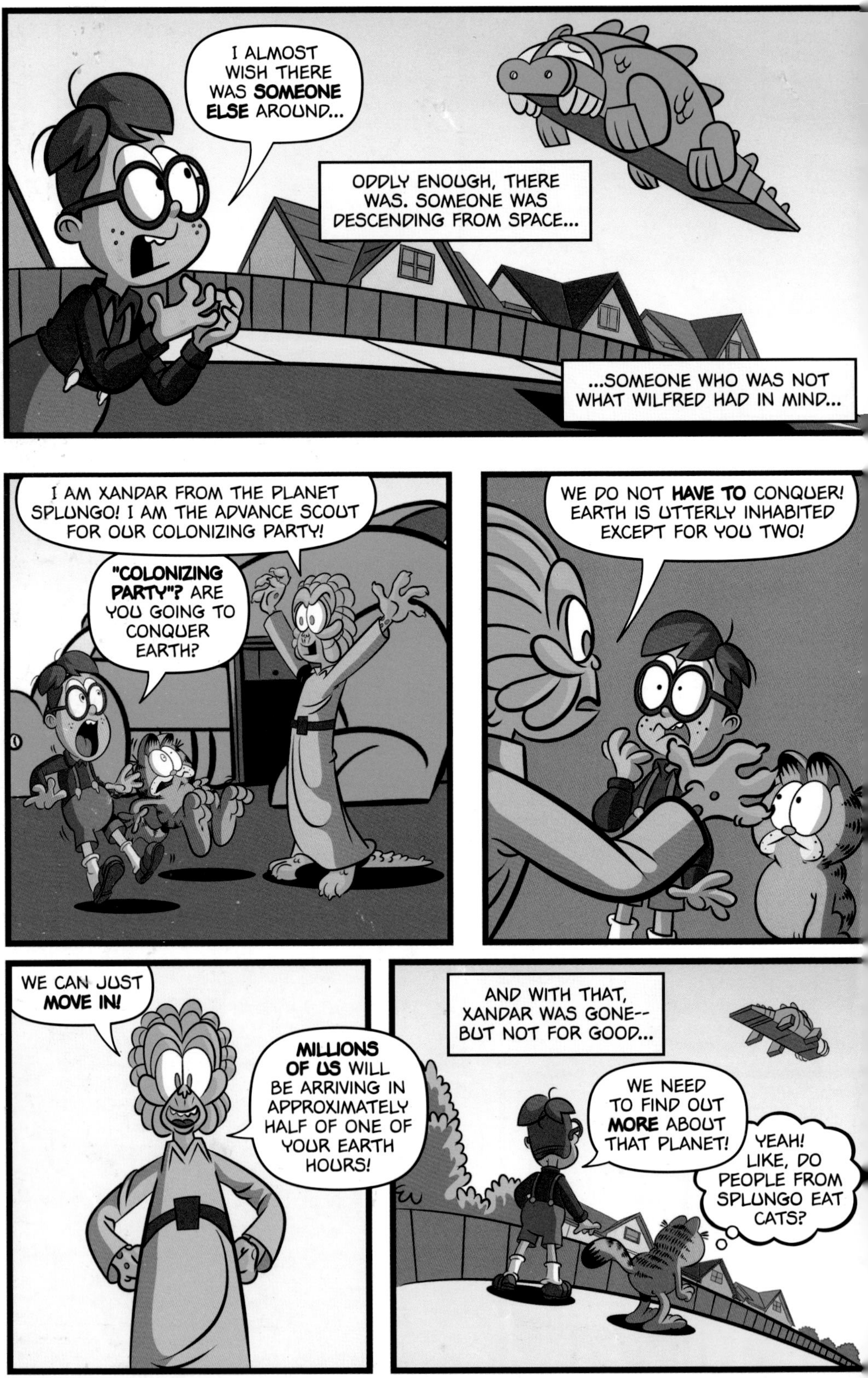
I ALMOST WISH THERE WAS **SOMEONE ELSE** AROUND...
ODDLY ENOUGH, THERE WAS. SOMEONE WAS DESCENDING FROM SPACE...
...SOMEONE WHO WAS NOT WHAT WILFRED HAD IN MIND...
I AM XANDAR FROM THE PLANET SPLUNGO! I AM THE ADVANCE SCOUT FOR OUR COLONIZING PARTY!
"COLONIZING PARTY"? ARE YOU GOING TO CONQUER EARTH?
WE DO NOT **HAVE TO** CONQUER! EARTH IS UTTERLY INHABITED EXCEPT FOR YOU TWO!
WE CAN JUST **MOVE IN!**
MILLIONS OF US WILL BE ARRIVING IN APPROXIMATELY HALF OF ONE OF YOUR EARTH HOURS!
AND WITH THAT, XANDAR WAS GONE-- BUT NOT FOR GOOD...
WE NEED TO FIND OUT **MORE** ABOUT THAT PLANET!
YEAH! LIKE, DO PEOPLE FROM SPLUNGO EAT CATS?

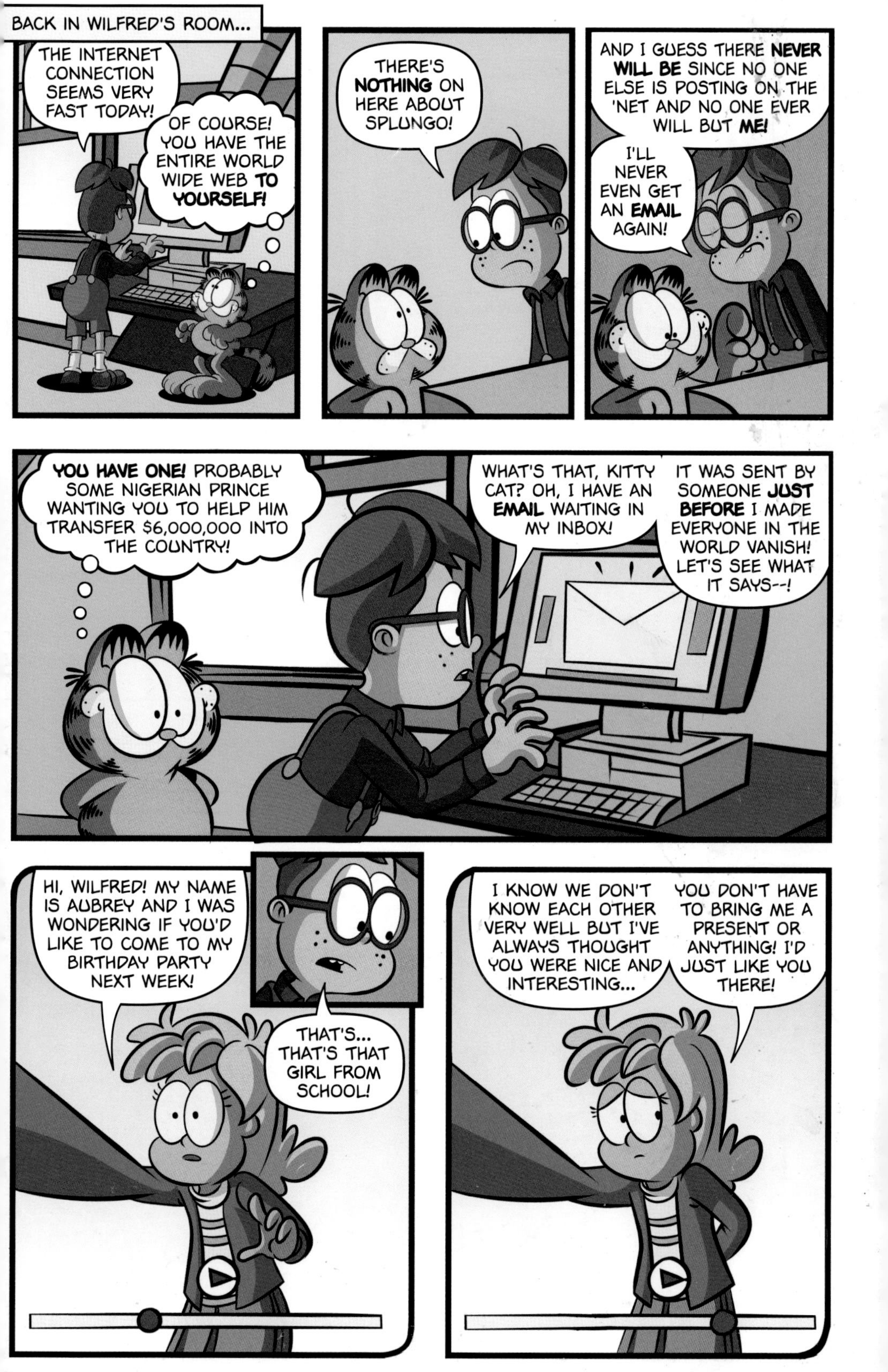
BACK IN WILFRED'S ROOM...
THE INTERNET CONNECTION SEEMS VERY FAST TODAY!
OF COURSE! YOU HAVE THE ENTIRE WORLD WIDE WEB TO YOURSELF!
THERE'S NOTHING ON HERE ABOUT SPLUNGO!
AND I GUESS THERE NEVER WILL BE SINCE NO ONE ELSE IS POSTING ON THE 'NET AND NO ONE EVER WILL BUT ME!
I'LL NEVER EVEN GET AN EMAIL AGAIN!
YOU HAVE ONE! PROBABLY SOME NIGERIAN PRINCE WANTING YOU TO HELP HIM TRANSFER $6,000,000 INTO THE COUNTRY!
WHAT'S THAT, KITTY CAT? OH, I HAVE AN EMAIL WAITING IN MY INBOX!
IT WAS SENT BY SOMEONE JUST BEFORE I MADE EVERYONE IN THE WORLD VANISH! LET'S SEE WHAT IT SAYS--!
HI, WILFRED! MY NAME IS AUBREY AND I WAS WONDERING IF YOU'D LIKE TO COME TO MY BIRTHDAY PARTY NEXT WEEK!
THAT'S... THAT'S THAT GIRL FROM SCHOOL!
I KNOW WE DON'T KNOW EACH OTHER VERY WELL BUT I'VE ALWAYS THOUGHT YOU WERE NICE AND INTERESTING...
YOU DON'T HAVE TO BRING ME A PRESENT OR ANYTHING! I'D JUST LIKE YOU THERE!

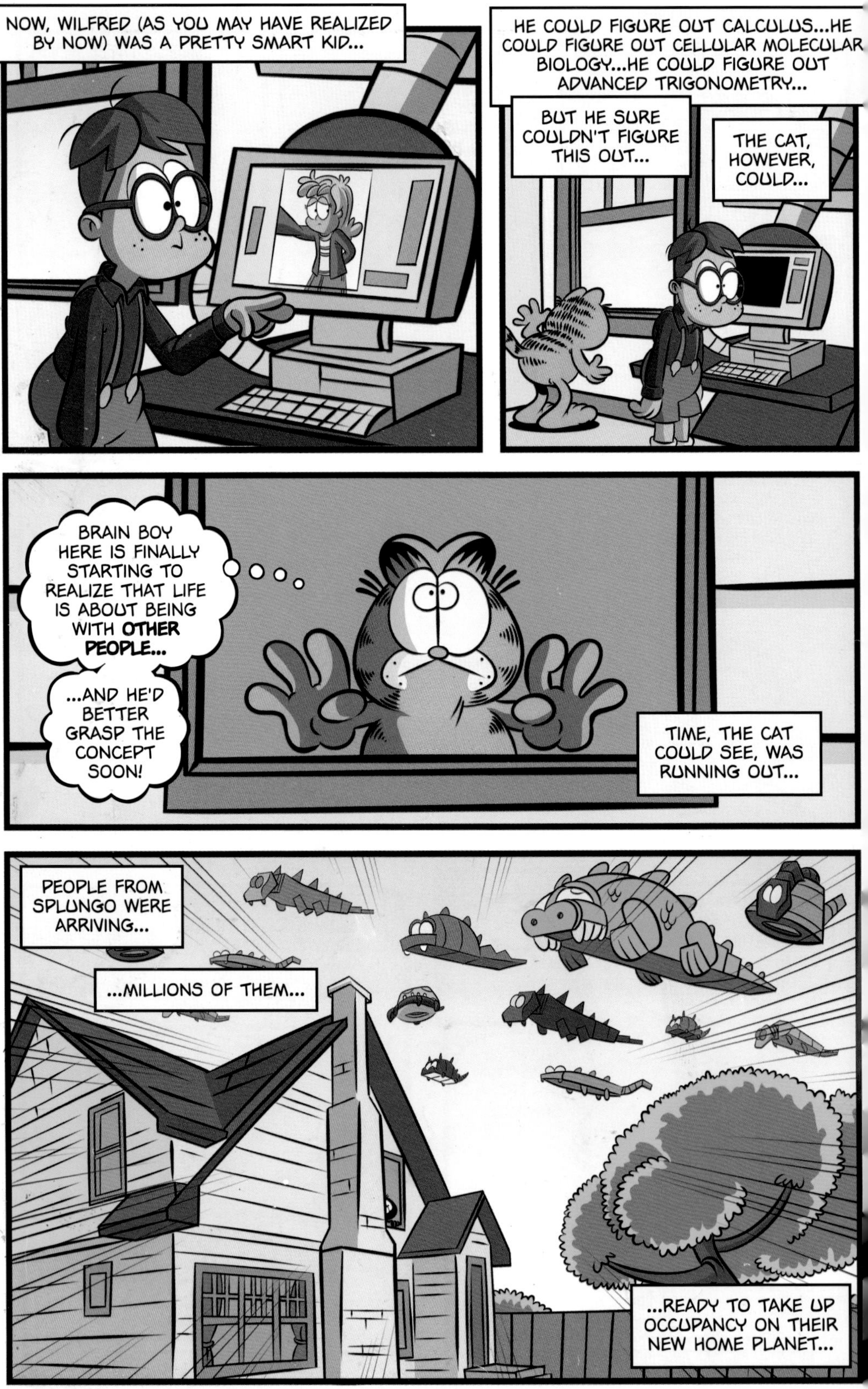

NOW, WILFRED (AS YOU MAY HAVE REALIZED BY NOW) WAS A PRETTY SMART KID...
HE COULD FIGURE OUT CALCULUS...HE COULD FIGURE OUT CELLULAR MOLECULAR BIOLOGY...HE COULD FIGURE OUT ADVANCED TRIGONOMETRY...
BUT HE SURE COULDN'T FIGURE THIS OUT...
THE CAT, HOWEVER, COULD...
BRAIN BOY HERE IS FINALLY STARTING TO REALIZE THAT LIFE IS ABOUT BEING WITH **OTHER PEOPLE...**
...AND HE'D BETTER GRASP THE CONCEPT SOON!
TIME, THE CAT COULD SEE, WAS RUNNING OUT...
PEOPLE FROM SPLUNGO WERE ARRIVING...
...MILLIONS OF THEM...
...READY TO TAKE UP OCCUPANCY ON THEIR NEW HOME PLANET...

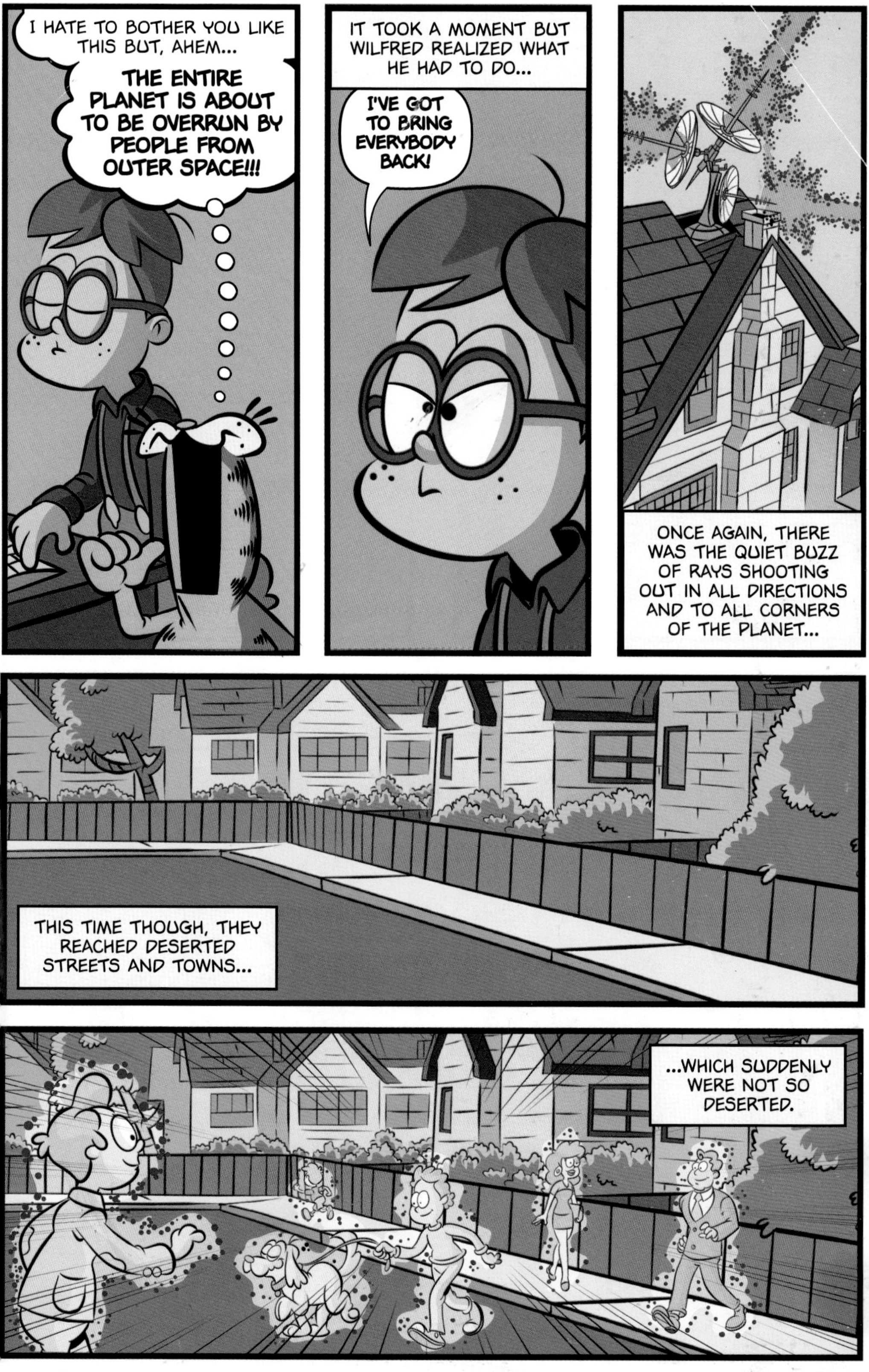

I HATE TO BOTHER YOU LIKE THIS BUT, AHEM...
THE ENTIRE PLANET IS ABOUT TO BE OVERRUN BY PEOPLE FROM OUTER SPACE!!!
IT TOOK A MOMENT BUT WILFRED REALIZED WHAT HE HAD TO DO...
I'VE GOT TO BRING EVERYBODY BACK!
ONCE AGAIN, THERE WAS THE QUIET BUZZ OF RAYS SHOOTING OUT IN ALL DIRECTIONS AND TO ALL CORNERS OF THE PLANET...
THIS TIME THOUGH, THEY REACHED DESERTED STREETS AND TOWNS...
...WHICH SUDDENLY WERE NOT SO DESERTED.

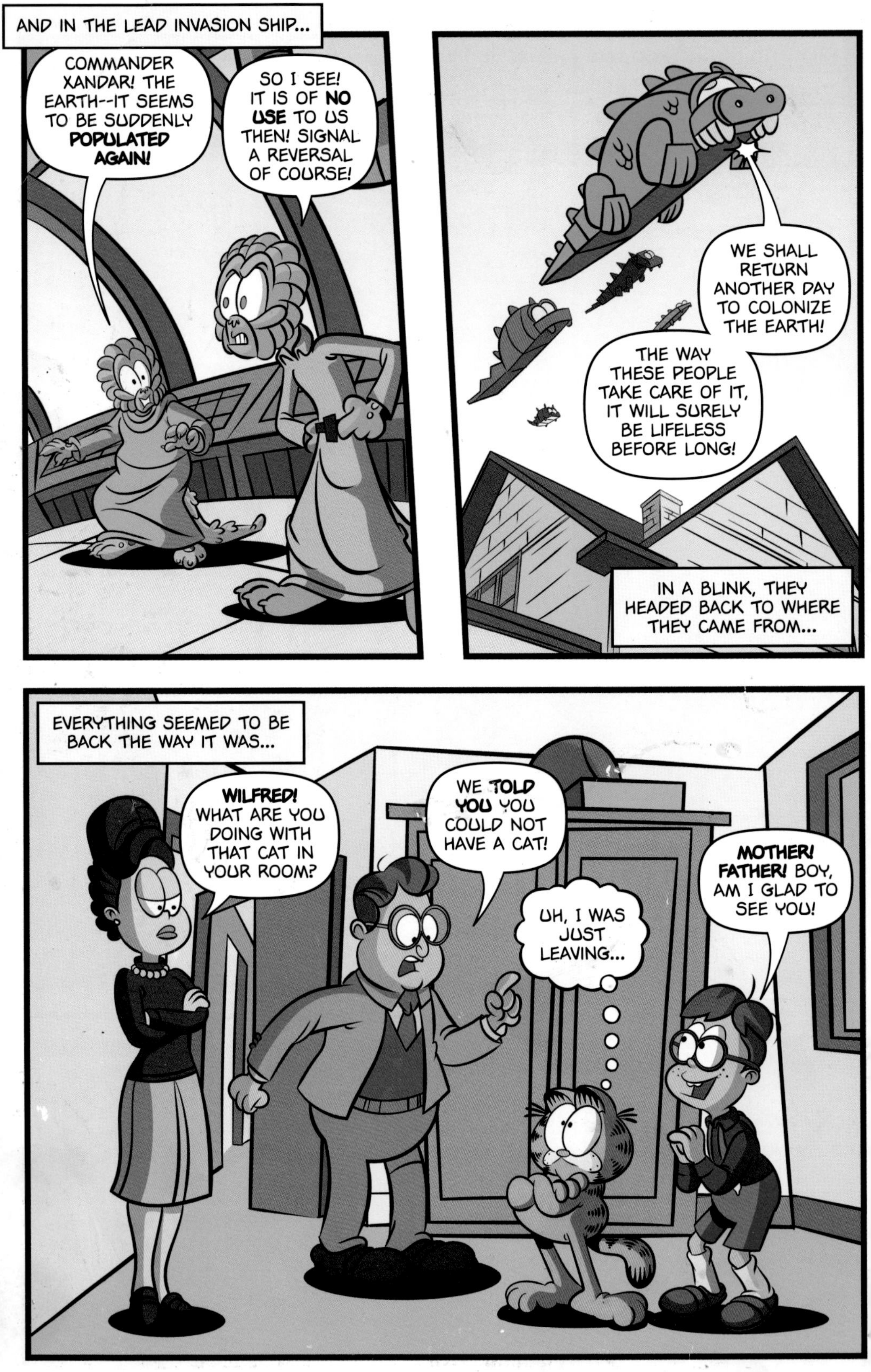

AND IN THE LEAD INVASION SHIP...
COMMANDER XANDAR! THE EARTH--IT SEEMS TO BE SUDDENLY **POPULATED AGAIN!**
SO I SEE! IT IS OF **NO USE** TO US THEN! SIGNAL A REVERSAL OF COURSE!
WE SHALL RETURN ANOTHER DAY TO COLONIZE THE EARTH!
THE WAY THESE PEOPLE TAKE CARE OF IT, IT WILL SURELY BE LIFELESS BEFORE LONG!
IN A BLINK, THEY HEADED BACK TO WHERE THEY CAME FROM...
EVERYTHING SEEMED TO BE BACK THE WAY IT WAS...
WILFRED! WHAT ARE YOU DOING WITH THAT CAT IN YOUR ROOM?
WE **TOLD YOU** YOU COULD NOT HAVE A CAT!
UH, I WAS JUST LEAVING...
MOTHER! FATHER! BOY, AM I GLAD TO SEE YOU!

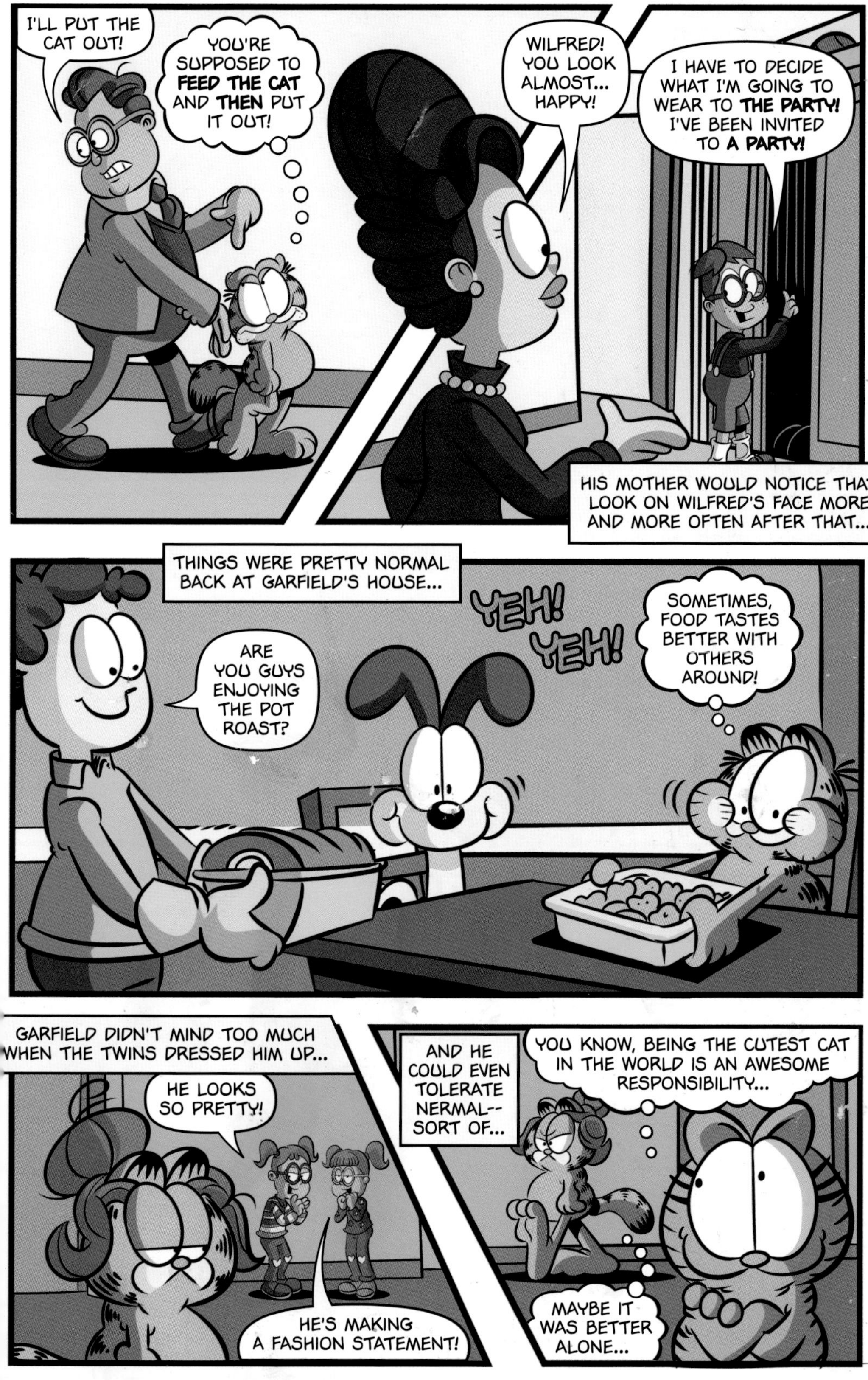
I'LL PUT THE CAT OUT!
YOU'RE SUPPOSED TO FEED THE CAT AND THEN PUT IT OUT!
WILFRED! YOU LOOK ALMOST... HAPPY!
I HAVE TO DECIDE WHAT I'M GOING TO WEAR TO THE PARTY! I'VE BEEN INVITED TO A PARTY!
HIS MOTHER WOULD NOTICE THAT LOOK ON WILFRED'S FACE MORE AND MORE OFTEN AFTER THAT...
THINGS WERE PRETTY NORMAL BACK AT GARFIELD'S HOUSE...
ARE YOU GUYS ENJOYING THE POT ROAST?
YEH! YEH!
SOMETIMES, FOOD TASTES BETTER WITH OTHERS AROUND!
GARFIELD DIDN'T MIND TOO MUCH WHEN THE TWINS DRESSED HIM UP...
HE LOOKS SO PRETTY!
HE'S MAKING A FASHION STATEMENT!
AND HE COULD EVEN TOLERATE NERMAL-- SORT OF...
YOU KNOW, BEING THE CUTEST CAT IN THE WORLD IS AN AWESOME RESPONSIBILITY...
MAYBE IT WAS BETTER ALONE...

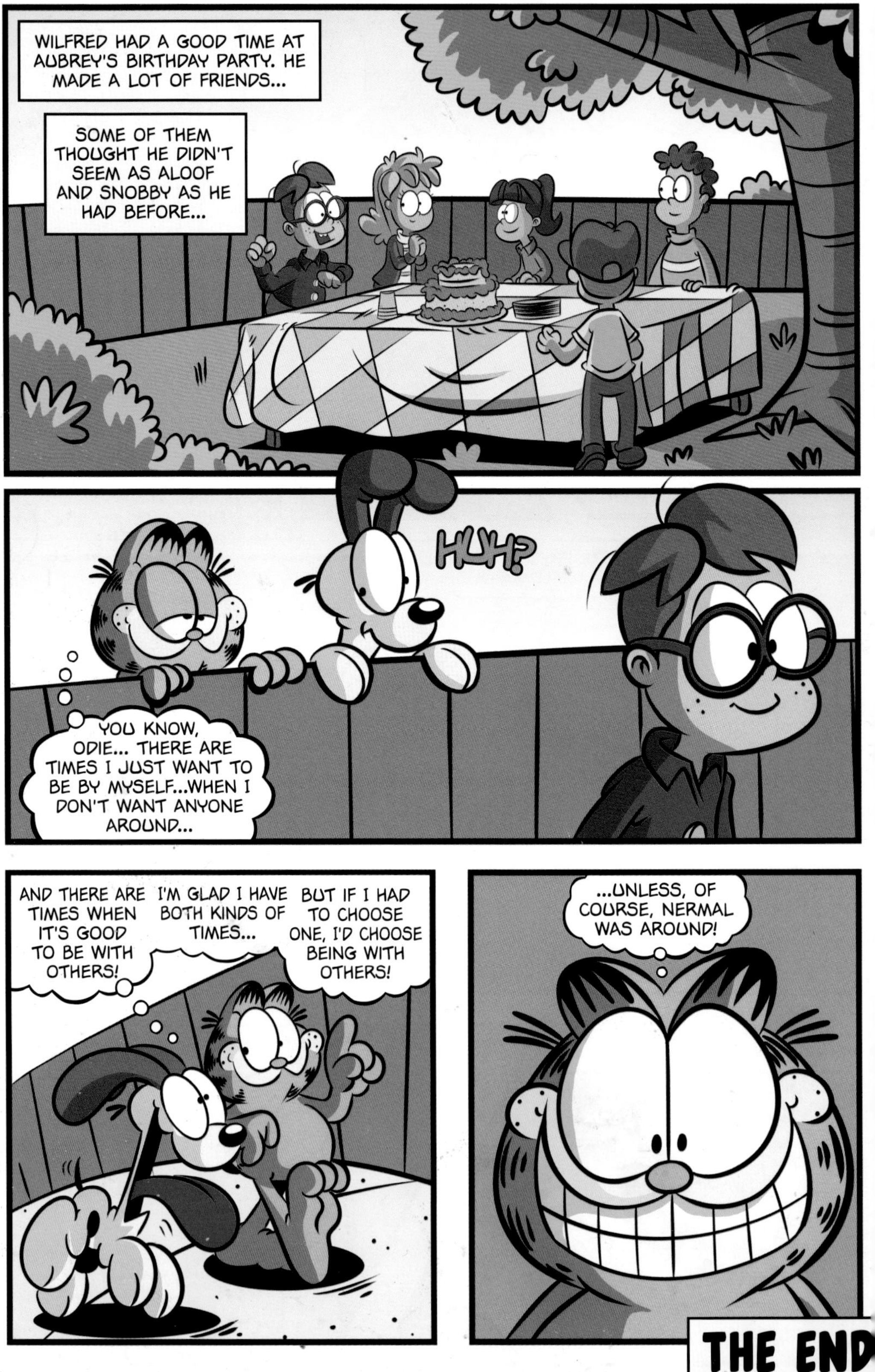
WILFRED HAD A GOOD TIME AT AUBREY'S BIRTHDAY PARTY. HE MADE A LOT OF FRIENDS...
SOME OF THEM THOUGHT HE DIDN'T SEEM AS ALOOF AND SNOBBY AS HE HAD BEFORE...
HUH?
YOU KNOW, ODIE... THERE ARE TIMES I JUST WANT TO BE BY MYSELF...WHEN I DON'T WANT ANYONE AROUND...
AND THERE ARE TIMES WHEN IT'S GOOD TO BE WITH OTHERS!
I'M GLAD I HAVE BOTH KINDS OF TIMES...
BUT IF I HAD TO CHOOSE ONE, I'D CHOOSE BEING WITH OTHERS!
...UNLESS, OF COURSE, NERMAL WAS AROUND!
THE END

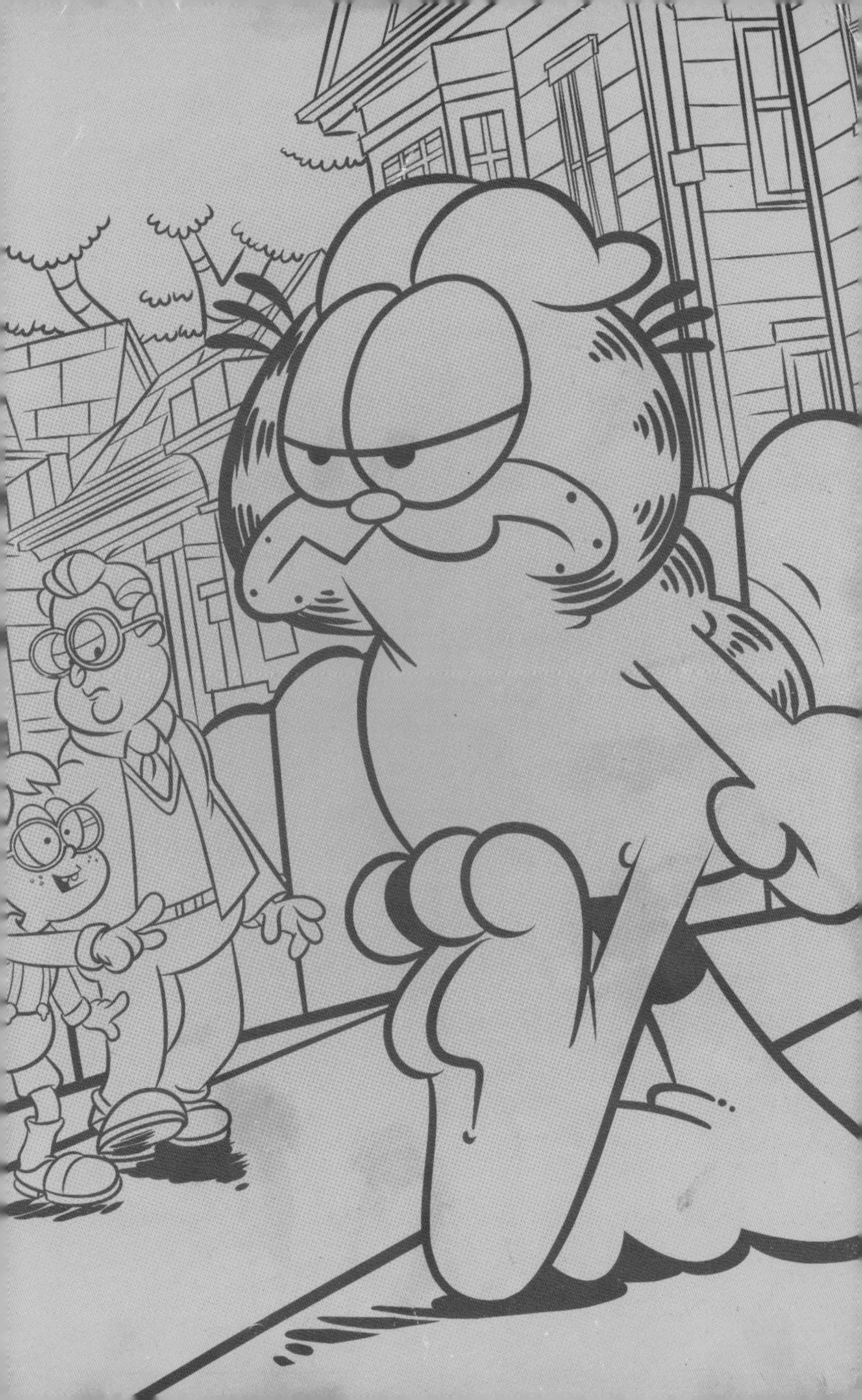

"HOW MUCH MONDAY CAN YOU TAKE?"

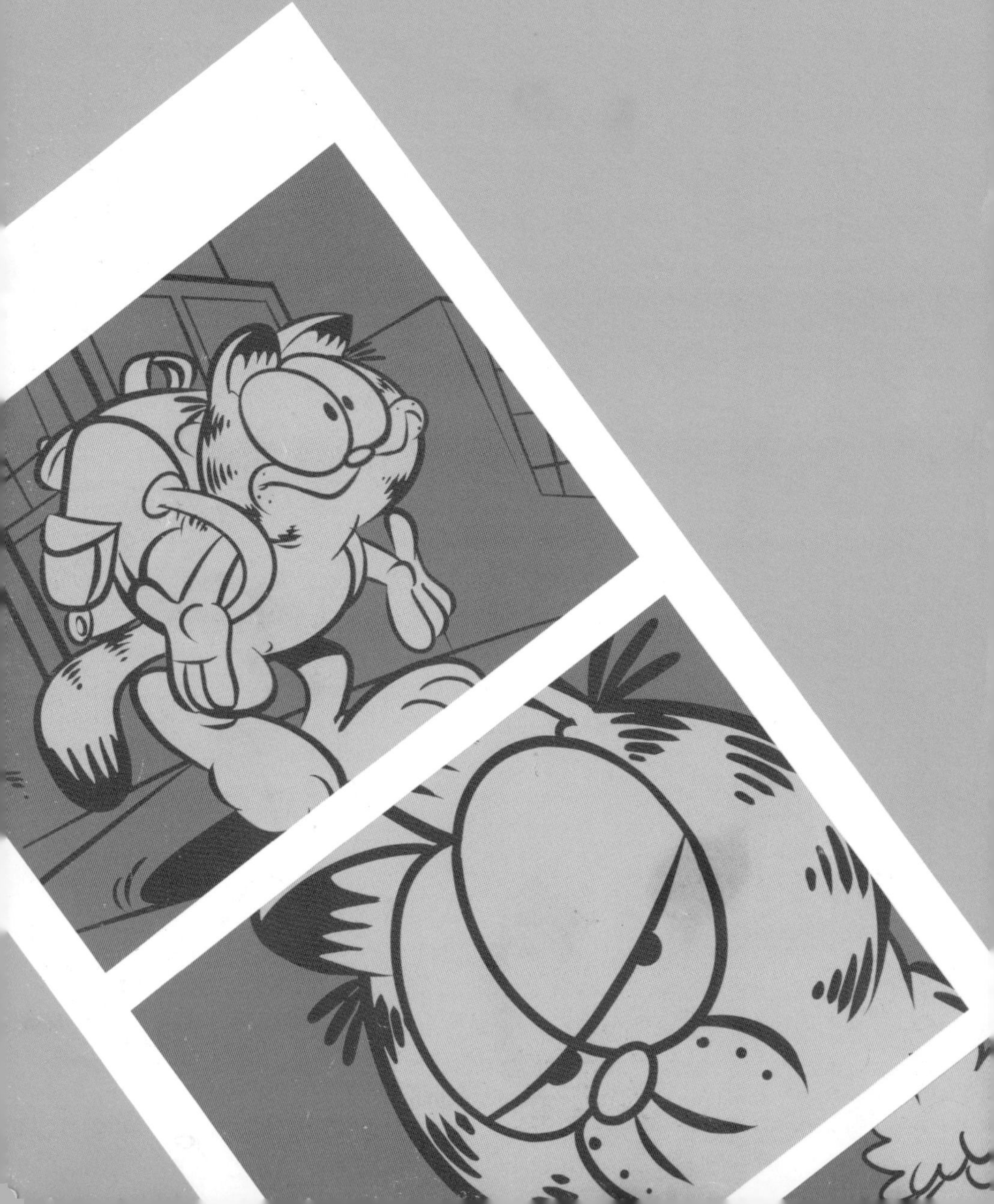

HOW MUCH MONDAY CAN YOU TAKE?

STORY & ART by LIZ PRINCE — COLORS by KYLE FOLSOM

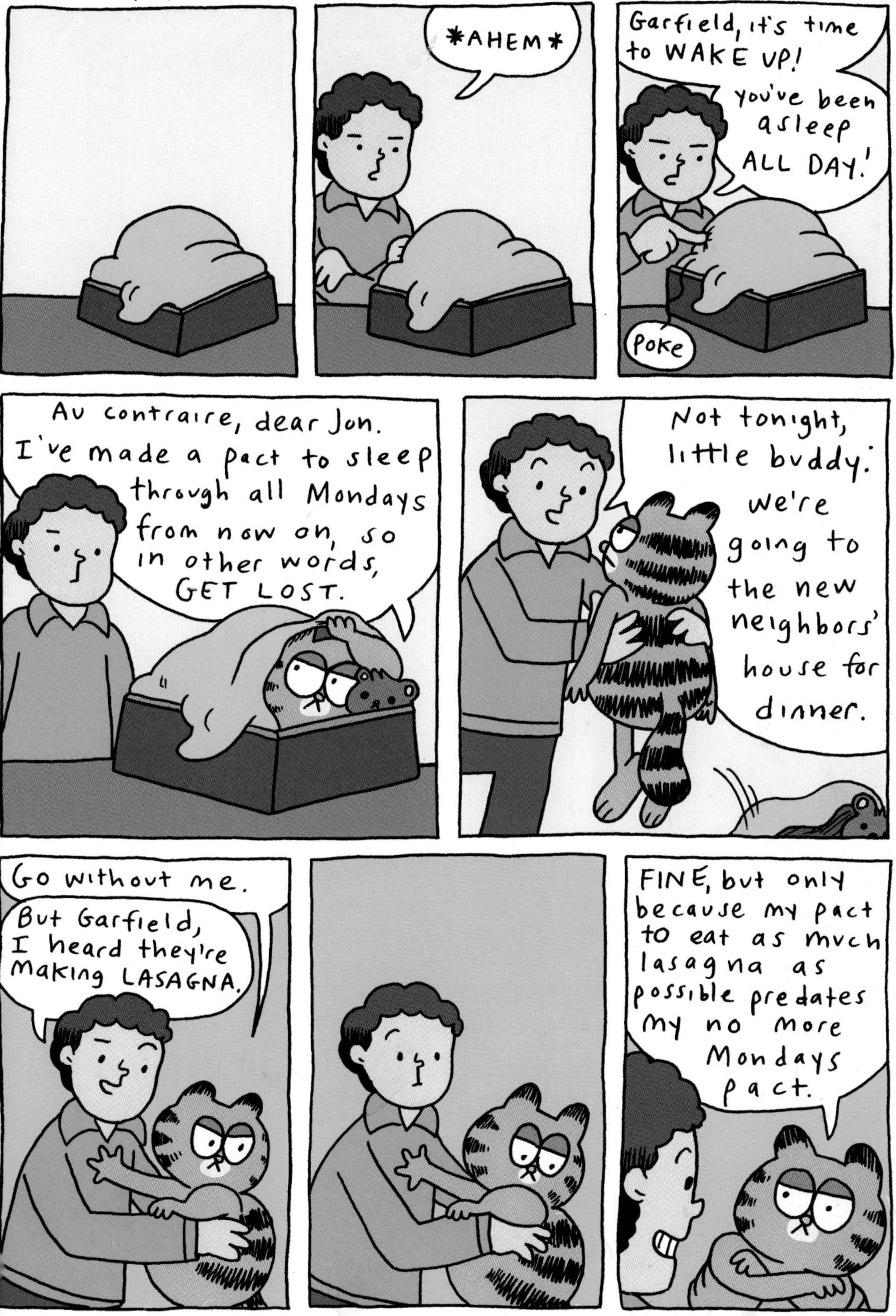
AHEM
Garfield, it's time to WAKE UP!
You've been asleep ALL DAY!
POKE
Au contraire, dear Jon. I've made a pact to sleep through all Mondays from now on, so in other words, GET LOST.
Not tonight, little buddy: we're going to the new neighbors' house for dinner.
Go without me.
But Garfield, I heard they're making LASAGNA.
FINE, but only because my pact to eat as much lasagna as possible predates my no more Mondays pact.

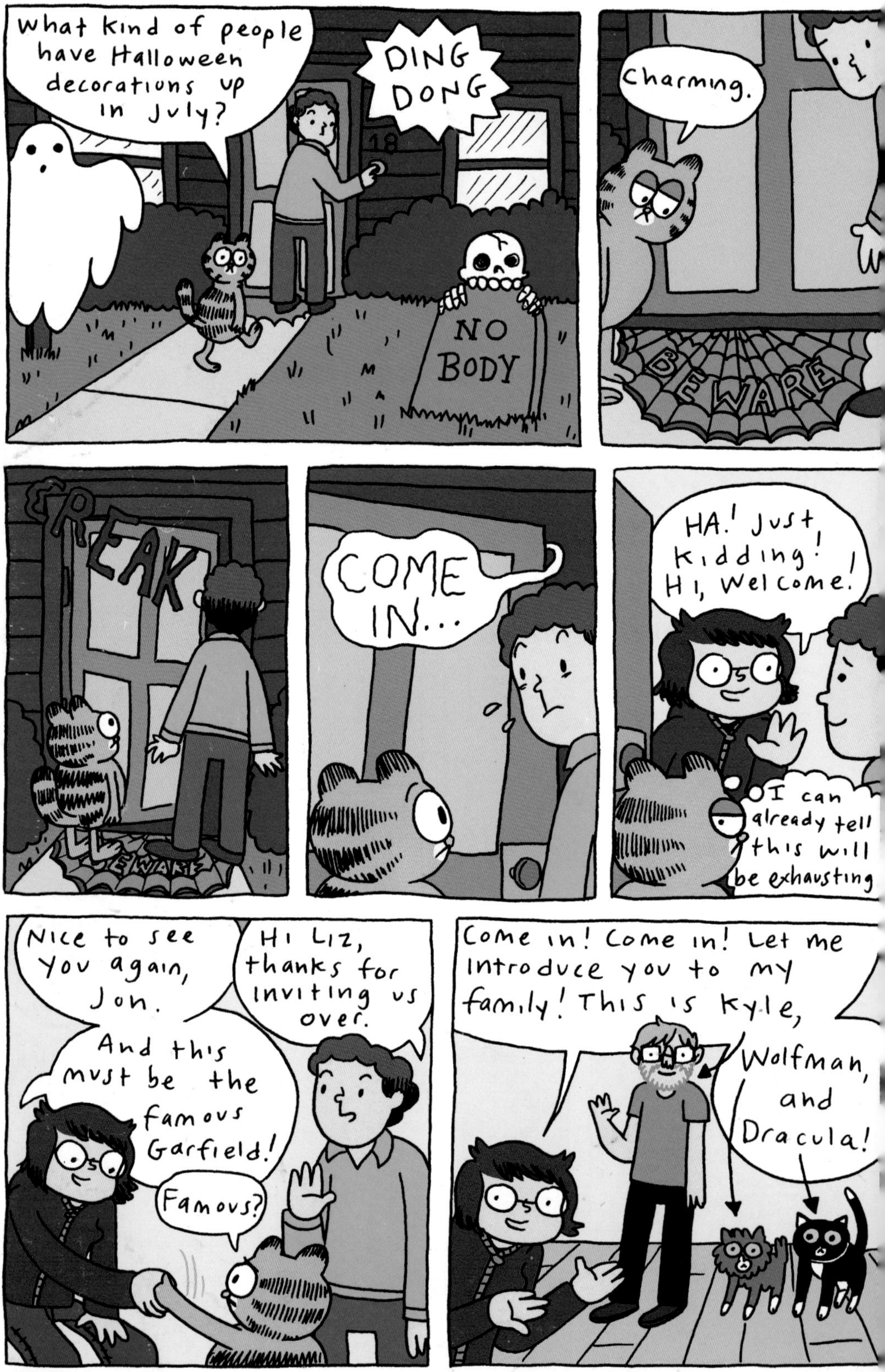
What kind of people have Halloween decorations up in July?
DING DONG
18
NO BODY
Charming.
BEWARE
CREAK
BEWARE
COME IN...
HA! Just kidding! Hi, Welcome!
I can already tell this will be exhausting
Nice to see you again, Jon.
Hi Liz, thanks for inviting us over.
And this must be the famous Garfield!
Famous?
Come in! Come in! Let me introduce you to my family! This is Kyle,
Wolfman,
and Dracula!

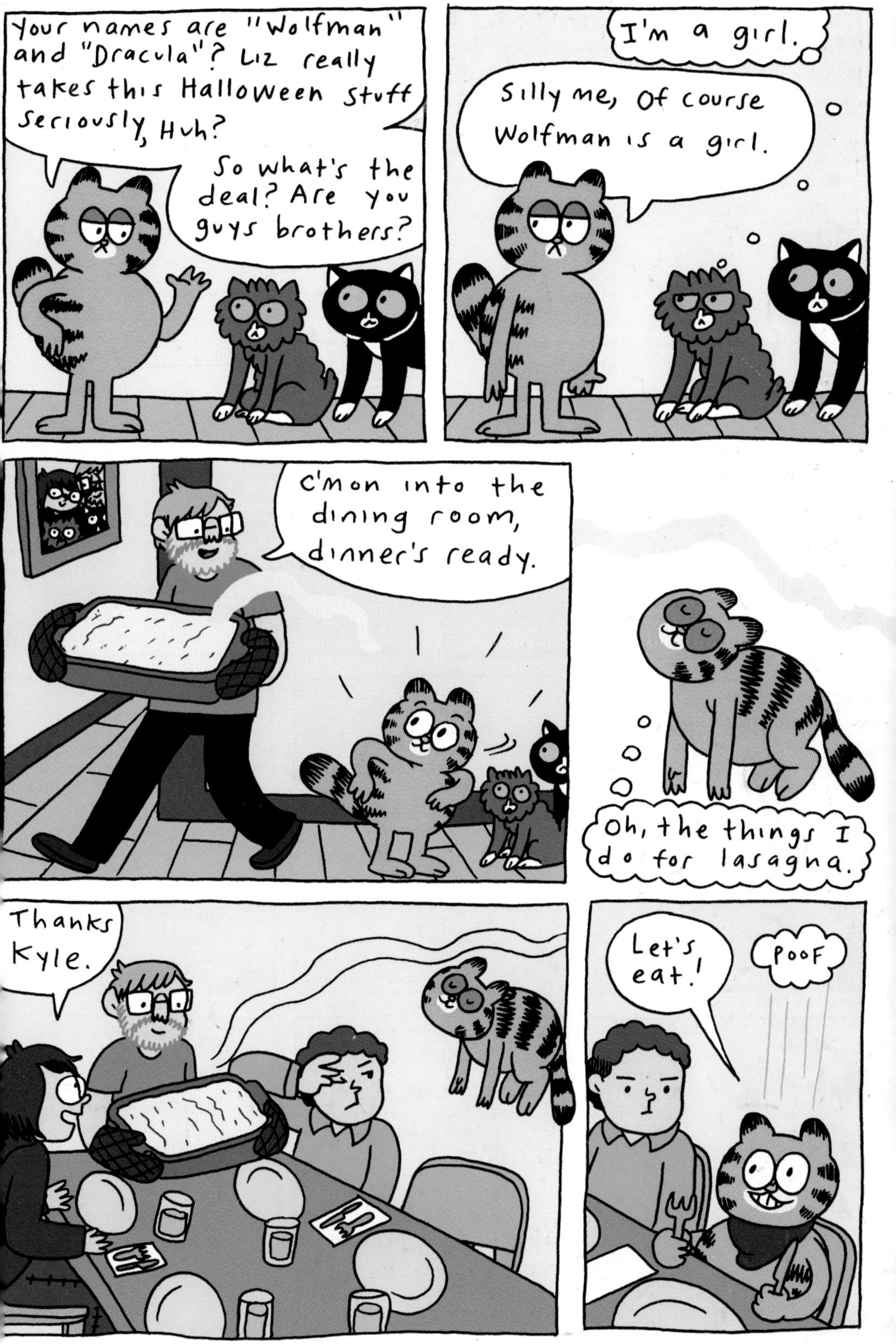
Your names are "Wolfman" and "Dracula"? Liz really takes this Halloween stuff seriously, Huh?
So what's the deal? Are you guys brothers?
I'm a girl.
Silly me, Of course Wolfman is a girl.
C'mon into the dining room, dinner's ready.
Oh, the things I do for lasagna.
Thanks Kyle.
Let's eat!
POOF

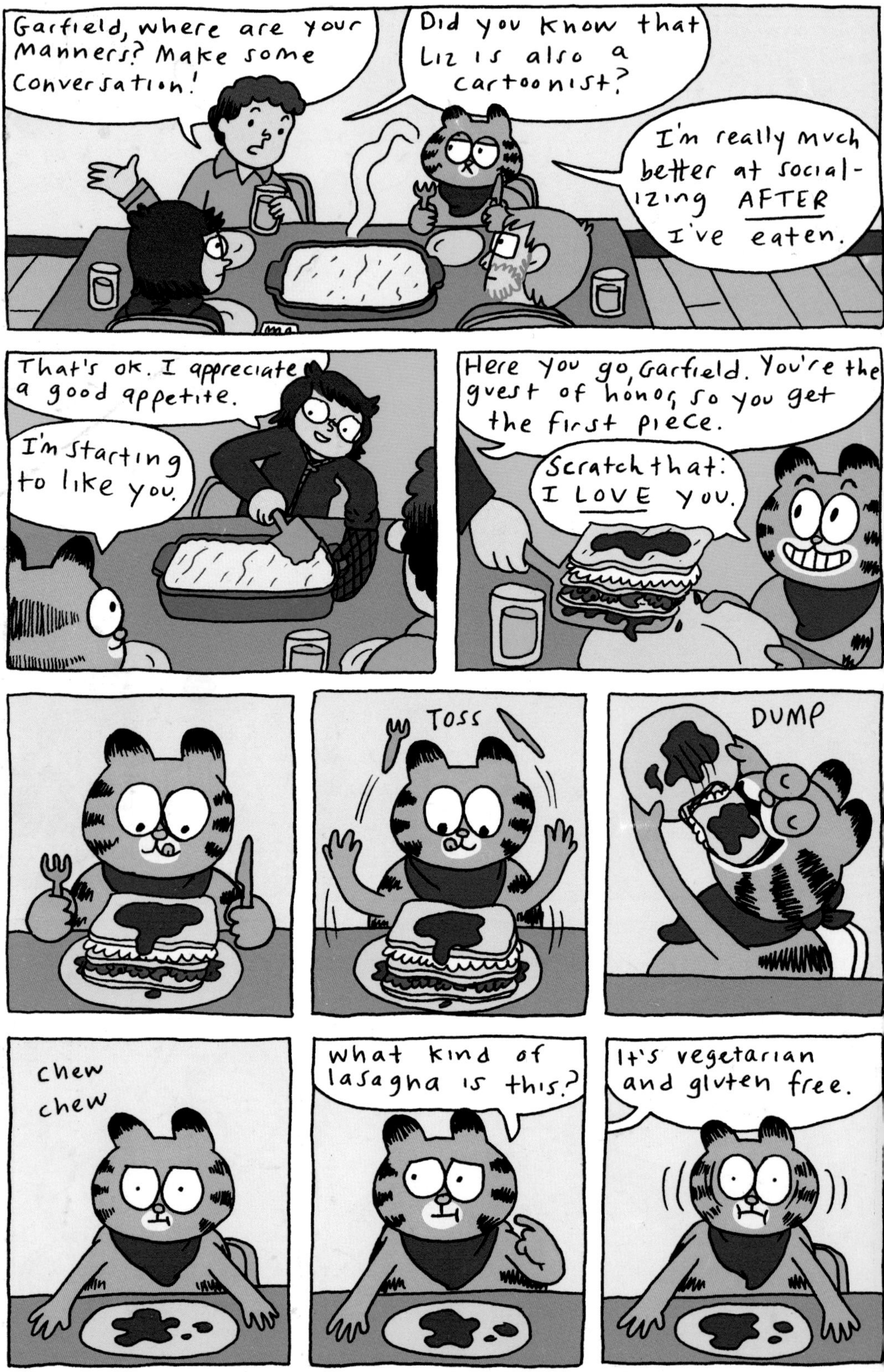
Garfield, where are your manners? Make some conversation!
Did you know that Liz is also a cartoonist?
I'm really much better at social-izing AFTER I've eaten.
That's ok. I appreciate a good appetite.
I'm starting to like you.
Here you go, Garfield. You're the guest of honor, so you get the first piece.
Scratch that: I LOVE you.
TOSS
DUMP
chew chew
what kind of lasagna is this?
It's vegetarian and gluten free.

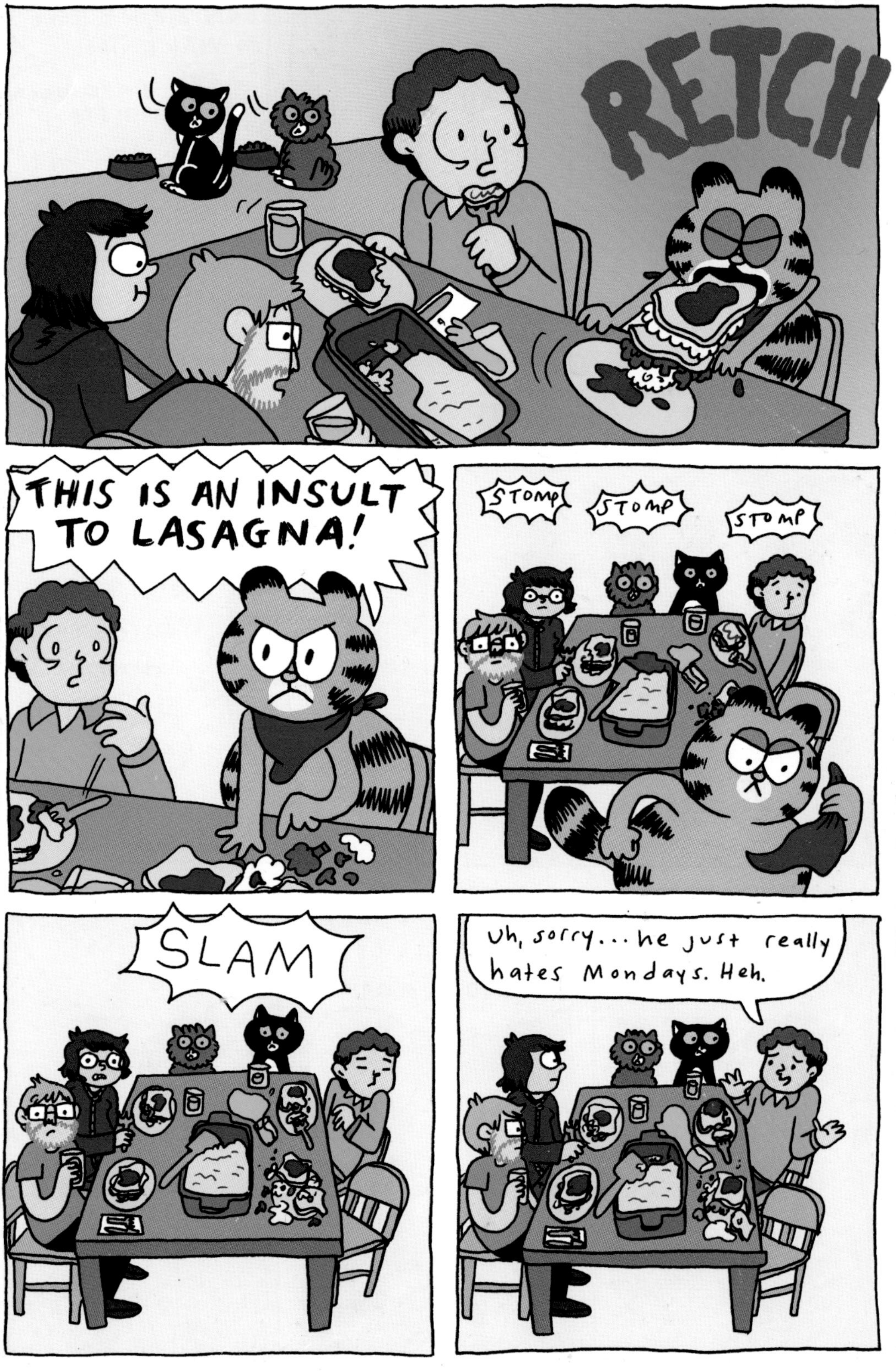
RETCH
THIS IS AN INSULT TO LASAGNA!
STOMP
STOMP
STOMP
SLAM
Uh, sorry... he just really hates Mondays. Heh.

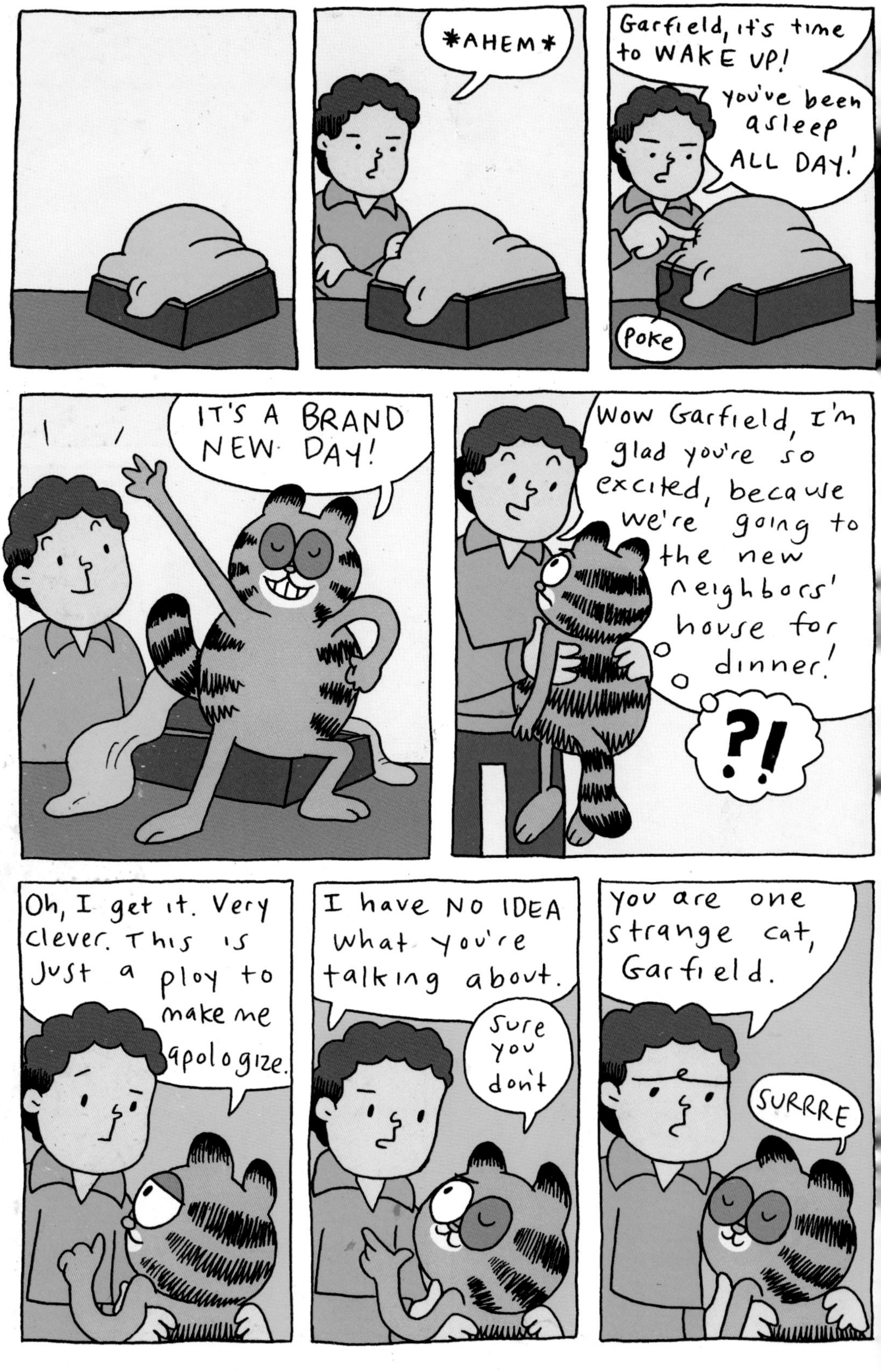
AHEM
Garfield, it's time to WAKE UP!
You've been asleep ALL DAY!
POKE
IT'S A BRAND NEW DAY!
Wow Garfield, I'm glad you're so excited, because we're going to the new neighbors' house for dinner!
?!
Oh, I get it. Very clever. This is just a ploy to make me apologize.
I have NO IDEA what you're talking about.
Sure you don't
You are one strange cat, Garfield.
SURRRE

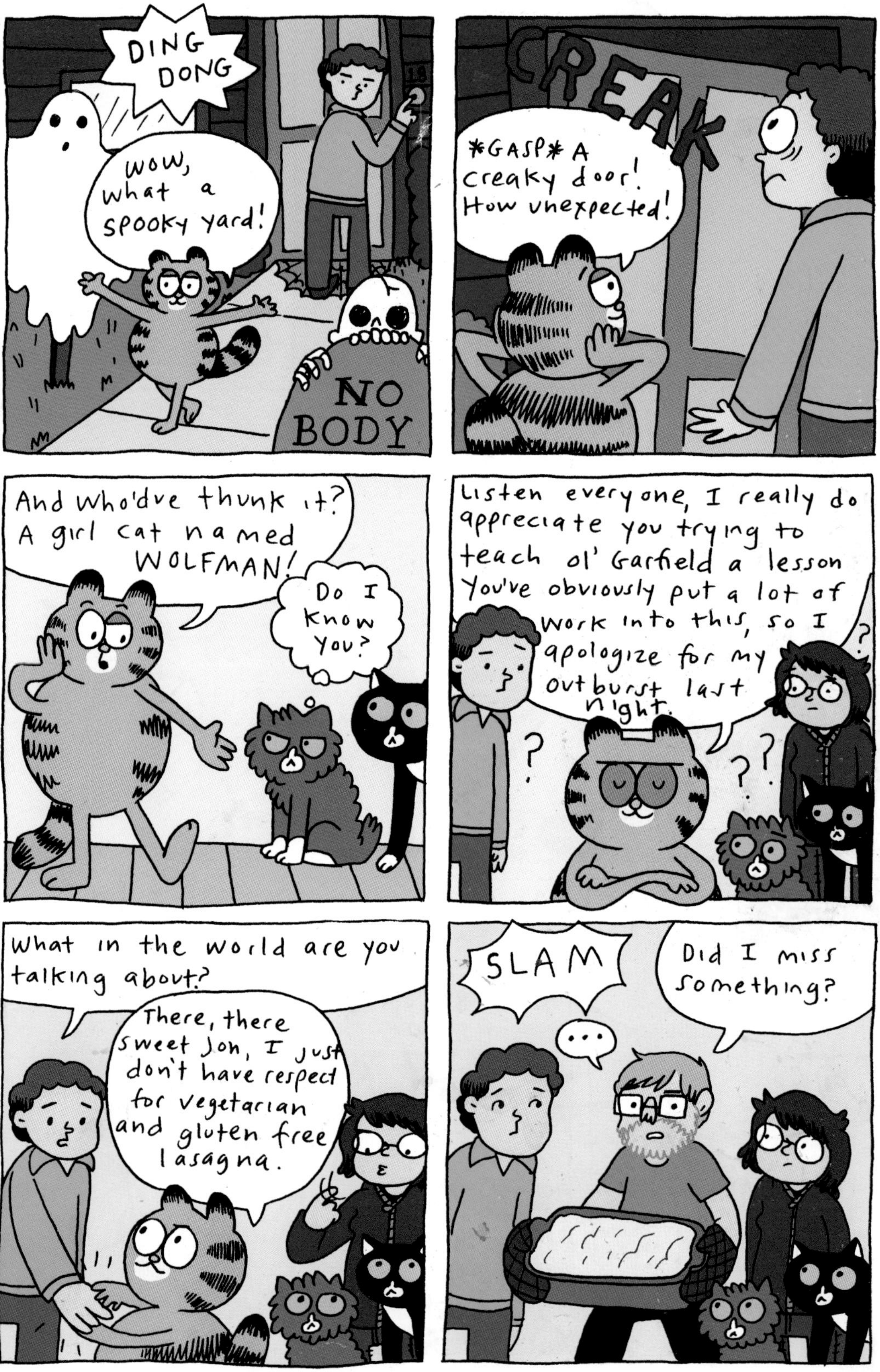
DING DONG
WOW, what a spooky yard!
18
NO BODY
CREAK
GASP A creaky door! How unexpected!
And who'd've thunk it? A girl cat named WOLFMAN!
Do I know you?
Listen everyone, I really do appreciate you trying to teach ol' Garfield a lesson. You've obviously put a lot of work into this, so I apologize for my outburst last night.
?
??
?
What in the world are you talking about?
There, there sweet Jon, I just don't have respect for vegetarian and gluten free lasagna.
SLAM
Did I miss something?
...

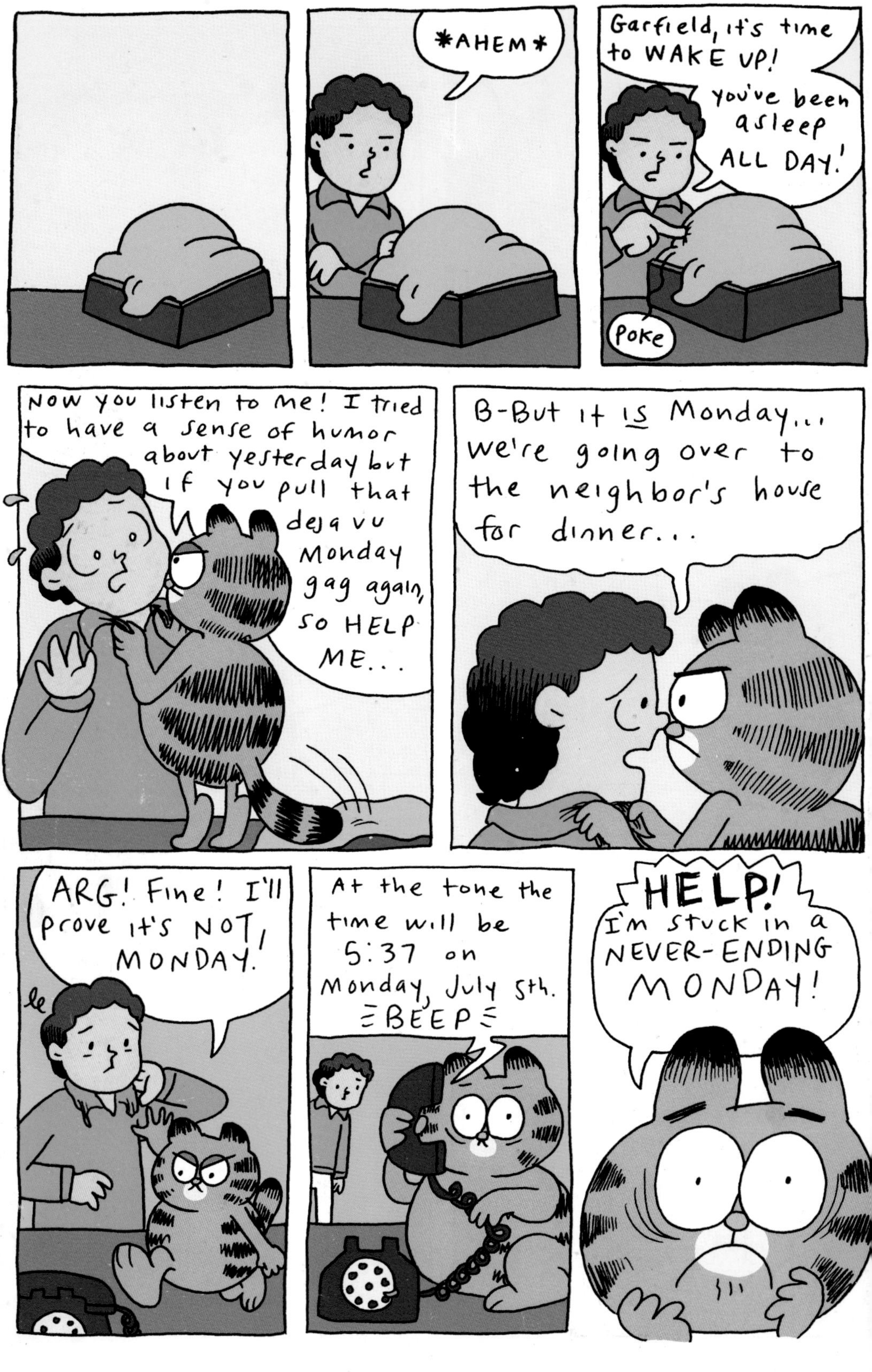
AHEM
Garfield, it's time to WAKE UP!
You've been asleep ALL DAY!
POKE
Now you listen to me! I tried to have a sense of humor about yesterday but if you pull that deja vu Monday gag again, so HELP ME...
B-But it IS Monday... we're going over to the neighbor's house for dinner...
ARG! Fine! I'll prove it's NOT MONDAY!
At the tone the time will be 5:37 on Monday, July 5th.
BEEP
HELP!
I'm stuck in a NEVER-ENDING MONDAY!

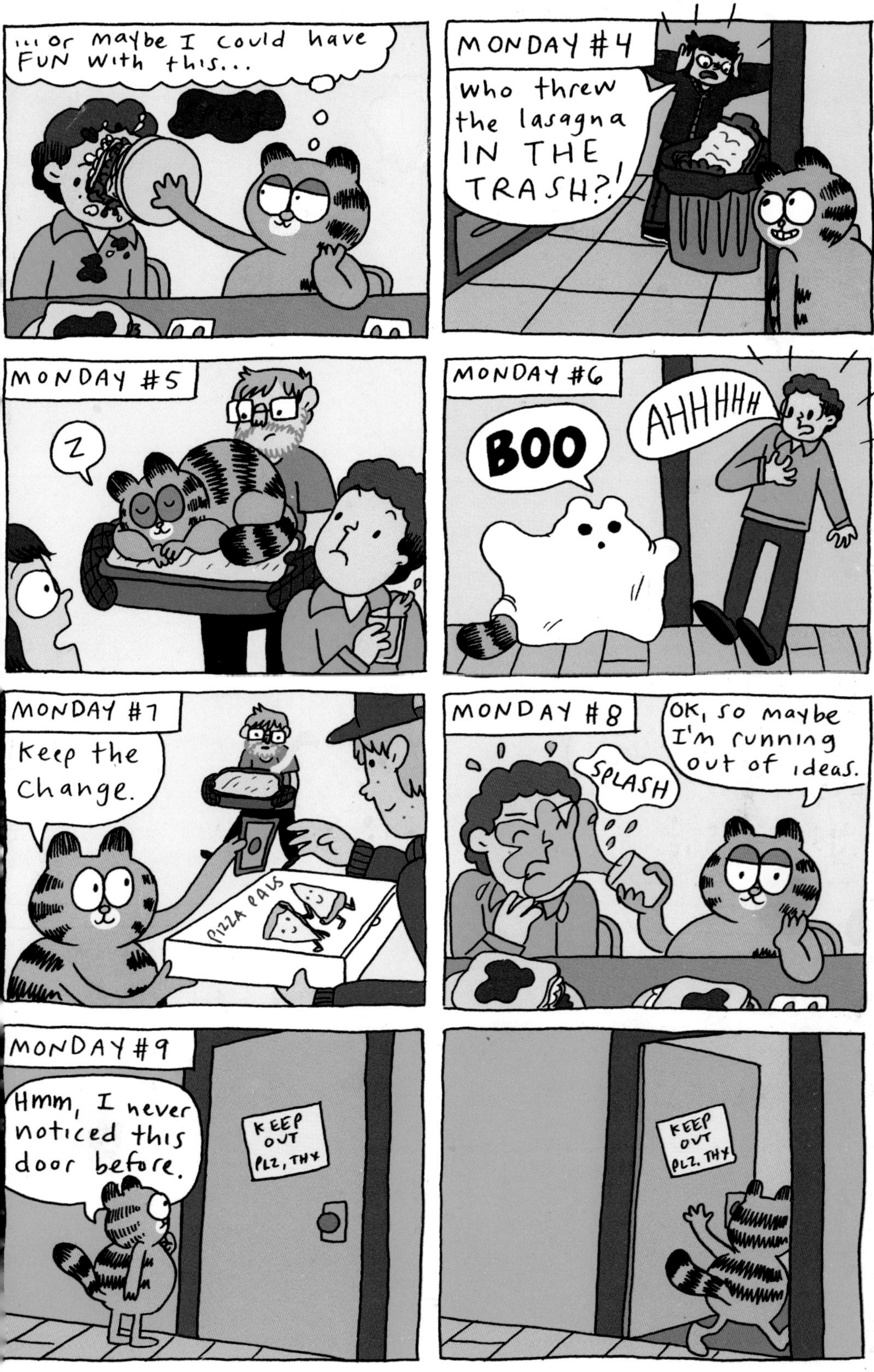
...or maybe I could have FUN with this...
SPLASH
MONDAY #4
who threw the lasagna IN THE TRASH?!
MONDAY #5
Z
MONDAY #6
BOO
AHHHHH
MONDAY #7
Keep the change.
PIZZA PAWS
MONDAY #8
SPLASH
OK, so maybe I'm running out of ideas.
MONDAY #9
Hmm, I never noticed this door before.
KEEP OUT PLZ, THX
KEEP OUT PLZ, THX

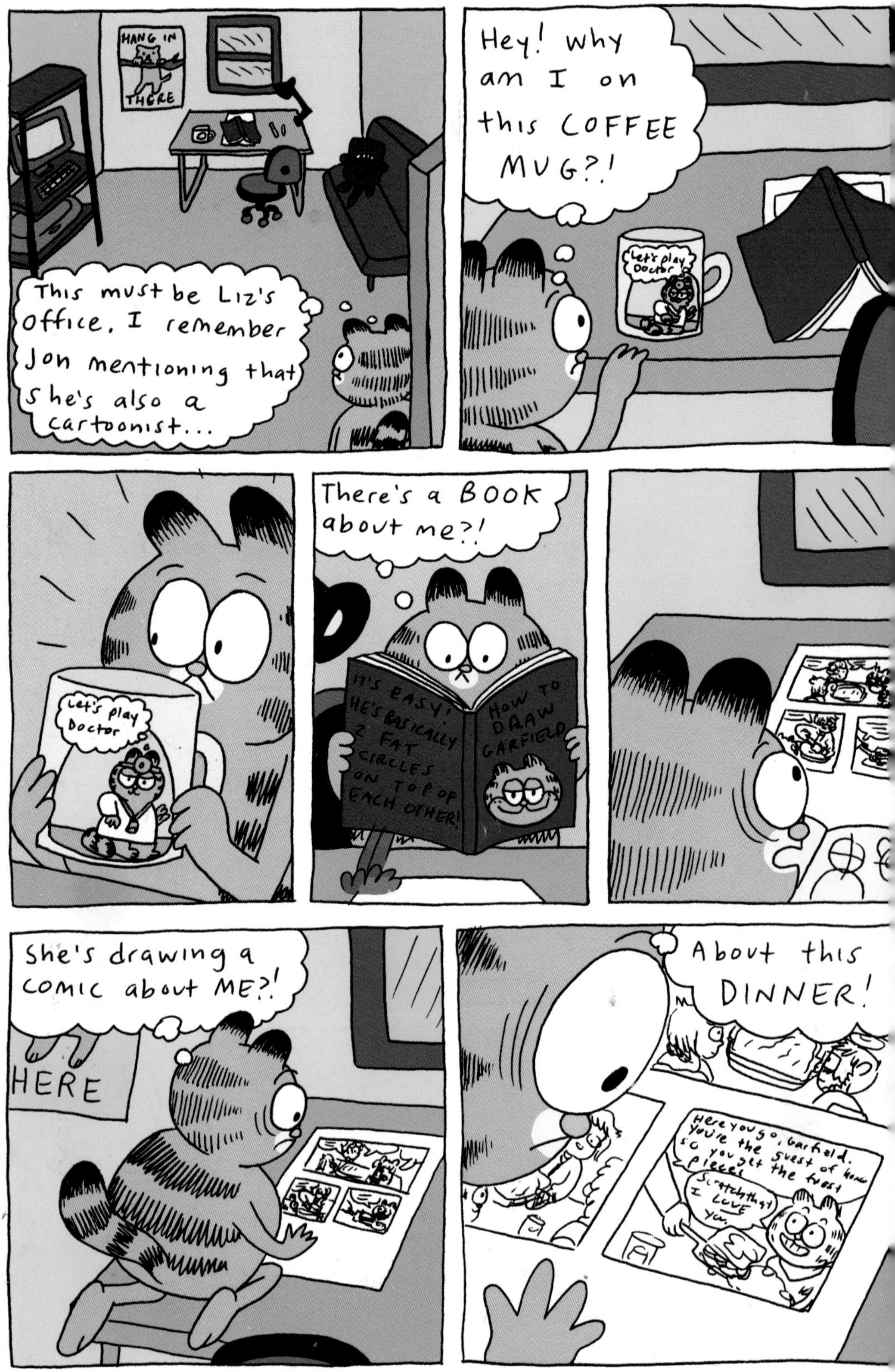
HANG IN THERE
This must be Liz's office. I remember Jon mentioning that she's also a cartoonist...
Hey! Why am I on this COFFEE MUG?!
Let's play Doctor
Let's play Doctor
There's a BOOK about me?!
IT'S EASY! HE'S BASICALLY 2 FAT CIRCLES ON TOP OF EACH OTHER!
HOW TO DRAW GARFIELD
She's drawing a comic about ME?!
HERE
About this DINNER!
Here you go, Garfield. You're the guest of honor so you get the first piece!
Scratch that I LOVE you.

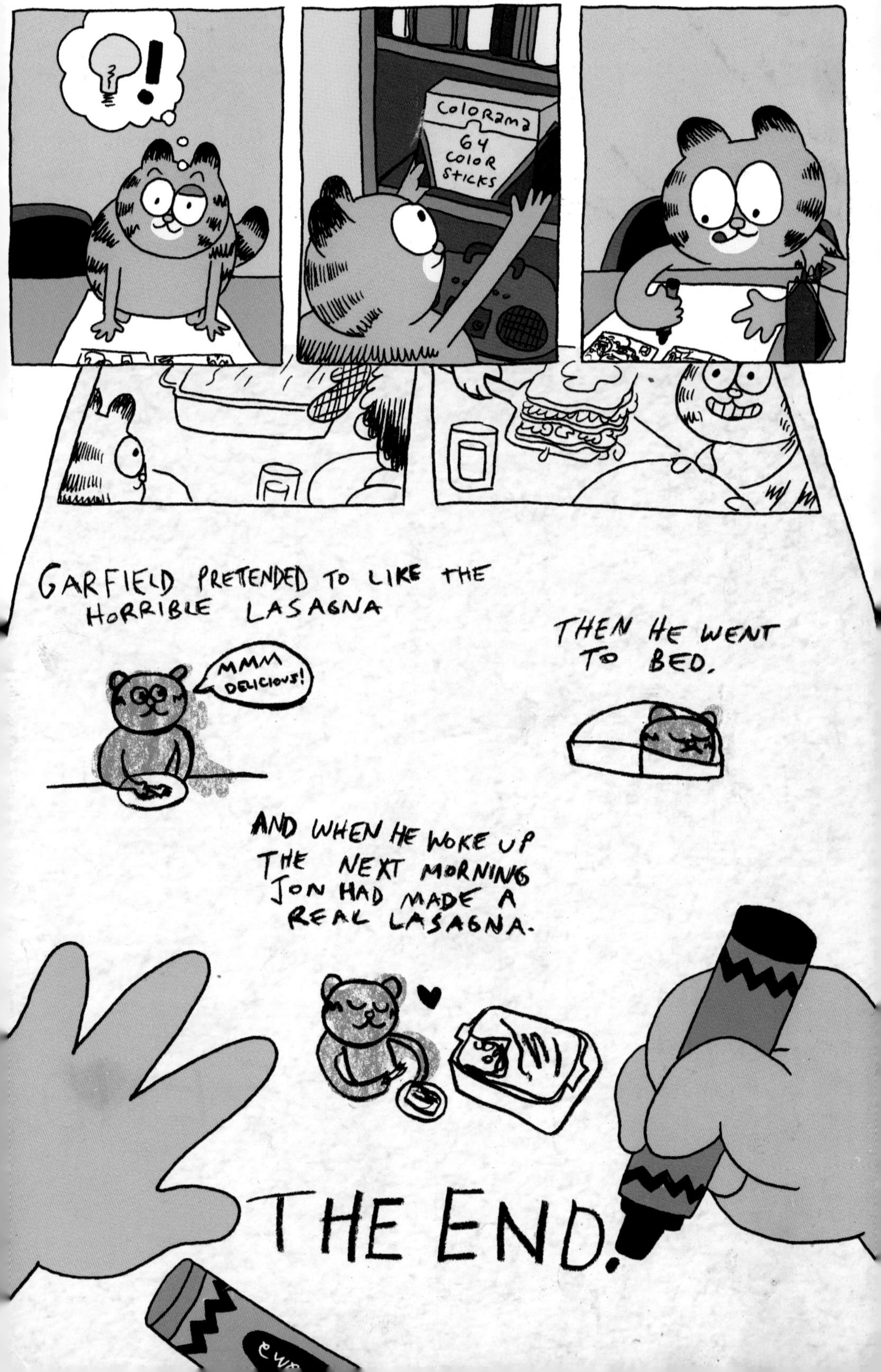
Colorama
64 COLOR STICKS
GARFIELD PRETENDED TO LIKE THE HORRIBLE LASAGNA
MMM DELICIOUS!
THEN HE WENT TO BED.
AND WHEN HE WOKE UP THE NEXT MORNING JON HAD MADE A REAL LASAGNA.
THE END.

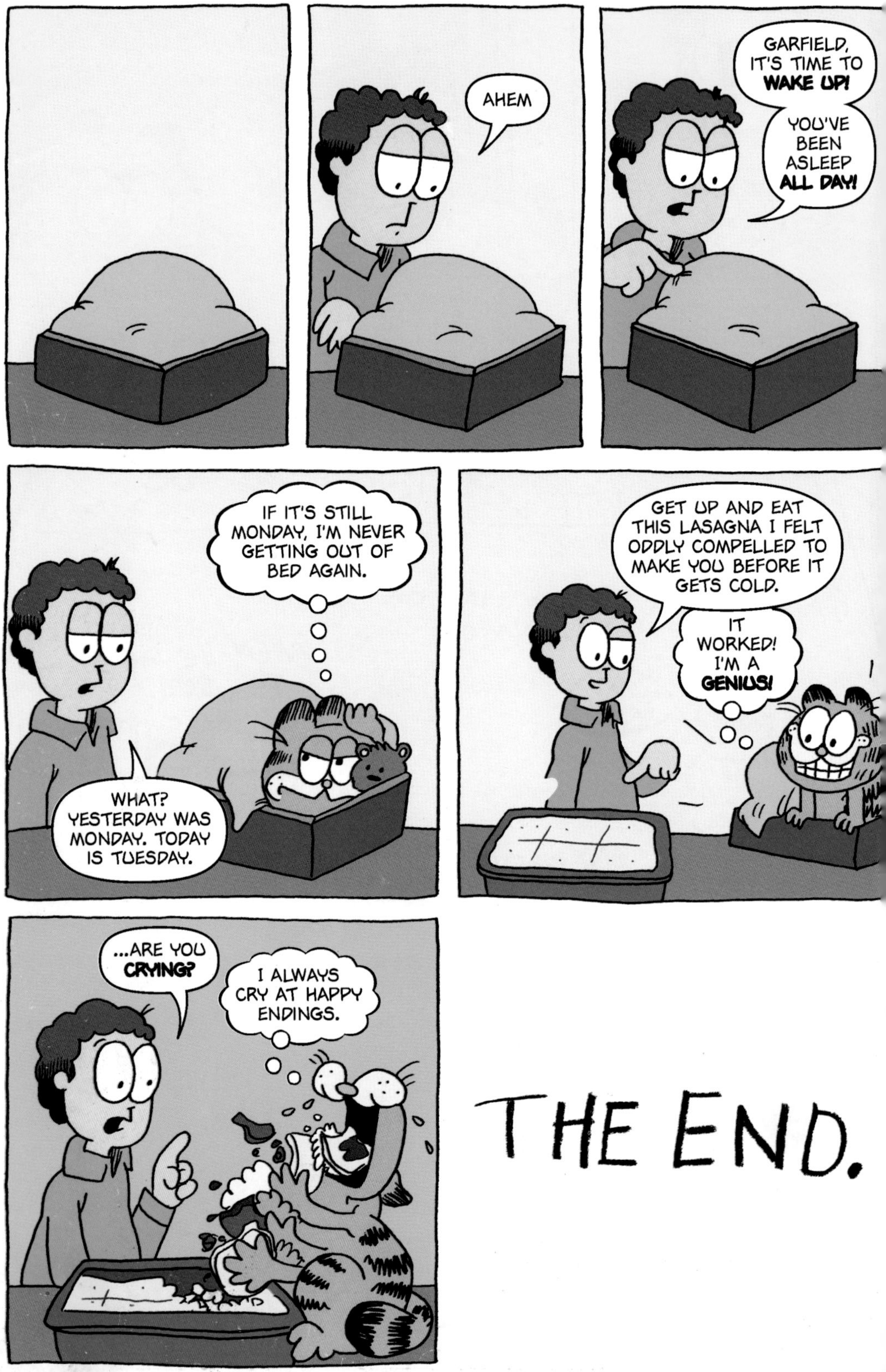
AHEM
GARFIELD, IT'S TIME TO **WAKE UP!**
YOU'VE BEEN ASLEEP **ALL DAY!**
IF IT'S STILL MONDAY, I'M NEVER GETTING OUT OF BED AGAIN.
WHAT? YESTERDAY WAS MONDAY. TODAY IS TUESDAY.
GET UP AND EAT THIS LASAGNA I FELT ODDLY COMPELLED TO MAKE YOU BEFORE IT GETS COLD.
IT WORKED! I'M A **GENIUS!**
...ARE YOU **CRYING?**
I ALWAYS CRY AT HAPPY ENDINGS.
THE END.

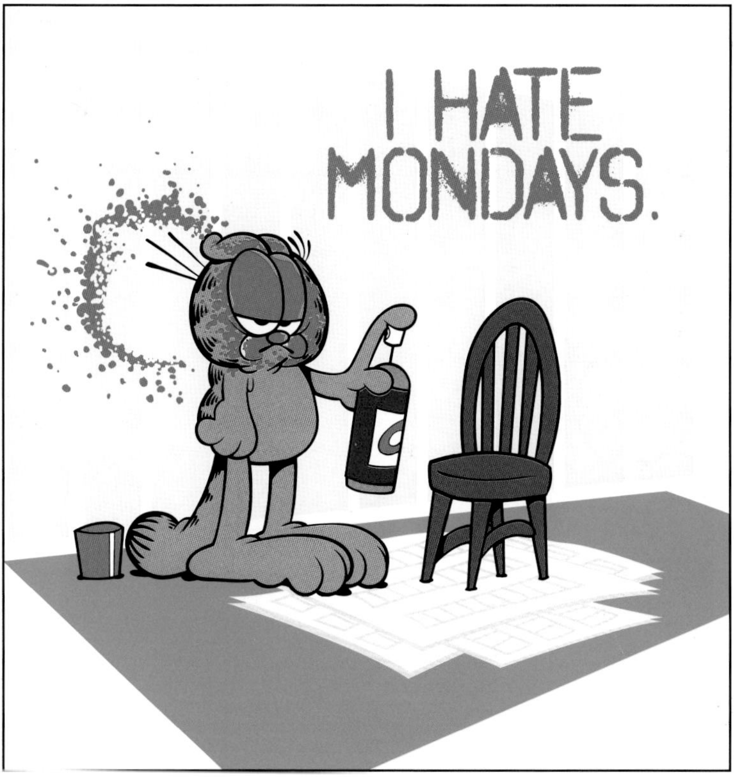
I HATE
MONDAYS.

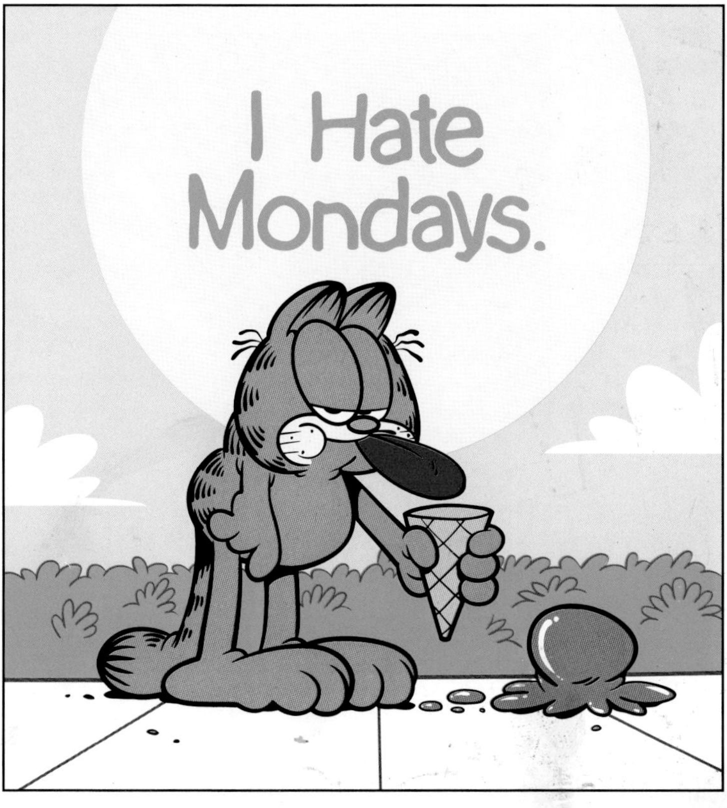
I Hate
Mondays.

Concepts:
Mark Acey,
Brett Koth

Concepts:
Mark Acey,
Brett Koth

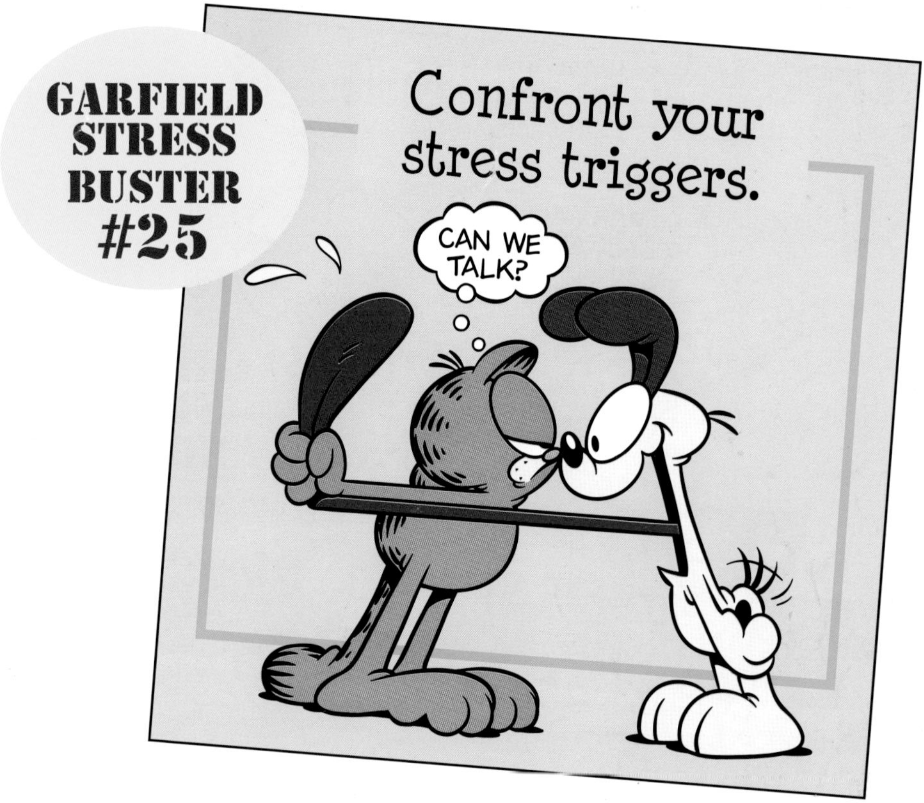
GARFIELD STRESS BUSTER #25
Confront your stress triggers.
CAN WE TALK?

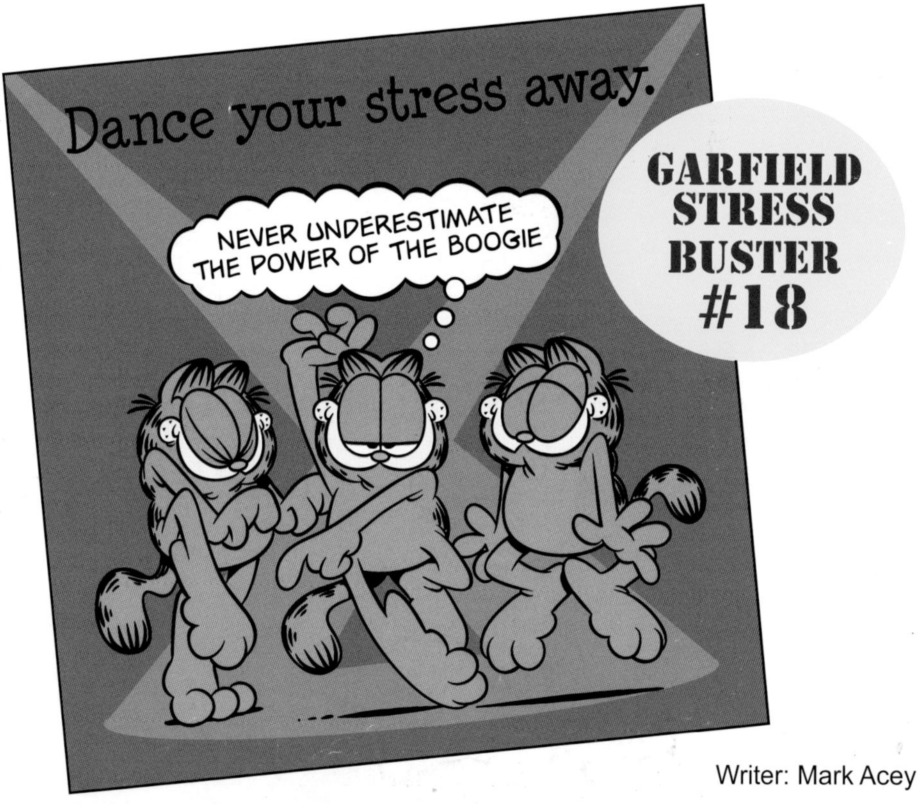
Dance your stress away.
GARFIELD STRESS BUSTER #18
NEVER UNDERESTIMATE THE POWER OF THE BOOGIE

Writer: Mark Acey

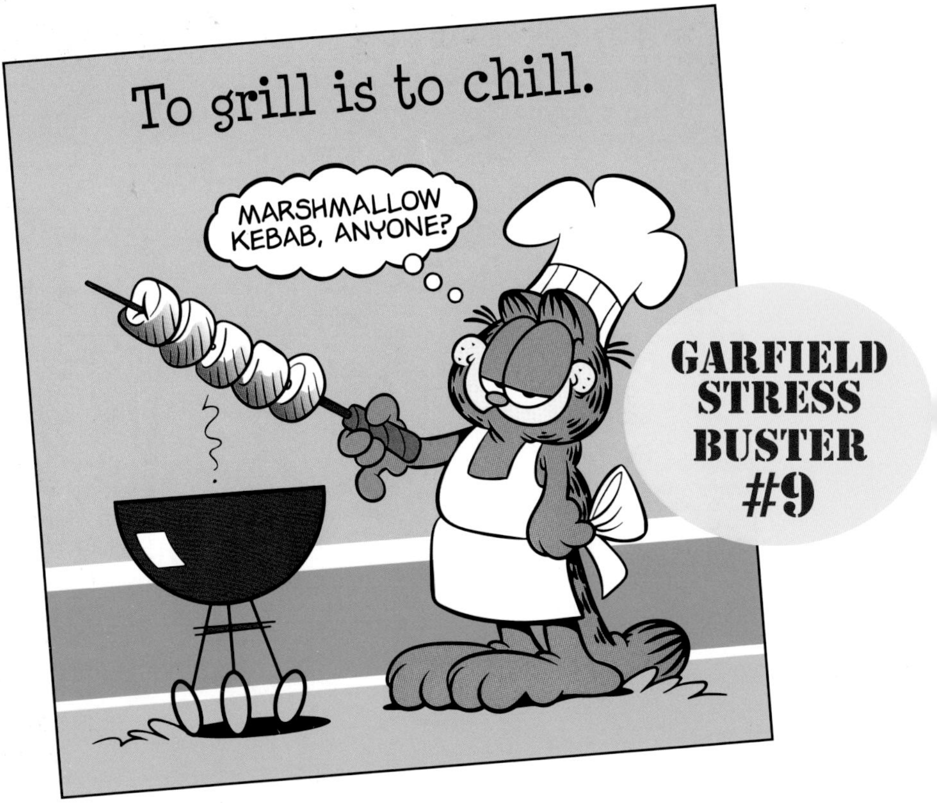
To grill is to chill.
MARSHMALLOW KEBAB, ANYONE?
GARFIELD STRESS BUSTER #9

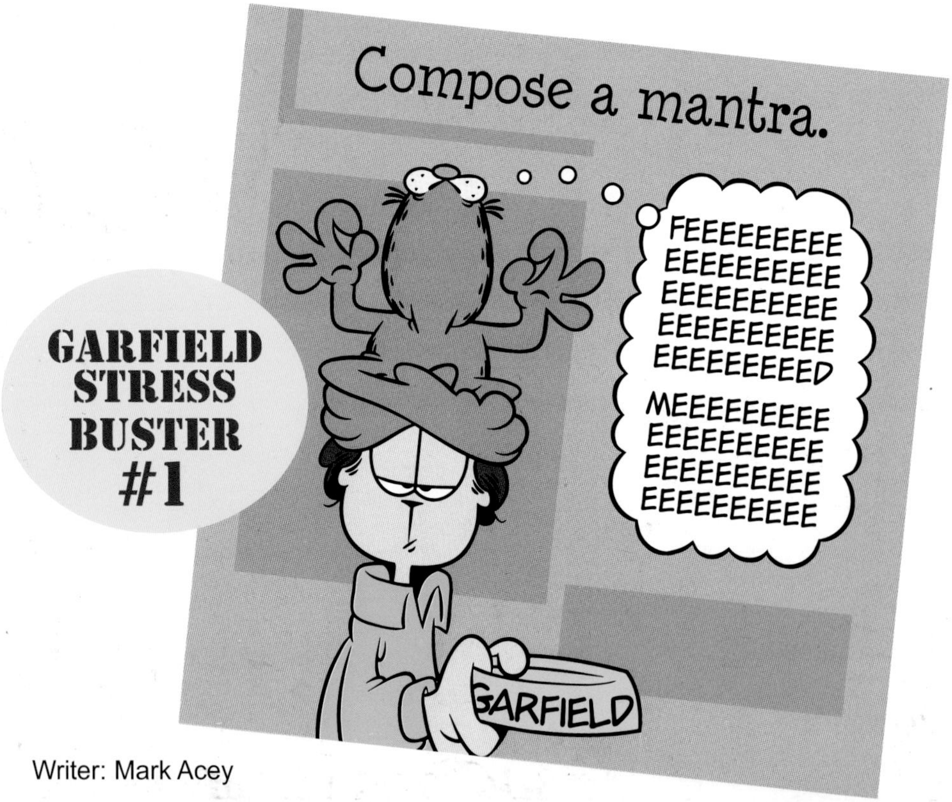
Compose a mantra.
GARFIELD STRESS BUSTER #1
FEEEEEEEEE EEEEEEEEEE EEEEEEEEEE EEEEEEEEEE EEEEEEEEED
MEEEEEEEEE EEEEEEEEEE EEEEEEEEEE EEEEEEEEEE
GARFIELD

Writer: Mark Acey

Garfield Sunday Classics

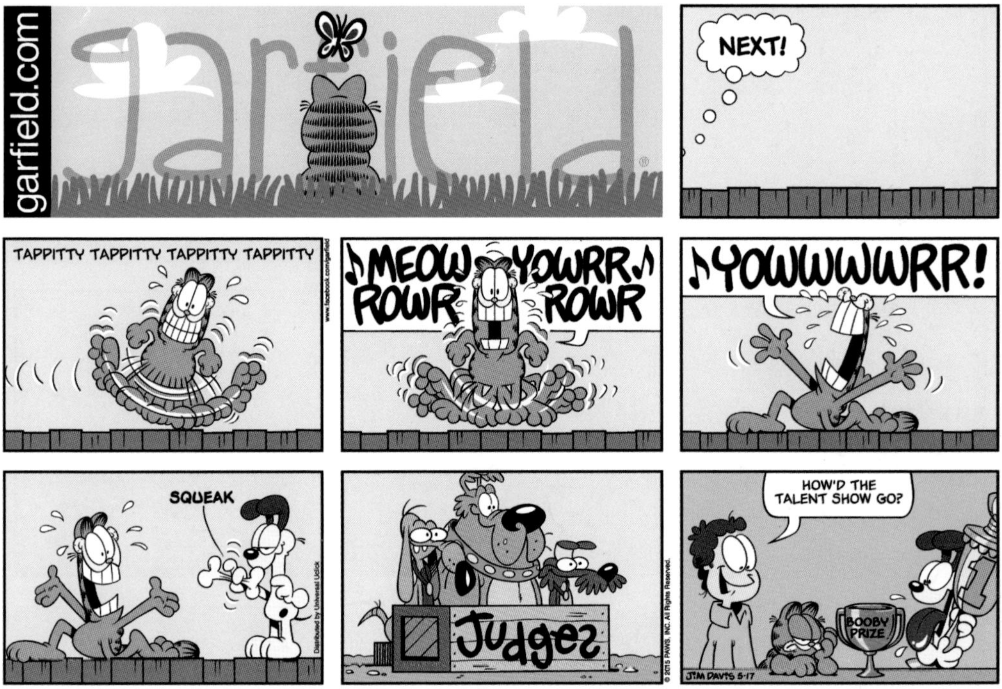
garfield.com
garfield
NEXT!
TAPPITTY TAPPITTY TAPPITTY TAPPITTY
www.facebook.com/garfield
♪MEOW YOWRR♪
ROWR ROWR
♪YOWWWWRR!
SQUEAK
Distributed by Universal Uclick
Judges
© 2015 PAWS, INC. All Rights Reserved.
HOW'D THE TALENT SHOW GO?
BOOBY PRIZE
JIM DAVIS 5-17

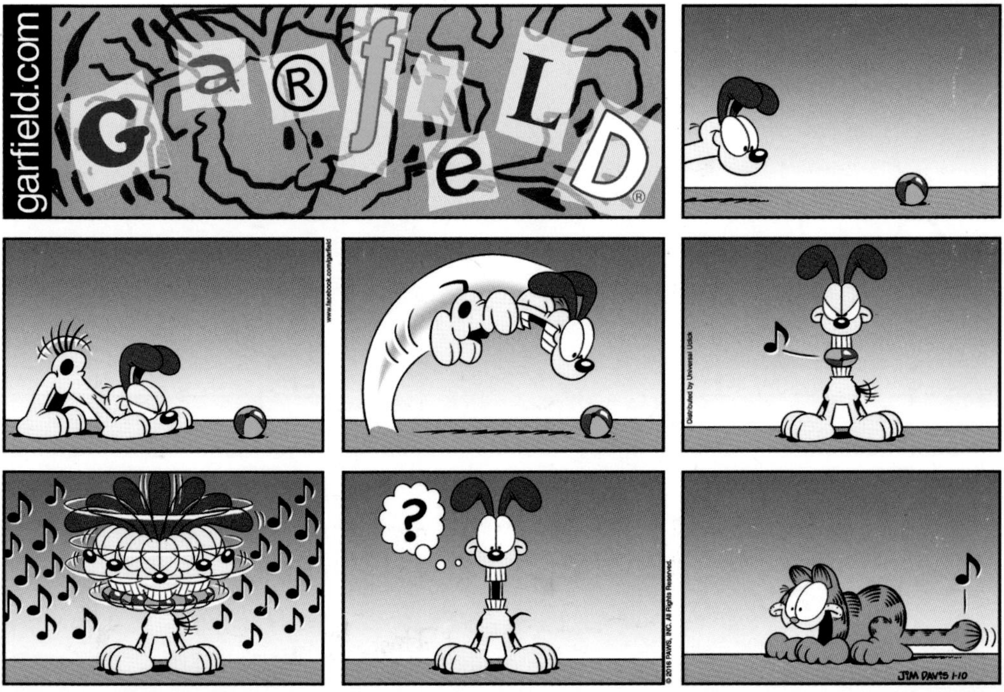
garfield.com
GaRfiLeD
www.facebook.com/garfield
Distributed by Universal Uclick
?
© 2016 PAWS, INC. All Rights Reserved.
JIM DAVIS 1-10

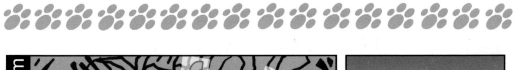

Odie Unleashed

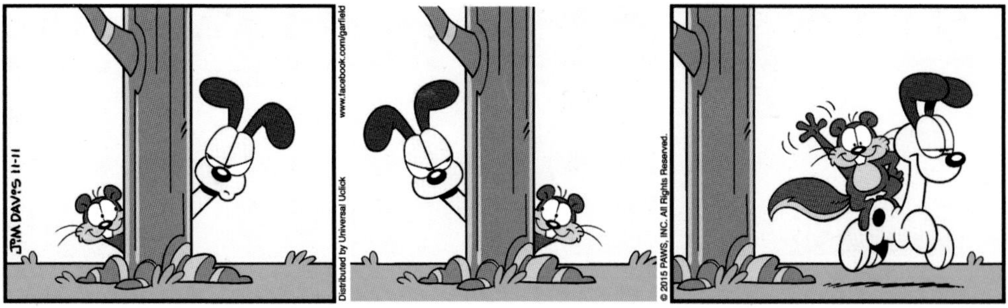
JIM DAVIS 11-11
Distributed by Universal Uclick www.facebook.com/garfield
© 2015 PAWS, INC. All Rights Reserved.

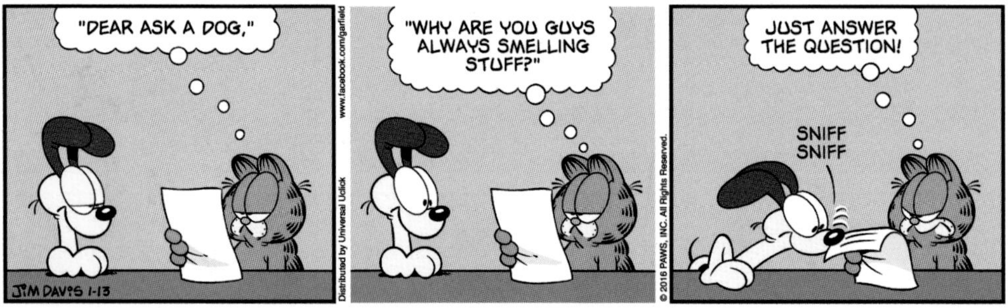
"DEAR ASK A DOG,"
JIM DAVIS 1-13
"WHY ARE YOU GUYS ALWAYS SMELLING STUFF?"
JUST ANSWER THE QUESTION!
SNIFF SNIFF
Distributed by Universal Uclick www.facebook.com/garfield
© 2016 PAWS, INC. All Rights Reserved.

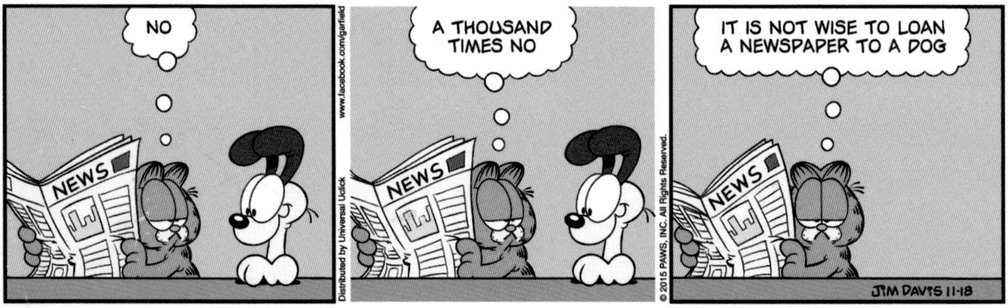
NO
NEWS
A THOUSAND TIMES NO
IT IS NOT WISE TO LOAN A NEWSPAPER TO A DOG
JIM DAVIS 11-18
Distributed by Universal Uclick www.facebook.com/garfield
© 2015 PAWS, INC. All Rights Reserved.

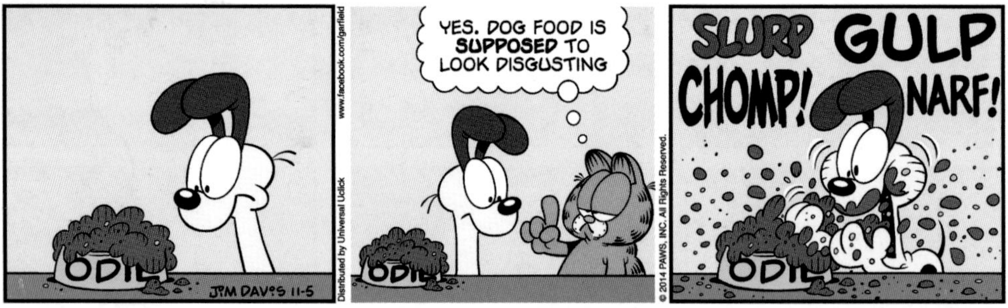
ODIE
JIM DAVIS 11-5
YES. DOG FOOD IS **SUPPOSED** TO LOOK DISGUSTING
SLURP GULP
CHOMP! NARF!
Distributed by Universal Uclick www.facebook.com/garfield
© 2014 PAWS, INC. All Rights Reserved.

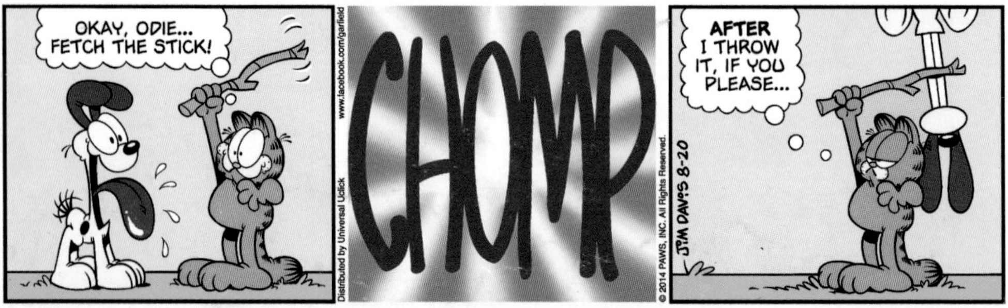
OKAY, ODIE... FETCH THE STICK!
CHOMP
AFTER I THROW IT, IF YOU PLEASE...
JIM DAVIS 8-20
Distributed by Universal Uclick www.facebook.com/garfield
© 2014 PAWS, INC. All Rights Reserved.